MIDNIGHT AT THE

ORPHEUS

By the Author

The Artist's Muse

Betting on Love

Midnight at the Orpheus

Visit us at www.boldstrokesbooks.com

For Josh,
Thank you for all the support!
Noir writers represent!
all the best, Alyssa

MIDNIGHT AT THE
ORPHEUS

by

Alyssa Linn Palmer

LIBERTY
EDITION

A Division of Bold Strokes Books

2015

MIDNIGHT AT THE ORPHEUS

ISBN 13: 978-1-62639-607-4

This Trade Paperback Original Is Published By
Bold Strokes Books, Inc.
P.O. Box 249
Valley Falls, NY 12185

First Edition: December 2015

Credits

Editor: Ruth Sternglantz
Production Design: Stacia Seaman
Cover Design by Jeanine Henning

Acknowledgments

Many thanks to my parents, who took me to Chicago to do research. Also thank you to the dedicated staff of the Newberry Library for all their assistance, and to the docents aboard the tall ship *Windy* for all their stories. And finally, thank you to Ruth, editor extraordinaire.

To my parents for all their support.

CHAPTER ONE

Chicago, Autumn 1925

"Just a prostitute," the young beat cop said, taking in the drowned woman's attire. The remnants of a thin dark dress clung to her waterlogged form, making her skin paler still in the light from the patrol car's headlights.

Detective Jack Lang lit a cigarette and stepped closer, leaving his ogling of the beat cop's bottom in its snug trousers to stare down at the body. Such a shame Jones was as straight as they came. Not that he would ever pursue another cop—it was just too dangerous. It might get him where this girl was now—cold, her throat mottled with bruises. Her head rested at an awkward angle. Jones began to shift the body onto the sheet lying nearby on the bank so they could take the body up the slope to where the morgue van waited. The girl's head turned toward him, and though her face was puffy and her eyes closed, he recognized her.

She should have been dancing the night away at the Orpheus. Just last week she had been, but now she was dead.

"Hurry it up, Jones," he snapped. He paced back to his sedan and left the beat cop and the coroner to deal with the corpse. How had she ended up in the river, so obviously murdered? She'd been on top of the world, popular, successful, and beautiful.

He stubbed out his cigarette and lit another. Important people would have to be told, and he didn't want to be the bearer of bad news.

❖

Cecilia Adeline Mills scraped the globs of leftover salad dressing into the garbage can before stacking the plates on the worn countertop by the wash sink. The conversations from the front room of the café were a sustained murmur that drifted back to where she stood, wiping her hands on her apron. The dishes were piled high and threatening to overflow the small space. This wasn't what she'd pictured when her ma told her they were moving to the city. Not at all.

A crash came from the café and conversation stilled. A woman laughed and the murmur started up again. Cecilia's boss, Paul, stormed into the back, his face red with anger.

"Get out there and clean it up!" he snapped. The front of his usually pristine shirt and vest was covered with stains in several shades of brown. He threw his tray into the sink. "What're you staring at?"

Cecilia bit her lip against the words she wanted to snap back. He could clean it just as well, and he didn't have a stack of dishes to wash. She grabbed a handful of rags from the pile nearby and took the broom and dustpan and went out into the café. The mess was easy to see; the customers gave one of the window tables a wide berth. White porcelain shards lay in a puddle of coffee. She hurried over and crouched by the mess. She swept the shards into the dustpan, trying to remove most of the porcelain before she could use the rags to clean up the spilled coffee.

When she pushed a half-moon of a coffee cup into the pan, a pair of dollar bills, mostly soaked with coffee, lay underneath. She glanced quickly over her shoulder. Paul hadn't returned, and none of the café's customers deigned to look her way. Of course they wouldn't—she was just the lowly drudge sent to clean up the mess.

Cecilia quickly peeled the bills from the tile floor and wrapped them in a small piece of rag before shoving them into the pocket of her apron. The money would be enough to buy bread at the bakery, and fixings for a proper dinner for herself and her mother. It'd be their first real meal in several days.

The check for the coffees was disintegrating in a puddle of coffee and porcelain, and she pushed it into the dustpan where it fell into sodden, illegible pieces.

She cleaned up the mess as quickly as she could, running a rag over the floor in long swipes. A pain shot through her finger and she gasped, dropping the rag. Blood welled from her fingertip, dripping onto the tile.

"Here." A slim hand with crimson nails held a white handkerchief in front of Cecilia's face. Cecilia took it and wrapped the cloth around her fingers.

"Thank y—" she began, glancing up. The words trailed away. A young woman, perhaps four or five years older than her, stood there, perfectly turned out in a cream-colored drop waist dress and pearls, over which she wore a wool coat with a fur collar. Red hair peeked out from under her cloche and her gray eyes were framed by dark lashes. She looked like a movie star from one of the pictures Cecilia had seen in a magazine.

"You're welcome," the woman said. She bent closer and Cecilia caught a hint of her perfume, a musky jasmine scent. "Next time be more careful."

"Yes ma'am, I will," Cecilia replied. The woman smiled, a slight lifting of the corners of her reddened lips.

"If you're going to steal the tab, you'll need to be more subtle," the woman replied, her voice dropping to a whisper. Cecilia felt her cheeks heat in embarrassment and her stomach roiled with nerves. The woman gave her a wink and straightened.

Cecilia stared as the woman strolled to the door, joining a pair of girls who waited for her. They left the café, piling into a black Packard touring car that idled at the curb. Before the driver closed the door, the red-haired woman looked right at her. A small, secret smile flittered across her features. The car door swung shut.

Cecilia dropped her gaze back to the floor. The rags had soaked up nearly all the coffee and she gave them a half-hearted swipe before placing them onto the dustpan. She picked up the broom, careful not to dislodge the handkerchief, and carried the mess back to the garbage.

Paul came out of his small office, now neatly attired in a fresh shirt and vest, as she dumped the pan's contents into the garbage bin. He seemed calm.

"Is it clean?" he asked. She nodded, propping the broom and dustpan in the corner of the galley kitchen. Standing at the sink, she turned on the cold water and unwrapped the handkerchief. Paul leaned in as she held her bloodied fingers under the tap. "Whose is that?" he asked, looking at the handkerchief.

"I don't know. A woman gave it to me." She held out the crumpled bit of cloth and he took it from her, spreading it out to reveal a delicate monogram stitched in light blue thread in one corner. *NP*.

"Rich? And red haired?" he asked. When she nodded, he looked gratified. "That's Miss Prescott. She told me she came here because our salads rival those at the Edgewater."

"Oh, I see." It didn't matter to her that Paul was obsessed with attracting a more sophisticated crowd by aping the pretentious meals served at the Edgewater hotel, but now she had the young woman's name. Miss Prescott. She hoped Miss Prescott would come back.

"Did you find the money in that mess?" Paul asked. She started.

"No, I didn't see it," she said lamely. She tried not to stiffen and kept her attention on her fingers, gently rubbing away the blood. Paul cursed under his breath about thieving customers and tossed the handkerchief down on the counter before striding out into the café. Cecilia turned off the water and reached for the handkerchief, bringing it up to her nose. When she breathed in, she could just catch a whiff of perfume. She wanted to see Miss Prescott again.

❖

"You still hanging round here?"

Patrick Sheridan looked up from where he sat on the steps of an old tenement, a cigarette dangling from his lips. He smiled. "What do you think? Unlike you, Dooley, I haven't found my racket."

No matter whether he was in New York or Chicago, the street was the same one he'd always been on: filthy, crowded, the poor mixed with the desperate. He wasn't desperate, but that was only a matter of another day or two.

Dooley stood out from the rest, wearing a three-piece brown suit. It made Sheridan feel as if he were indeed the poor relation. His dark trousers and white shirt had seen better days, and his woolen coat had a patched elbow and a rent in the sleeve. He knew he looked as poor as he was, nearly as filthy as all the rest. He had three days' worth of dark unshaven beard and it was a wonder Dooley had recognized him. He had just enough cash to last him until the end of the week, but he'd have to find something soon.

"How'd you like to make some money?" Dooley asked, hooking his thumbs in his belt.

"Doing what?"

"Friend of mine could use a guy like you. It's lifting boxes, but it'll be steady. Maybe you could get yourself out of this shithole."

Dooley wrinkled his nose as he gazed down the street, and Sheridan knew Dooley was seeing his own past as well as the sagging tenement houses with laundry draped on fire escapes and hung from windows. A couple of homeless fellows stood around a barrel that smoked, warming their hands on the burning garbage. The air was rank from the stockyards to the south. It had been his neighborhood once, but no more.

"Whereabouts?" Sheridan asked. He could make a few bucks, and if it turned out to be lousy, he could skip out.

"It's on North Clark, near the Old Rose Distillery," Dooley replied. "You'll be working for a fellow named Sal."

"Thanks, pal. Why me?"

Dooley shrugged, taking a cigarette case from his pocket. "Figured you wouldn't be too proud to refuse. And you're one of the few who didn't kick the shit out of me in juvie." He laughed, but it was a tight sound, not joyous at all.

Sheridan remembered Dooley then, the skinny one, always picked on. He'd been smart, but it hadn't made him any friends. Of their entire cohort of delinquents, he was the only one who'd ever got out and into someplace nicer.

"I wouldn't have come back here, if I'd done as well as you," Sheridan replied.

"Neither would I, but my mother's too stubborn to move," Dooley said with a snort of disgust. "But since I'm here, whaddya say?"

"Much obliged." Sheridan flicked the butt of his cigarette into the street. He rose and came down the steps to shake Dooley's hand. Dooley patted him on the back, an incongruous gesture given that Sheridan was half a foot taller and easily outweighed him.

"You'll be working with dagos," Dooley confided as they moved down the street toward the nicer end, away from the worst of the filth. Dooley's mother lived on the second floor of one of the better-kept buildings in the area.

"If I have to," Sheridan said, "but a job's a job. And anyway, I wouldn't work with the North Side gang again. Not after what they did to me."

"Now that O'Banion's dead, they'll be as good as useless," Dooley agreed. "The Italians run everything on the South Side, anyway. Sometimes I think we'd do better in New York, around more of our own."

Sheridan chuckled. "Thought about it, but never had enough coin to get there. And after that last spell in the clink, definitely not. Got an uncle there, and a couple of cousins."

Dooley paused outside the door. He held out his hand. "Been good seeing you. Be sure you get there by eight o'clock. I'll tell Sal to look out for you."

Sheridan shook Dooley's hand firmly. "Thanks for the favor. See you around?"

Dooley grinned. "I'll stop by. Gotta give us micks an edge in the South somehow."

❖

Cecilia hunched her shoulders and tucked her work-roughened hands into the pockets of her jacket. The weather had turned cold and the wool of her jacket was worn thin in places. The wind sliced through the fabric, chilling her to the bone. She caught glimpses of the setting sun between buildings when she crossed the many streets on her way home, but it wasn't enough to warm her.

She held tight to the two dollars in her pocket as she crossed into the district south of the Union stockyard. The smell of penned cattle and manure filled the air, but she hardly noticed it anymore. Every once in a while the scent reminded her of the farm, but out there it was cleaner, nicer somehow. Her ma's hired hand had kept the barn clean. She wanted to go back, sit under the apple tree and read, but that was gone now, and she was stuck here. She glanced over her shoulder as she walked. Some of the tenement gangs wouldn't hesitate to take what they thought was their due, especially when the light was fading.

If only she'd had time to reach the bakery before it closed. Her mouth watered at the thought of a warm, fresh loaf of bread. In her dreams, she'd spread a thick slice with creamy butter, like the kind her mother used to make. She went past the dark bakery and the small tailor's shop, and crossed over West Forty-Seventh Street, heading south. The tenement houses here were weathered and sagging, worse than their counterparts to the east, but it was all she and her mother could afford.

Cecilia trudged up the creaking stairs of the old house. The air inside the wooden building was a mix of smoke and cooking smells, and her stomach growled. When she reached the third floor, she unlocked the door to number twelve and pushed inside.

A low light burned within and her mother sat slumped on their one upholstered chair, her face lined and pale. She coughed into her handkerchief.

"How was work?" she asked, her voice raspy.

Cecilia took her time hanging up her jacket on the peg by the door. She took the money and the fine cotton handkerchief from the pockets, tucking the handkerchief into the pocket of her dress. She went to the small sink, reaching for the old tobacco tin on the shelf above.

"There's soup," her mother continued, "and day-old bread. I was able to get the last loaf from Mrs. Wharton at the bakery before they closed."

"Thanks, Ma," Cecilia replied. "I made a few tips at work today. It was a good day." It was a lie, but her mother didn't need to know where the money had come from. Paul hardly paid her enough to survive on, and he didn't need those two dollars like they did. She took down the tin and pried open the lid, intending to put the money in and add to their meager savings.

The tin was empty.

She turned, tin in hand. "Ma, what happened? I thought we had money."

Her mother sighed and rose from the chair, shuffling to the bed to unfold her nightgown. She smoothed the thick material with a gnarled hand. "I didn't get paid today—they're late again—and the landlord was by for the rent." Slowly, as if the movement cost her great effort, she began to undress, carefully folding her clothes.

"I'll have to make more," Cecilia said. She put the money into the tin and replaced it on the shelf. She went to the woodstove and served herself a bowl of soup. At the small kitchen table, the bread lay atop the checkered grease-paper tablecloth, and she cut herself a slice, dipping it into the soup to soften the hard crust.

"Will you get a chance to waitress instead of just washing dishes, now that you've been there awhile?" her mother asked. She sat on the bed and took down her graying hair, brushing it out carefully for one hundred strokes. She did it every night without fail.

"Doubt he'll let me, even though he could use the help." Cecilia thought of the tips she could earn, the money she could bring home. She knew she could do as good a job as he did with the customers, better even. She pushed the remainder of the bread slice into the last few drops of her soup.

"He'll let you," her mother said confidently. "When you come to bed don't forget to turn out the lamp. We'll need to get more kerosene this week."

"Yes, Ma." Cecilia took her bowl to the sink and washed and dried it before putting it away. She was tired, but she didn't want to go to bed just yet. She took up her mother's copy of Byron's poems and settled into the chair, bringing the lamp close. It wasn't the apple tree, but it would do.

She squinted in the dim light. The book fell open to a familiar page, the poem she always read. *She walks in beauty, like the night / Of cloudless climes and starry skies, / And all that's best of dark and bright / Meet in her aspect and her eyes...* Gray eyes under dark lashes. She let the book fall into her lap and leaned back, resting her head on the back of the chair. The stuffing there had flattened from years of use and she could feel the wood underneath the upholstery.

Miss Prescott wouldn't be spending her evening in a tenement room, Cecilia thought. She'd be out dancing, or at home in a cozy and well-heated apartment, where a maid cooked her dinner and turned down the bedcovers. Did she think of today at all? Would she remember?

Cecilia rose without reading the rest of the poem. She knew it by heart. There was no point in thinking of that woman. She was rich, and Cecilia herself was no better than a maid. Cecilia changed into her nightgown and put out the light before crawling under the covers. She fell asleep, dreaming of that small, secret smile on those red lips.

CHAPTER TWO

Sheridan stood in front of the warehouse door at a few minutes to eight. He knocked. And waited. Just as he thought to knock again, the door swung inward. A man, gone to seed, with a shock of gray hair and dark eyebrows looked him over. His suit jacket hung open and Sheridan wondered if it would close over his protruding belly, but his shirt was clean and pressed, pristine. Looked like a rich fellow that should be out schmoozing in some fancy hotel. Must be the owner, Sal.

"You the one Dooley sent?" the man asked, his words thickly accented. Sheridan held out his hand.

"Patrick Sheridan, sir."

The man gave the briefest of shakes. "Salvatore di Benedetto," he replied. "Just Sal to you. Come along."

Sal led him through a short corridor, past an office where a man sat smoking a cigarette and looking through a ledger, and into the warehouse proper. A truck stood, its back doors open, empty and ready. A lean dark-haired man in worn coveralls stood nearby, sizing up an extensive pile of boxes that stretched to the far wall.

"This here's Angelo. He'll show you what to do. Lunch break at twelve, and you're free to go at five." Sal returned to the office, leaving him with the surly looking Angelo.

"So you're the Paddy," Angelo said derisively. He pointed to the truck. "When that's full, we'll do the next, and so on. Not much to it."

Sheridan shucked his coat, hanging it on a hook by the door. He rolled up his sleeves as Angelo had done.

"It's Sheridan," he corrected. Angelo shrugged.

Sheridan strode over to the nearest stack of crates. "Which first?"

Angelo pointed at three stacks nearest to Sheridan.

"Those ones. And be quick about it, Paddy." He strolled over to talk to the truck driver in Italian, leaving Sheridan to work.

❖

By lunch, Sheridan was ravenous and he didn't think the meat pie he'd bought from a street vendor nearby would be enough. Angelo had helped him with a few crates, just enough to make a show for Sal, leaving most of the work for Sheridan.

He passed the office on his way back to the floor and paused just beyond when a raised voice caught his attention.

"The speakeasies on State will buy from us or they'll regret it. I'll have the boys round."

"There's new owners, they don't know how it is." He recognized Sal's voice.

"Be ready for fifty cases to go out for them tomorrow," the other voice said. "Cap'll take care of them tonight."

Sheridan sucked in a breath. Before he could move, Sal came into the corridor. His dark brows rose and he gestured for Sheridan to go ahead of him.

Sheridan obeyed, tensely waiting for a shot to ring out. He'd overheard, and he knew too much.

❖

Cecilia gathered the dirty dishes onto her tray, carefully stacking the cups and saucers, arranging the porcelain to carry as much as she could. The check still lay on the table and the customers had paid in a pile of small change. The total came to just under a dollar and they had left a dollar in quarters and five nickels.

With quick fingers, she scooped up the check and the change, setting it on the tray, but letting one of the quarters slide under the edge of her cleaning rag. Paul wouldn't notice and it still left a ten-cent tip. She carried the tray back to the sink, stuffing the rag into her apron pocket. She started to clear the tray. When Paul came by, she gave him the check and the handful of change. He sifted the coins through his fingers and frowned.

"Cheapskates," he muttered, shoving the cash into his pocket. He continued out to the café without stopping. Cecilia pulled out the rag and heard the quarters clink against the change at the bottom of her pocket.

She'd become smarter in the past few days, not wanting a repeat of the first time, where the woman had spotted her theft. She could feel the woman watching her when she came into the café, and she'd held off taking anything else when she was around. But that still left her a few opportunities. Paul didn't seem to notice that some of his tips were smaller than usual, or if he did, he blamed the customers' tightfisted ways. He should know, after all—he was one of the most miserly people she'd ever known.

She scrubbed the dirty cups and saucers in the soapy water, then rinsed and set them in the racks to dry. Her shift was nearly over and she itched to leave. When she got home she'd put the seventy cents she'd managed to lift into the tobacco tin. There were a few dollars' worth of change in there now; her mother hadn't questioned her after she'd fibbed that Paul had started letting her waitress on occasion.

She felt a twinge of guilt for lying to her mother, but her pitiful wage and her mother's small wage from the factory were hardly enough to live on. She wanted out of the tenement, and that wouldn't happen without money.

Cecilia dried her hands on her apron and picked up her tray. She had time for another round of the café before the end of her shift. As she left the back, she heard a laugh and her gaze fastened on the red-haired young woman from the other day. She stood at the door, flirting with Paul, who seemed to soak up the attention like a sponge in water. She tore her gaze away from Miss Prescott and started toward the table she'd been sitting at. The white porcelain cup sat there neatly, red lipstick marring the rim. She placed it on her tray and gathered up the cloth napkin next to it.

A glint of blue from the floor caught her eye. She rested the tray on the table and bent to scoop up the sapphire earring that lay on the tiles. For a moment she was tempted, but she knew she could never go through with it. Not to someone who had been so kind. She hurried over to the door, where Miss Prescott lingered.

"Pardon me," Cecilia said, trying to catch her attention.

Paul gave her a stern look. "You got work to do," he snapped. "Get on with it."

"But—" She held up the earring. Miss Prescott's gloved hand went to her ear.

"Oh my." She gave Cecilia a brilliant smile and reached for the earring. Cecilia caught her breath as their fingers brushed. The white gloves reminded her of the grocer's daughter back home, who'd showed off her Sunday best. She'd been blond, though, with blue eyes and a lazy smile. Cecilia thought she'd been the most beautiful girl ever. Except she hadn't met Miss Prescott then. "Thank you."

Miss Prescott's gaze caught hers, and Cecilia felt her cheeks flush. Paul nudged her aside, monopolizing Miss Prescott's attention once more. If she could, she'd shove him out of the way, and make him go do the dishes. If only she didn't need the money so much.

She turned away and saw that a table of older women had just risen, leaving their dirty dishes on the table.

What a mess, she thought, reaching the table. It had been a large group and a big order—coffees all round and a selection of pastries. Her eyes widened when she saw the check.

A small pile of bills and change sat atop the check. She nudged the dollar bills aside to see the total and realized the party had tipped generously. A dollar would buy her and her mother a good meal. She hesitated, taking a moment to stack the dirty dishes on her tray. Just one wouldn't hurt.

She slid a dollar off the top of the stack and folded it in her hand, tucking it into her palm before continuing to place the dirty teacups onto the tray.

A hand came down on her wrist and the tea cups tinkled against one another as the last cup fell from her hand. She stared up into Paul's angry face. A sick feeling grew in her stomach, twisting and churning.

"So this is how you repay me?" His fingers dug into her wrist and he pulled her away from the table. She dug in her heels but he was far stronger and her resistance made no difference as he dragged her toward the back.

"I'll teach you to steal from me, you little guttersnipe," he barked. "My friends on the force just love beating some sense into little thieves like you."

Paul pulled her into the office and shut the door, shoving her down into a chair.

"Give it up." He held out his hand and she reluctantly dropped the folded dollar into his palm.

"You've made a mistake," she said, but her voice sounded lifeless even to her own ears. She'd be thrown in jail, and then who would take care of her mother?

"Give me the rest." Paul seized her by the shoulder and shook her. "All of it."

Cecilia dug into her apron pocket and brought out the change she'd managed to pilfer earlier that day. Paul snatched up the coins and tossed the cash onto his desk. He lifted the receiver of the black phone.

"You, sit there," he commanded, pointing at her. "And don't you dare move. Hello, yes—give me the police station." He watched her hawkishly and Cecilia twisted her hands in her apron. The distance from the chair to the door was short, but she wouldn't make it far.

"Send me someone over," Paul said into the phone. "I have a thief in my establishment." He listened, then smiled. "Thank you, Officer."

The desk sergeant poked his head around the half-open door. "Finally, someone."

Detective Lang looked up from his file, setting down the witness statements on the Lina Saverino case. Or the drowned prostitute case, as everyone else called it. He had liked Lina; he felt protective of her, of her situation. Her ignominious end was something he wanted to keep hushed as long as he could.

"What is it?" He closed the folder.

"Paul over at the Café Parisien caught one of his staff stealing," the sergeant replied.

"And? Send one of the boys. I'm busy." He laid a hand on the folder.

"There's no one else," the sergeant said, looking sheepish. "They're all on other calls."

Lang sighed and stood, grabbing his trench coat and fedora from the rack. "All right. If Navarra asks, tell him where I've gone." He needed a break and some fresh air. Collaring a little ragamuffin thief would do.

"Of course."

Lang took one of the unmarked cars over to the café. He wasn't in uniform and he hated the attention bystanders gave the marked cars, crowding about as if they were about to see some famous gangster get taken in.

The café was half-full when he walked in, mostly women lingering over cups of tea and coffee. Judging from the bags at their feet, a bunch of rich ladies who'd been out shopping.

Paul came out from the back, carrying a tray of cookies and cakes. "In my office," he said as he passed. "Go on back—I'll be right there."

Lang strolled back past the small kitchen and the sink piled with dishes. He pushed open the office door. He was startled to see the offender was a young woman, slender and dark haired, and very pale. Her hands clutched the spattered white apron she wore and she looked up at him with obvious trepidation.

"So, what did you steal from Paul?" he asked, leaning against the desk. The girl looked down at her hands, her pale cheeks flooding with color. When she didn't answer, he asked again and added, "If you tell me now, I'll see if I can get him to go easy on you."

Her shoulders rose and fell as if she'd taken a deep breath. "I took some of the tips," she said, finally raising her head to look at him. "I was going to use the money to buy food." Her eyes were glassy with unshed tears.

"You could end up in prison," Lang remarked. He knew Paul wouldn't want to go easy on this girl—he wasn't the type. He could be gentlemanly with the ladies that frequented his café, but among the thugs of the area he had a reputation for violence. They respected him for it and as a result he paid much less in protection money. Word had got around about the last lowlife who'd tried to shake him down. Lang knew the police gave him preferential treatment because of it.

Before he could say anything more to the girl, Paul came in, already raring for a fight.

"Take her back to the station and lock her up," Paul said. "I won't have anyone stealing from me, least of all some little girl." He reached over and slapped the girl, who took the hit with more courage than Lang had expected. Her head rocked back but she glared at Paul, even as the tears spilled down her cheeks. Paul moved to slap her again but Lang raised his hand.

"That's not necessary," he said, staring at Paul until he backed away. "How much did she take?"

"At least twenty dollars. I don't know how long she's been skimming from me," Paul said, moving around the desk to drop into his chair.

Lang glanced at the girl. The imprint of Paul's hand reddened on her cheek. She gazed back at him, still courageous despite the pain.

"What's your name?"

"Cecilia Mills."

"How about you call it even, Paul?" he suggested, reaching out with a careful hand to lift Cecilia's chin and turn her battered cheek toward him. "That slap is enough."

"No." Paul snorted.

Lang sighed. "I'll take her back to the station. Get your things, Miss Mills."

Cecilia stood shakily and he let her precede him from the office. As she took off her apron and gathered up her coat, Lang stood in the door of Paul's office.

"I'll let you know if it goes to trial," he remarked. Paul rose from his chair.

"It'll teach her not to steal," he snapped.

"Of course." Lang took Cecilia by the arm and led her through the café. Some of the patrons turned and stared. Paul followed them to the door. Before he could open it, someone pulled the door open from the outside.

Lang came face-to-face with Nell Prescott.

She was done up in her usual elegance, her hair in a careful twist, wearing a white wool coat that looked brand new and white gloves. Her dress underneath was a dark royal blue and it looked like silk. Did she know about Lina? Did she wonder where Lina was? He wanted to say something, but now was not the time. She hardly noticed him, or his surprise. Her gaze slid past him to Cecilia, and then to Paul.

"What's going on here?" she asked, her voice surprisingly curt.

"Miss Prescott, I didn't expect to see you back here so soon," Paul said ingratiatingly. "Did you want a pastry for later?"

"I saw the detective here," she said. "What is going on?"

"Nothing for you to worry about, Miss Prescott," Paul answered. "The detective's just taking care of a thief on my staff. They'll be out of your way in a moment."

Nell didn't move aside. Rather, she shifted and blocked the doorway. Lang bit back a smile. He'd seen that look on her face before, when she'd been determined to get her way at the Orpheus. He'd known her long enough and knew Paul wouldn't be getting out of this unscathed. But why Nell would put herself out for this girl, he had no idea.

"How much do you pay her?" she asked Paul, her voice sharp. She skewered him with a glare. Paul bristled.

"Enough," he said. Nell gave an unladylike snort.

"I doubt that. How much did she take?"

Lang released Cecilia's arm and the girl shot him a look of surprise.

"Paul says she took twenty dollars," Lang informed Nell, who dug into her purse and pulled out a trim leather wallet.

"Here." She held out a twenty-dollar bill toward Paul. It looked dirty in her pristinely gloved hand.

Paul tried to refuse the cash. "That's not the point," he blustered.

Lang's brow rose and Nell winked at him.

"Double, then?" she asked Paul. She took another bill from her wallet. Cecilia stared at her in bewilderment.

"Well, I suppose we could let bygones be bygones," Paul said, trying to sound magnanimous. "You're such a good customer, after all. Detective, let her go—this time."

"You're too kind." Nell's tone was dry.

Paul took the money and Nell glanced at Lang and then at Cecilia. "Shall we?" She turned on her heel. Lang followed her out, taking Cecilia by the arm when she didn't move.

"You're lucky," Lang remarked to her. She nodded, though her gaze was fixed on Nell.

"Want to come for coffee with us, Detective?" Nell asked with a laugh. Lang checked his watch.

"I have places to be," he said. An image of Lina's sodden corpse flashed through his mind. He couldn't tell her, not yet.

❖

"I don't like snoops," Sal remarked. He dropped a hand on Sheridan's shoulder as they emerged into the warehouse.

"No, sir." Sheridan bit out his reply, his entire body tense, wanting to flee.

"Sit down." He indicated a crate. Sheridan sat and Sal took a seat across from him after waving Angelo away. Angelo climbed up into the cab of the last truck for the day and they watched him pull out, hearing the gears grind as he shifted. Sal winced.

"Stupid boy." He shook his head.

"You're not going to kill me, are you?" Sheridan had to know. No point in prevaricating.

Sal threw back his head and laughed. "No, Irish, I'm not. I'd rather you stayed on. You're a better worker than Angelo, and you're honest at that." He gave Sheridan a hard stare. "But you need to also be able to keep your mouth shut."

"Yes, sir."

Sal seemed satisfied with that. He pulled a roll of bills from his jacket pocket and Sheridan tried not to gape. Sal held more money than Sheridan had ever had in his life.

Sal noticed his surprise. "This business is very profitable," he said, undoing the rubber band and counting out a dozen bills. "Prove yourself to me, and one day you could be the one with the full pocket." He held out the bills, waiting patiently for Sheridan to take them.

"Thank you, sir."

"Just Sal. Save the scraping for Capone, or his lieutenants." He chuckled.

Sheridan folded the bills and closed his hand over the cash.

"Go on," Sal said, rising. "Same time tomorrow."

Sheridan grabbed his coat from its hook and slung it on, shoving his fist into one pocket. He knew exactly what he wanted. Instead of heading straight back to his room, he stopped in at a tailor—Evans—that he'd spied on his daily walk. He eyed the clothes in the window before he went inside. A bell jangled over his head.

"What can I do for you?" An older man came out from the back room, his clothes covered in a long smock. His hair had been slicked back and a pair of spectacles perched on his beaky nose. From under the smock, a pair of wingtip shoes gleamed.

"I need a suit," Sheridan said simply.

"Indeed you do," the man remarked dryly, stepping around him, eagle eyes taking in his worn clothes. "And soon."

"Do you have anything that I can have right away?"

"I'll measure you, and we'll see." The man led the way into the back room, a large workroom with several suits in various states of completion.

"I have a nice brown serge that would fit you," the tailor said as he took Sheridan's measurements, noting them in a ledger. "The man who ordered it never came back for it."

"Only brown?" It seemed so sensible a color, and he wanted something remarkable.

"It'll do you for now," the tailor replied. "Unless you want to order a second?"

"Brown will do." He couldn't afford another, not just yet.

The tailor bustled about, pulling a suit from a large closet that ran along the back wall. From what Sheridan could see, it did look to be about his size, but then, he was no tailor.

"New job?" The tailor turned back.

"Is it obvious?"

"Easy guess. Now take those off, and we'll see how well this fits." He waited until Sheridan had stripped down to his underclothes. His nose wrinkled. "For another few dollars I'll make sure you have some new cotton undershirts."

Sheridan pulled on the trousers and buttoned them up. They sagged at the waist, but the bottom hem lay perfectly around his ankles.

"Not bad," the tailor mused. "Now the jacket."

The jacket felt bulky, and Sheridan knew immediately that it would need more adjustment.

"Must have been a big fellow," he remarked to the tailor as he waited for the man to make more notes in his ledger.

"He was. Not a very nice one either." The tailor unbuttoned the front of the jacket and slipped his hand over the seams before turning the edge out. He eyed the lining. "This will take a few days. One of my girls will make the adjustments."

Sheridan took off the jacket and handed it to the tailor, then stripped off the trousers and laid them flat on the worktable. He got back into his regular things, already missing the feel of the serge.

"When should I come back?" he asked.

"Friday."

They returned to the front of the shop and the tailor figured the total on a pad of paper. "I'll let you have it on a discount since I've had it so long. Thirty dollars."

Sheridan counted out the money and handed it over. He had just enough left to pay his rent on the room and buy some food, but soon he wouldn't have to look like he was tenement born—he could stroll around in his new suit just like Dooley. He'd move to a better part of town, meet women…

He shook the tailor's hand and left the shop, grinning to himself. He was getting ahead of things, but he was on his way up, he knew it.

❖

"Now that's settled," said Miss Prescott, "you need to come with me for a cup of coffee. I've not seen you all week." She took Cecilia's arm and they left the detective behind.

"But—" Cecilia protested in a low tone, even as she let Miss Prescott lead her away. The absurdity of it made her laugh.

"Hush. We don't want Paul to change his mind," she said, pulling them into a small café. "I've glimpsed you for several weeks, working too hard and likely not getting paid what you're worth. And I'm Nell Prescott, by the way. Pleased to meet you."

A waiter came to take their order. "Two coffees," Nell said and Cecilia didn't think to object. She had no money to pay for a coffee, but she couldn't say no to Nell, not now.

"Do you always go around helping the less fortunate?" All the clothes Cecilia had on, in fact, her entire wardrobe, weren't worth even the shoes Nell wore. She didn't want to admit it, but Nell's poise and confidence intimidated her.

"Hardly ever, but I thought you deserved a hand up." Nell grinned. "The detective would never say no to me, you see. He knows better."

The waiter brought their coffees in stark white cups and saucers, along with a plate containing a small pitcher of cream, a sugar bowl, and a selection of biscuits.

"He's related to you?" Cecilia asked.

Nell's laughter was as bright as her presence. "Not at all. But I know some people."

Cecilia's brow furrowed as she tried to decipher the meaning. Who did she know?

"So, do tell me your name," Nell said as she pulled off her gloves and set them on the table. She poured cream into her coffee and added a heaping spoonful of sugar. "It's only polite that I know the lovely girl I've saved from Paul's clutches."

"Cecilia Mills."

"That's all? Nothing about yourself?"

"What is there to say? I'm not very interesting." Cecilia copied Nell's movements and readied her own coffee.

"Not true. Start with why you're working at that café. Is there no sweetheart to take care of you?"

There had been boys, but none that interested her very much. "No sweetheart. And I need the job because I need the money." She didn't want to admit where she and her mother lived. Surely Nell had never seen a tenement house with its cold and dingy rooms, or had mice scurry over her pillow. "But why help me?"

Nell leaned forward. "I like you," she whispered almost

conspiratorially. "I want to get to know you." She gave Cecilia another wink as flirty as the first. Cecilia felt herself flush. Surely Nell was teasing her.

"I'll bore you."

"I doubt that. You're different." Nell brushed the top of Cecilia's hand, the delicate touch making Cecilia tremble.

"Not so different," she stammered.

"Beautiful," Nell murmured.

A group of girls bustled into the café, chattering loudly. Nell frowned and moved back. Cecilia felt a pang of disappointment. With just the two of them in the café, it had been their own little world.

Nell laid down some change from her purse, enough for both coffees. "Let's split," she said. "I can't hear myself think in here."

Once outside, she took Cecilia's arm. "My place is nearby."

Her place was like nothing Cecilia had ever seen. The uniformed doorman nodded to them and the elevator boy tipped his cap as he deposited them on the third floor. Nell pulled a key from her purse and opened the door, leading Cecilia into a richly decorated sitting room.

A brilliantly colored rug covered the floor and Cecilia paused at the edge, not wanting to ruin something so beautiful by treading upon it. She didn't even want to sit on the brocaded sofa. A girl like her didn't belong here; she knew she'd long to see such opulence once she went home to her tiny room.

Nell took off her jacket and tossed it negligently over the back of the sofa.

"Don't be shy," she said, striding through the door and into a small kitchen, the heels of her black Mary Janes clicking on the parquet floor.

Cecilia unbuttoned her jacket but didn't take it off. She moved hesitantly to the kitchen entryway, glancing down at her much-repaired shoes. The toes were starting to look scuffed and she needed to polish them to hide the wear.

"Do you want a proper drink?" Without waiting for an answer, Nell poured liquor into two delicate glasses. She gave one to Cecilia, who sipped it cautiously. "It's sherry."

Cecilia took another sip. The sweet stickiness filled her mouth and she savored the taste, her tongue darting out to catch the drops on her top lip. She glanced up from her glass and found Nell watching her.

"What is it?" Was she doing something wrong?

"Just you." Nell caught at Cecilia's free hand, pulling her closer. "You're beautiful."

Cecilia opened her mouth to object, but Nell's soft mouth brushed hers and she froze, uncertainty overriding her desire to kiss back.

Nell stopped, pulling away. "I thought surely..." she began, frowning.

Cecilia found her voice. "I just didn't expect it." She closed the distance between them, angling her face up to Nell, who stood several inches taller.

Nell cupped Cecilia's cheeks. Her hands were soft, hands that didn't have to clean or work, hands that knew nothing beyond their life of ease.

"I kept seeing you, but I couldn't think of how to make myself known until today." Nell kissed her again, and this time Cecilia let herself relax and respond. Nell tasted of sherry and Cecilia thought she would never get enough of those soft lips, the tongue that teased and touched, fluttering in her mouth.

They broke apart, breathing heavily. Cecilia hadn't felt this way since she'd first realized she could give herself pleasure. Her fingers had clutched at Nell's curves during their kiss and she loosened her grasp on the light silk of Nell's dress.

Nell took the glass from Cecilia and pushed her jacket off her shoulders. It fell to the floor. Nell's hand on her breast was gentle, caressing, and Cecilia leaned into the touch.

The door buzzer rang and they parted abruptly. Cecilia's heart pounded.

"Damn it." Nell said some other words that Cecilia had only ever heard the roughest of men use. Nell stalked toward the door. Cecilia gathered her coat from the floor and slipped it on, trailing behind Nell.

Nell tugged open the heavy door, revealing a dark-haired man whose smooth olive skin was broken only by a scar that ran across his forehead near his hairline. His thin lips parted in an amused smile.

"We're going to be late, my dear," he said, stepping inside. He gave Nell a kiss and Cecilia's spirits sank. Here was Nell's real love. "Who's your friend?"

"Cecilia, this is Franky. Franky, this is Cecilia."

Franky looked her over and she felt as if he'd undressed her with his eyes.

"I should be going," Cecilia said, edging around him to the door. "It was nice to meet you." She buttoned her coat as she went.

"You could come with us," Franky offered, catching her arm. She looked at Nell.

"I'll see you soon," Nell told her, giving her a reassuring smile. He let go of her arm and Cecilia returned the smile.

"See you."

As the door closed behind her, she heard Franky chuckle and Nell's answering laugh. She wanted to go back in and demand her time with Nell, but she didn't dare. Nell already had a sweetheart. She was the outsider here.

CHAPTER THREE

"Whaddya think I am, a miracle worker?" The coroner strode into the morgue, leaving Detective Lang to follow. "I have a body from some damned brawl, two gangsters from the South Side, one little old lady, and the chief on my back. Your little girl is gonna have to wait."

"Can't you just take a look?" Lang asked. He wished he'd had a coffee with Nell and her beneficiary now. He rubbed his eyes.

"Look, Detective, you know as well as I do that she died from strangulation. The bruises on her neck—hell, her broken neck—all point that way. Probably her boyfriend did it. Now scram—I got work to do."

"She didn't have a boyfriend."

The coroner snorted. "You sure? Why don't you go ask some questions. Come back sometime next week—I might have something for you then."

Lang retreated the way he'd come, leaving the cloying smell of the morgue behind. When he got out into the street he took a deep breath. A marked police car idled at the curb and he opened the door.

"Back to the river, Jones," he said.

"What do you expect to find?" Jones asked as he put the car into gear. "The boys have been over the place and they talked to the neighbors. They got nothing."

"I saw the statements. They weren't trying hard enough."

Chastised, Jones kept his eyes on the road. When they reached the crime scene, he pulled over and killed the engine.

"You search the bank," Lang commanded. He eyed the apartment building across the street. Someone had to have seen something. He strode across the street and entered the lobby. The superintendent, a middle-aged woman with droopy eyes, gave him a curious look.

"I'd like to talk to your tenants," he said.

"What for?" She eyed him with suspicion now. He sighed and produced his badge, flashing it for her perusal.

"I'll start with the apartments facing the river," he said and started toward the stairs.

"Your boys already came through here," she called after him, but he was already climbing to the second floor.

There was no answer at the first door, but the name slot over the buzzer was empty. He put an ear to the door. Nothing stirred. He continued down the corridor.

At the next door, he heard footsteps in answer to his knock and saw the momentary flash of darkness over the peephole. The door creaked open half an inch and stopped, the inner chain going taut. A pale eye in a mottled face stared back at him.

"I'd like to ask you a few questions."

The eye glanced down at his badge, and up again to his face. "I ain't talking to you, copper." The door slammed shut and he heard the chain rattle. He pounded on the door.

"Buzz off, copper!"

"Bastard," Lang muttered to himself, making a note of the number on the door. He'd check the statements later for that one.

The next door read *Kowalsky*. He buzzed and waited. He was about to buzz again when he heard the shuffle of feet and the scrape of a bolt being drawn back. The door swung open to reveal an elderly lady hunched over her cane, her wispy white hair framing a delicate face. Her rheumy eyes took him in.

"What do you want?"

He went through his usual introduction and she waved him inside.

"You're much nicer than those young officers that came around the other day," she remarked as she settled into a brocade armchair.

"Mrs. Kowalsky, did you see anything on the night in question?" Lang asked, drawing a high-backed chair from her small dining table.

She gave him a cautious glance. "It's not safe to see anything, Detective," she said. "You know that."

"Can you give me anything at all?" Lang asked, leaning forward in his chair. "Completely off the record?"

She paused, her gaze drifting toward the window, where the weak sunlight filtered through the lacy drapes.

"I had trouble sleeping," she said. "And I got out of bed and came to the kitchen to get a glass of water. Didn't turn the light on—I know this place like the back of my hand.

"Anyway, I went back to bed, but there was a screech, like someone hit their brakes too hard—you know the sound. I can just see out my windows without pulling the drapes, and I saw a dark car out there, about a block down. Can't tell you what sort—they all look alike to me. Not like the old days where I could tell you about horses." She smiled.

"Did you see anyone get out of the car?"

"Couldn't see well enough to know who, but the one fellow was carrying something. I saw a flash of white, or so I thought."

"Anything else?"

She shrugged, looking at him once more. "Detective, it's hard to see at night. And you know as well as I do that if even this got out, I'd be in trouble. I need this place. My husband owned it and I haven't got any family. I don't want to rock the boat."

Lang rose. Someone had been here with Lina's body—it had to have been. "Thank you, Mrs. Kowalsky," he said, taking her hand. "I won't say a word."

"You won't get much help out of anyone else," she observed. "They're mostly gone to work at this time of day."

She showed him to the door, and he found himself out in the dim corridor once again. He knocked on all the other doors in the row, but it was as she'd said. He went up the stairs to the next floor, but there was no answer at any of the doors.

He went back downstairs and saw Jones waiting for him by the car.

"Anything?"

"Nope," Jones replied. "Where to now?"

"Back to the station."

❖

"I'll need you longer today," Sal told Sheridan as Sheridan loaded a box onto the bed of a small truck. "I'm short a hand for the Orpheus delivery."

"All right." Sheridan wiped his forehead with a faded handkerchief. His workday had nearly ended, but he wanted this chance to show Sal he could do something other than lug boxes.

"Good lad." When he was pleased, Sal often spoke to Sheridan as if he were still a youngster. Sheridan didn't mind, but he knew it rankled Angelo, who never received such gentility from Sal. "The truck's waiting outside. Tony's driving and he'll tell you what's to be done."

Sheridan pulled on his jacket and went to find Tony. He could hear Angelo jabbering away in Italian to Sal, and he didn't sound happy. When he climbed into the truck's cab, Tony gave him a nod.

"Angelo not coming?"

Sheridan could hardly understand him, talking in heavily accented English around the butt of a thick cigar.

"Sal sent me," he replied. Tony shrugged.

The truck trundled down the street, shuddering and clanking as Tony shifted gears. Soon they'd come into the area just north of the Levee, idling in the rush of traffic. Tony muttered to himself, leaning over the steering wheel and peering up the street. When the traffic shifted, he made a sharp right into an alleyway. Brick walls enclosed them and Tony drove slowly, finally shuddering to a stop in front of a nondescript metal door. He honked the horn and the door flew open.

"About time," hollered a man from the stoop. He was dressed in a fine suit, and his undone tie dangled about his neck. Something about him seemed familiar, but Sheridan couldn't place him. "Bring it in."

"Unload as fast as you can," Tony said. "The boss don't like stragglers."

Sheridan leapt down from the cab and set to work, opening the back door and hauling the first box to the edge. Tony joined him, and Sheridan followed the man into the back of the club. A clatter of dishes came through a swinging door, but they turned to the right, coming to the top of a staircase. The man from the stoop waited at the bottom, propping open the door to a large storage room.

"In here," he said, quite unnecessarily. As Sheridan passed him, he snuck a glance. The man was olive skinned, with dark, hard eyes. His mouth was fixed in a contemptuous smile, and a silvered scar ran across his forehead. That scar gave him away. Sheridan knew exactly why the man had seemed so familiar. It was a memory he would never forget. Flames flashed in front of his eyes, and he could still hear the screams, smell the smoke that had billowed from the old wooden-frame house. His whole life had gone up in that moment.

Tony nudged his back with the edge of the box he carried, and Sheridan picked up his pace.

After they'd placed the first boxes inside and gone back upstairs, Tony thumbed toward the door.

"Get the rest," he said. "I need to have a chat with Franky."

Sheridan lugged box after box of liquor from the truck to the storeroom. He caught bits of the conversation between Tony and Franky, enough to work out that business was picking up daily and Tony would be providing more deliveries.

"I'll see how sales go, but we'll need double this, I expect." Franky lit a cigarette and shook hands with Tony. Sheridan waited, doffing his cap to blot at his forehead. His arms ached and his legs wanted to shake from climbing and descending the stairs, but he kept his knees locked. He wouldn't ever show weakness.

"Franky, are you done yet?" came a strong feminine voice. A curvaceous redhead flounced into view, and Sheridan couldn't help looking her over, from the tips of her black patent-leather heels, up her slim, stocking-clad legs, and over the sequined dress that dipped low in the front, revealing her pale cleavage.

Franky drew her close. "Almost done, baby," he said, his tone relaxed

She glanced at the two other men with disinterest, then back to Franky. She pouted.

"You're always so busy," she said.

"I'll have a dance for you," he replied and gave her derriere an affectionate pat. "Now, go on. Make sure all the girls are ready."

"All right." She continued to pout.

"You know I rely on you," he added.

"Of course you do." She gave him a brilliant smile and sauntered down the hallway. Franky watched her go and Sheridan thought his bemused smile was an affectation for her sake. When Franky turned back, his eyes were hard, and his disdain became apparent.

"Women," he muttered, taking a drag of his cigarette. He gave them a wave. "I'll call if I change the order."

"Of course." Tony headed for the door. "Come on, Paddy."

Sheridan replaced his cap and went out to the truck.

"That's Franky Greco," Tony said as they drove away. "He's got the ear of the big boss, so make sure you treat him well."

"Right."

Sheridan's reply must have sounded too casual for Tony's taste, but he knew exactly who Franky was, and it took all he was worth not to head back in and strangle the man.

"If you piss him off, he's mean as a viper," Tony added. "And don't go fancying his girl Nell, either. Last man who did that ended up in Lake Michigan." He guffawed. "She led him on a pretty chase though, the fool."

"She's not my type," Sheridan replied.

"Sure she isn't. The way you were looking at her, she'd be your type if you could."

Sheridan snorted. "I'd like to stay dry."

Tony chuckled, tapping his hands on the steering wheel as he drove. He turned into the lane and pulled up behind the warehouse. "Good night, Paddy."

Sheridan climbed down from the cab and watched Tony drive away. He buttoned his jacket and cursed the rent in the wool that let the chill night wind cut through the fabric.

The Orpheus. One day he'd be there, dressed elegantly like Franky had been, with a woman like Nell hanging off his arm. He'd be better for her than that dago.

He couldn't forget the vicious, nasty boy Franky had been, and now the man was just as bad. Franky had been responsible for his stint in juvie, but that wasn't even the worst of it. To get back at a defeat from the gang Sheridan had joined as a boy, Franky had burned their meeting place to the ground. They'd met in the basement, below his mother's small apartment.

They'd fought, as the house burned and his mother screamed. He'd managed to defeat the older boy, finally striking him across the forehead with a board, but he'd been too late to save his family.

One day. Franky would regret what he'd done.

❖

"Any leads on that drowned prostitute?"

Lang sat back in his chair, lighting a cigarette while he considered his words. His boss, Vince Navarra, a short and balding man who was firmly in Capone's pocket, waited impatiently.

"Nothing new, but you know as well as I do that she wasn't drowned," Lang said finally.

Navarra snorted. "You've never been able to lie to me, Lang," he said. He'd worked with Lang since he'd been a beat cop and knew him better than anyone.

"I know who she is," he said. "I would pursue it, but the public won't care anyway. One more fallen woman, after all."

"You didn't tell me that before," Navarra snapped. He leaned forward. "So, who is she, and how long have you known?"

"Lina Saverino. That's why."

Navarro swore. "Have you told Miss Prescott yet?"

Of course Navarra would know about Nell and Lina's association. Something wasn't right. Lina shouldn't have been in the river; she was too well-known for that. Something—no, someone—had to have happened.

"No. Not until I knew more."

"Don't tell her."

"Why not?"

"She's a woman. They get emotional." He shrugged. "Tell Franky Greco first. He can decide how far this goes, and he'll be glad we've kept this hush."

Lang looked up from where he'd been brushing cigarette ash from his trousers. "Will he now?"

"Of course he will. He likes a heads-up."

"You've told him already."

"I haven't. But that's your job." Navarra made a sour face. "The less I have to deal with him on this, the better. Tell him, Lang, and then her body can be moved from the morgue and open up some space." He waved a hand, dismissing him.

"Whatever you say, boss. Anyway, Miss Prescott's moved on, found another girl." Lang rose. He hadn't missed the slight shudder of fear. Navarra dreaded disappointing Franky, more than any other gangster he'd done business with. Torrio at least had been predictable, wanting results from his graft. Franky, on the other hand, played by his own rules, just like Torrio's successor, Capone, and they deviated from Torrio's with deadly effect.

"Has she now? Well, she's always had another on the string, from what I've heard. Still, don't tell her," Navarra warned. "I don't want her in my office in tears."

Lang nodded. There was more to this, and Navarra knew. "What have you heard?"

"Nothing." His expression gave nothing away, except Lang knew him well enough to know that face only came out when he knew more than he was letting on. He was paid not to know. So much for cops being defenders of the weak, and of the truth. Bastard. "Make sure this doesn't get out. Last thing I need is the papers and Greco breathing down my neck."

"I'll let you know how it goes with Franky." He slammed the door behind him, taking some satisfaction from hearing the noise echo in the hallway.

CHAPTER FOUR

Cecilia lingered outside the shop window, her hands bundled into the pockets of her threadbare coat. Light snow dusted the ground and a crisp breeze slipped through the fabric to chill her skin. Beyond the reflection of her thin and red-cheeked face, she could see a trio of young women paying for their purchases. The shopkeeper, a rotund older man, smiled.

The *Help Wanted* sign, in small bold print, made her shift her feet impatiently. Finally the young women moved toward the door. She stepped back from the window, taking her hands from her pockets and smoothing down her coat. She needed to look presentable. She needed this job, needed it desperately. With luck she'd be able to convince the shopkeeper that she would be the perfect assistant.

She'd wanted to try for a job in another café, but though Paul had excused her thievery, it hadn't stopped him from passing along the word to other restaurateurs. Perhaps this shop, selling ladies' accessories, wouldn't have heard about her.

The girls piled out, going straight to the car that idled at the curb, ignoring her altogether. The driver helped them with their parcels, a bland face under his fedora, and then he held the doors for the young women. She couldn't even imagine what it would be like to have a life like that, one of such ease.

Cecilia took a breath and entered the shop, trying to focus on her original errand. The shopkeeper looked at her with some disdain as she approached the counter, his gaze flicking over her and taking in her worn yet clean clothes.

"Can I help you?"

"I'm here about the advertisement." Cecilia gestured to the sign in the window.

"I don't think you're suited," he replied.

"I have experience," she countered.

The shopkeeper shrugged. "It doesn't matter."

"I can balance the register and wrap parcels," she persisted. "I'd even work a day for free, to prove it."

"No." His tone was unbending. "You should find somewhere closer to home."

"Somewhere less fancy, you mean."

"If you like." He straightened the pen and paper resting near the cash register. "If you want to work with clothes, I know the factories are hiring lots of girls."

Cecilia couldn't hide her shudder. She wouldn't work in a factory, hunched over a sewing machine for hours on end, penalized for every error, squinting in the low light. She knew what it did; she saw it every day in her own mother.

"Thank you for your time," she said. She tried not to drag her feet as she left. There were lots of other shops between here and home; surely she'd find work.

❖

With Navarra's warning ringing in his ears, Detective Lang entered the Orpheus. How he'd investigate without letting slip that Lina was dead, he didn't know. Absently he handed his coat and fedora off to the coat-check girl and tucked his claim ticket in his pocket. It was early yet and the club was practically empty, with only a few stalwarts in attendance. Lang lit a cigarette and wandered over to the bar, taking in the lean shoulders of the bartender's assistant as he shifted bottles of champagne from a crate into a tub of ice behind the bar.

The young man had rolled his sleeves to the elbow and Lang watched the flex of muscles in his forearms, the olive cast of his skin dark against the crisp white of his shirt.

"What can I get you, Detective?" Tomas, the Orpheus's longtime bartender, asked. "Champagne?"

"Whiskey," Lang replied, "and a splash of tonic. That bubbly stuff you call champagne is awful."

Tomas chuckled as he set a tumbler on the bar, pouring two fingers from a bottle with a plain label. Lang put down a bill and Tomas tucked it into his pocket. "You're here early tonight," he observed.

"If I stayed at the station, I'd have to tackle the paperwork," he said by way of excuse.

"Better to be here and admire the pretty girls," Tomas replied, drawing himself up to his full height, his smile widening as one of those girls, a petite blonde in a costume more sequins than fabric, sauntered up to the bar. "What can I get you, Scarlett, *cara mia?*"

The blonde pouted. "Soda water. Enzo will have my head if I start in before my act. What a stick-in-the-mud."

Lang glanced over again at the assistant, tuning out Scarlett's complaints to Tomas. The young man had finished with the champagne and was gathering up the crates. He turned, and Lang saw him straight on. Dark brown eyes, a full mouth, and dark, curly hair. He let his gaze linger, moving over the black vest and trousers, noting the bulge. Delicious. His gaze moved upward again and he caught the man's eye.

A quirk of the corner of the young man's mouth gave him hope, but Lang had no chance to make his acquaintance. The young man turned away again, lifting the stacked crates. Lang had one more glimpse as he pushed open a door to the back of the club, and then he was gone.

Lang turned his attention to his drink. The first sip burned, but it didn't last long. Scarlett strolled away from the bar and Tomas went back to his preparatory work.

Enzo, the manager, came over to the bar. "Don't give Scarlett any booze until after midnight," he said to Tomas. "Last night she was half-cut and made a mess of her routine."

"Yes, boss," Tomas said. "She had soda water."

"Good."

"Is Lina around tonight?" Lang interjected before Enzo could leave. The manager paused.

"She's been away," he replied. "Went to visit relatives—a sick grandmother." Enzo shrugged.

"Do you know when she'll be back?"

"She's been gone a couple of weeks already and I hadn't heard. If you'll excuse me." Enzo strode away, shaking an angry finger at a member of the orchestra who had dared come onto the dance floor with his tie still undone.

A sick grandmother. Oldest excuse in the book. What had really happened?

He tossed back the rest of his whiskey. Talking to Franky Greco would be his next step.

"Mr. Greco in tonight?" he asked Tomas.

"Not yet," Tomas replied. His assistant came back with another crate. "Can I get you another drink?"

"Please." Lang pushed the tumbler forward and Tomas filled it again. If he had to wait, at least he'd have something pretty to look at.

❖

"You coming?"

Sheridan took his coat from the peg. "Where?"

Angelo and one of the truck drivers, Donato, hovered near the door.

"For a drink." Angelo rolled his eyes and Sheridan knew he would next mutter something in Italian about the stupid Paddy, but instead, he smiled. "It's a Friday tradition."

"Come on." Donato grinned and gestured to the door.

Sheridan shrugged on his coat. One drink wouldn't hurt. Maybe they knew a place where they could get a proper drink instead of the swill sold to the desperate. He hadn't had a glass of good whiskey since 1919. He couldn't afford it. But now, with his week's pay in his pocket—aside from the money he'd secreted in his shoe—he could get himself a glass.

"All right."

They took him to a small restaurant, where the tables were crammed close together in the front room. Angelo nodded to the woman serving pasta to a dour-faced old man and continued through, pushing open the swinging door. Sheridan and Donato followed him through a small kitchen. Angelo paused at a scarred wooden door.

"Tell no one, eh?" he said with a wink. Sheridan nodded and Angelo pushed open the door. Cigarette smoke wafted out with the sound of voices. Inside, a cluster of tables much like the ones in the front room were snugly arranged, half-full with patrons. Most had mugs of beer, but some drank wine, and others, Sheridan was gratified to see, had whiskey.

Angelo strolled up to the bar, greeting the bartender by name and ordering a beer. He turned to Sheridan.

"What'll it be?"

"Whiskey, neat."

"No soda?"

Sheridan glanced at the bottle. "That depends."

The bartender smiled and set a glass on the bar, and Sheridan watched him pour two fingers of whiskey. It glinted invitingly. He lifted the glass and sniffed, then closed his eyes. Real. He'd know the scent of Jameson anywhere. The alcohol burned pleasantly in his mouth and he savored the taste.

Angelo nudged him. "Pay the man, Paddy," he said with a laugh. Sheridan handed the bartender a five. Donato grabbed a beer and they found a table.

Other men trickled in as work finished for the day, and soon the room was packed full. Angelo kept up a steady stream of Italian to a man at the next table, but Sheridan was content to sit and drink. He had a second whiskey, and a third. When he stood up to get himself a fourth glass, he staggered. The room spun.

He could hardly believe it. It had been so long, he'd lost all head for liquor. Shameful. He was just glad none of his brothers were here to see him, drunk as a boy on his first beer.

Angelo clapped him on the back. "Come with me," he said, leading Sheridan toward the door. "We should go." He burped.

Donato waved them on, lifting his beer in farewell.

They exited into an alleyway that reeked of refuse, even in the gathering chill.

"Ugh." Sheridan wrinkled his nose and tried not to breathe too deeply. He wanted to remember the subtle flavors of the whiskey, not this. He buttoned his coat.

"How far do you have to go?" He turned toward Angelo.

A fist connected solidly with his cheek. He landed on his backside, his ears ringing and his vision blurred.

"Go home, Paddy." Angelo towered over him, grabbing his jacket. Sheridan blinked and his vision started to clear. He could taste blood. "Go back to the North Side and your own kind." His fist came down on Sheridan's jaw, snapping his head back.

Sheridan threw up his arm and blocked the next blow, and then pulled Angelo down with him. They grappled for several minutes, neither man gaining the upper hand.

"What the hell?" Sheridan tried to ask, but Angelo spat at him.

"You took my job," the other man snarled. "I'm the one Sal always came to—until you came around." He gave Sheridan one last shove, breaking his grip. He pulled himself up, grabbing at the brick wall.

"I work hard," Sheridan shot back, wiping a hand across his bloodied mouth.

"Find another job," Angelo demanded. "Or else you'll regret it."

"Go to hell."

Angelo spat at Sheridan's feet before going back into the speakeasy.

Once he was alone, Sheridan rose to his feet, straightening his jacket and brushing off some of the filth that had gotten down all of one sleeve. He touched his jaw experimentally, then his nose. Nothing broken. He spat blood onto the pavement. He wasn't going to give up that easily.

❖

He'd had too much to drink. The first whiskey had gone down easily, and so had the second and the third. At least, he thought it had only been three. When Tomas departed to help out the front bar, Lang had a chance to finally speak to his assistant.

"Have you worked here long?"

"Not very." The young man glanced over to the front bar, but Tomas was occupied. Lang could see him relax.

Lang's head swam. He wanted to ask the young man out for a drink later, or maybe something more, but his whiskey-sodden brain kept him from blurting out the question.

"Can I get you a cab?" the young man asked.

He couldn't talk to Franky Greco in the state he was in, either. He nodded and the young man waved over a waiter to give his request.

"Follow me," the waiter said. Lang pushed away his glass and gave the bartender's assistant one last glance. The young man met his gaze and smiled. Next time, he thought. Next time.

❖

Cecilia woke to the sound of her mother coughing. The old iron bedstead shook with her mother's convulsions, and even if she had been able to sleep through the noise, she never would have managed to sleep through the movement. She turned over and rubbed her mother's back. She could feel her mother's spine and ribs through the fabric of her nightgown, and it shocked her. She'd grown so thin, and Cecilia hadn't hardly noticed.

"Ma, are you okay?" She rubbed in small, soft circles. "Do you want me to get you some water?"

Her mother nodded and Cecilia crept out of bed, scurrying across the cold floor in her bare feet. She poured a bit of water from the wash pitcher into a teacup and brought it over to the bed. With effort, her mother sat up and held out her hand for the teacup. She sipped the water slowly, and finally her coughing ceased.

"You're not all right," Cecilia said, sitting next to her mother on the bed. "I know you said you'd be fine, but you're not."

"Not much we can do," her mother replied hoarsely. She finished the water.

"I could find a doctor," Cecilia said.

"No doctors," her mother insisted. "We can't afford it. I'll get better. I always do. It's just the early frosts that are keeping me from recovering quickly."

"I'll get another job, and then we can pay for a doctor."

"I'll get better soon." Her mother patted her hand.

Cecilia rose from the bed. She knew what she had to do today.

Dressed in her best clothes, Cecilia turned the corner. The apartment building where Nell lived was just up the street, but she lagged. Would Nell help her? She hated asking for charity, but she didn't know what else to do. And Nell had seemed sweet on her, and even Lang had said she would help.

She drew closer, then stopped in her tracks.

Franky came out of the building, Nell on his arm. They were richly dressed, and Nell leaned into him, smiling affectionately. He grinned down at her and said something that made her laugh.

She couldn't do it.

If Nell had been on her own, she could have gotten up the courage to ask, even to beg. With Franky there…She shuddered. He'd ask for a favor in return, she was sure of it. The way he'd looked her over before, like she was a piece of meat, made her wary.

As it was, she was too late.

Franky handed Nell into the black Packard idling at the curb, and then closed the door before walking around to the other side. The car rumbled off down the street away from her. Her heart sank.

Monday morning dawned bright and clear, a dusting of snow settling over the city, adding a deeper chill to the breeze. Sheridan huddled in the doorway of a shop across the street from the warehouse, his lean form tucked as far into the deep recess as he could manage. He waited.

Sal arrived, unlocking the door and letting himself in as he did every morning, but Sheridan didn't move. The sun brightened and the snow began to disappear from the pavement. He breathed on his hands to warm them before tucking them back into the pockets of his worn coat.

Angelo came striding up the street and Sheridan froze. He was in Angelo's direct line of sight, but the man didn't notice the extra shadow in the doorway. He was too busy greeting Tony, clapping him on the back, nattering something that gained only a shrug in response.

Sheridan heard the door slam and he relaxed, rolling his shoulders and stamping his feet to loosen muscles gone stiff from waiting. He waited awhile longer, lingering outside the shop. He wanted Angelo to be complacent, unprepared. By now he'd have decided that he'd scared off the Paddy and would be heartily congratulating himself, all the while explaining to Sal that some men just couldn't be relied upon.

The shopkeeper turned over his *Closed* sign and stared hard. Sheridan knew he looked a mess, with a bruise running along his jaw and a scrape across his forehead. The pain would be worth it in the end. He started across the street. It was time.

The door opened with a creak as it always did, but that didn't matter. The short hallway was empty. He glanced into the office, but Sal wasn't there. He unbuttoned his coat as he walked the last few feet, drawing himself up to his full height.

At first, his entrance onto the floor of the warehouse went unnoticed. Sal spotted him first and gave him a nod. He stood with Tony, a clipboard in hand, counting the inventory waiting to be distributed.

Sheridan stood. And waited.

Finally Angelo came around a stack of crates, a box of liquor in his arms. When he saw Sheridan, he swore, dropping the box. The glass bottles inside shattered, and Sal cursed Angelo, who didn't pay him the least attention as he came toward Sheridan. This time, Sheridan wasn't drunk, and he was ready. He dodged Angelo's first blow and returned it with a solid right jab that sent Angelo staggering away.

It was almost too easy. Angelo managed a few hits, but Sheridan was sharp, clearheaded, and out for blood. At the end, Angelo lay writhing on the floor, his shoulder dislocated and his nose broken.

"Well done." Sal stood near, a small smile on his fleshy lips.

Angelo groaned. "Shut up, you fool."

Sheridan tried to keep from smiling.

"Tony needs a hand with some deliveries," Sal continued on as if he witnessed such violence every day. Maybe he did. "I was going to send Angelo, but I don't think he'll be very useful today."

"Yes, sir." Sheridan turned to go. Tony waited, leaning against the door of the truck's cab.

"Don't be late again, eh?" Sal said. He tapped his clipboard. "Lots to do on Mondays, you know?"

"It won't happen again." As he took his spot in the truck, Sheridan heard Sal curse at Angelo.

"You've just cost him his job," Tony remarked as they pulled out of the warehouse.

"Too bad." Sheridan rubbed his knuckles. They were already starting to swell. "He deserved it."

"Maybe." Tony shrugged. "You impressed Sal, though. It'll help."

"Help how?"

"You're here, aren't you? Sal will find another guy to haul boxes."

Sheridan grinned, watching the streets roll by. He was on his way up.

CHAPTER FIVE

I'll call her for you." The doorman picked up a phone, turning away. Cecilia couldn't hear what he said, but he'd looked her over with some contempt when she'd requested to see Nell. This time, she couldn't lose her courage. She needed a job, and more days of pounding the streets hadn't panned out. She hoped Franky wasn't there.

The doorman turned back, unconsciously straightening his collar. "Go on up," he said, gesturing to the elevator. She smiled at him and walked past his desk, knowing that he watched her the entire way, as if she'd strip the chrome detail from the lobby and sell it for scrap. She wasn't the usual sort of visitor here, all dolled-up and escorted.

The elevator boy let her out on Nell's floor, and she paused on the threshold. Anxiety pooled in her stomach, making her nauseous. She swallowed. There was no going back.

The door opened and Nell poked her head out.

"Cecilia!" She gestured Cecilia forward and clasped her hand, pulling her into the apartment and kissing her cheek. "What a surprise." She closed the door and her fingers worked on the buttons of Cecilia's coat.

"I was in the neighborhood," Cecilia said, "and thought I would stop by. I'm not interrupting anything, am I?" She glanced around, searching for Franky.

"Never. I've missed you this week," Nell replied. She hung Cecilia's coat in the front closet. "I meant to get in touch and see how your job search was going, but I just couldn't get away."

Cecilia followed her into the living room, perching on the edge of the brocaded settee, her hands in her lap. Nell sank to the cushion beside her.

"Not well," Cecilia said. "I don't have any references."

"You don't have anything else? What did you do before working for Paul?"

Cecilia glanced down at her hands. Before moving to Chicago, she'd only ever worked on the farm. "I wondered if you knew of anywhere else I might find work. I will keep looking, of course, but you know so many places I don't."

"Can you dance?"

The question was completely unexpected.

"I can. I think."

Nell grinned. "Then I know just the job for you. How would you like to work at the Orpheus?"

Cecilia stared at her. "Doing what?"

"Dancing with the customers, of course," Nell replied as if she could hardly believe Cecilia didn't know. "A dollar a dance, or more, if the man likes you. That's how I started out, and now look at me." She gestured at the room and its nice furnishings. "It did help that I knew Franky, but I got here on my own."

"I don't know if I could," Cecilia replied. She imagined all the men, all those hands, all the leering. "What about a coat-check girl?"

"You'll make more money dancing, especially if you're good," Nell assured her, gently squeezing her fingers. "It'd be worth it."

"What if I'm no good at it?"

"I doubt that." Nell rose. "Come with me. We have to find you a dress. You can't come with me tonight dressed like that." She grasped Cecilia's hand and led her into the bedroom. It was done up in a similar brocade, but in a pale blue. The four-poster bed was as yet unmade, and cosmetics cluttered the vanity. A pot of face powder sat open and its dust spilled over onto the light-colored wood.

"Don't mind the mess. Ella hasn't been in yet. She won't until I leave." Nell threw open her wardrobe and began riffling through the clothes. Cecilia stood watching until a dark blue gown caught her eye. She grasped it, stopping Nell's search.

"What about this one?"

Nell pulled the dress from the mass of fabric, smoothing it with her hand. "It'll be perfect," she said. "It was always a bit short on me. Try it on."

Cecilia held the dress. "Here?"

Nell laughed. "Of course here. Let me help you." She pushed Cecilia's hands aside and began to unbutton her plain blouse. Cecilia averted her gaze and knew she was blushing.

"Don't be shy," Nell told her, her voice uncharacteristically gentle. She stroked Cecilia's exposed skin, her fingers moving lower as she undid more buttons. Cecilia shivered. "We have lots of time before we need to leave." Her breath was warm on Cecilia's cheek.

Cecilia turned her head and their lips met. The blue dress puddled on the floor, forgotten. At that moment, nothing else mattered, only the sweet softness of Nell's body against hers, the questing hands stripping her of her skirt and blouse until she stood in just her underwear and slip. She slid her fingers into the gaps between the buttons of Nell's dress, the skin surprisingly bare and warm.

Nell broke off their kiss. "Undress me," she whispered.

Cecilia undid the buttons one by one and pushed the dress off Nell's shoulders. Her pale flesh had a dusting of light freckles that followed her collarbones and descended into the shadow of her cleavage, hidden partly by a simple lace bra. Cecilia hadn't seen anything so beautiful in her life. Her fingers brushed over the lace, and down the bare expanse of skin, white as milk, to the lace ties at the top of Nell's satin tap pants.

"Go on," Nell encouraged. Cecilia undid the ties, pushing the satin down Nell's hips. Nell drew the bra over her head as the tap pants dropped to the floor. She stood naked, and Cecilia was in awe.

"Beautiful," she whispered, and Nell smiled.

"You haven't been with a woman, have you?"

"Not with anyone," she replied. Back home, she wouldn't have dared, and even when she first came to Chicago, she was too overwhelmed with the change to even think about it. And how to explain? She wouldn't know what to say.

Nell took her hand. "We'll go slow."

Cecilia sat on the edge of the bed. Nell was naked before her, gloriously naked. Her mouth went dry. She wanted so much but didn't know how to ask.

Nell reached for the hem of her slip, dragging it up, forcing Cecilia to stand again so she could pull it over her head and off. Her plain cotton bra and panties were next. Nell cupped her face and tilted it upward, planting kisses on Cecilia's forehead, eyelids, and, finally, her mouth.

"Lie back," Nell murmured, pressing her into the coverlet. The patterned brocade felt almost rough against her skin. Nell's hands ghosted over her torso, feeling like a light breeze tickling her. They became solid and warm on her hips and Cecilia drew in a sharp breath.

"Do you trust me?" Nell asked. She had lowered herself to her knees and she parted Cecilia's thighs.

Cecilia hesitated, thinking of the last time she'd been here in the apartment. She blinked. Nell was between her thighs. She wasn't going to ruin it. "Yes," she breathed.

"Good."

She felt Nell's breath on her thighs and when her tongue traced a damp trail up the sensitive skin, she trembled with need.

❖

Cecilia woke from her doze when Nell threw back the covers. The cool air from the window chased away the grogginess and raised goose bumps on her skin. She snuggled in close to Nell's warmth, enjoying the lazy stroke of Nell's hand on her back. "I wish we could stay like this forever," she murmured.

"If only," Nell agreed. "But we have to work." She sat up and stretched, sliding out of bed and heading toward the bathroom. Cecilia could hear water running and she reluctantly left the bed, feeling self-conscious in her nudity.

Nell stood under the shower spray, her red hair darkened with water and clinging to her scalp. If anything, she was more beautiful than before.

"Come in," she beckoned and made room for Cecilia under the spray. The hot water was heavenly and Cecilia closed her eyes, tipping her head back. Nell moved around her, dropping a kiss on her shoulder. She opened her eyes and reached for Nell, drawing her close. She could never get enough of her, the slender limbs, the swell of her breasts, the curve of her hip, and the hollow her hipbone created...

Nell kissed her again and moved out of reach. "Don't take too long," she teased, stepping from the shower and wrapping herself in a large white towel.

Cecilia washed her hair, and by the time she'd stepped out and dried off, Nell was nearly dressed, bent over a drawer in her vanity, choosing her jewelry.

The blue dress lay on the bed, along with underwear and a thin, filmy slip and a pair of dark stockings. Cecilia fingered the garments. She hadn't expected this—the underwear revealed more than she was used to. What would she do with her own clothes in the meantime? When she voiced her concerns, Nell smiled in amusement.

"Leave them here. We'll come back."

Cecilia drew on the undergarments and the slip, then sat on the bed to pull on the stockings. Once the dress settled on her frame, she stood in front of the vanity's large mirror and stared at herself in awe. The dress fell from her shoulders and clung to her hips before falling in an uneven beaded hem to her knees. She'd never worn something so lovely.

"I knew it would suit you," Nell said, pleased. "Sit down and I'll do your hair and makeup." She reached for the face powder and Cecilia closed her eyes.

When Nell had finished, Cecilia hardly recognized herself. Her face was pale, with a dusting of pink along her cheekbones and a slash of vermilion on her lips. Her eyelids were darkened and made her think of the photos of Egyptian statues she'd seen in the newspaper once. Her dark hair had been taken up in the back and the front had careful finger-waves that shone with pomade. Nell had begun powdering her own face, and she smiled at Cecilia's awe.

"Next time I'll teach you how to do it yourself," she said as she carefully applied rouge. "It's easier than you think."

Cecilia watched Nell for a few moments, then turned and paced to the window, moving aside the heavy drape to look outside. The sky had darkened and the wind rustled the trees. Leaves gathered in the gutters. The earlier pleasant weather had gone. She shivered, thinking of the walk to the Orpheus in her thin dress.

A dark car pulled up to the curb and a man got out, coming around the hood and heading into the building. She couldn't see his face, but he seemed familiar. She let the curtain drop.

Nell had transformed herself, and she shimmied into a pale cream dress with thin shoulder straps and plunging cleavage. She hung a ruby pendant about her neck and two long strands of beads.

"Our ride should be here soon," she said, leaning close to the mirror to check her lipstick. The doorbell chimed and Nell smiled. "Speak of the devil." She went into the living room and Cecilia followed.

Franky stood in the doorway, his fedora in his hand, his overcoat open to reveal a crisply tailored black suit. He kissed Nell soundly, then drew back, his eyes moving over Cecilia.

"Who's your friend?" he asked, gazing at her appreciatively. Nell dabbed at the smudge of lipstick on his mouth.

"You remember Cecilia, don't you? I introduced you last week."

He grinned and held out his hand to Cecilia. "My apologies. I didn't recognize you." He gallantly kissed her hand before turning his attention back to Nell. "Is she coming with us?"

"I thought I'd introduce her to Enzo tonight. He said he was looking for a few more girls, especially since my lovely Lina is away."

"He'll appreciate that. Who knows when Lina will return."

"Visiting family can't possibly take that long," Nell replied, pouting.

He shrugged. "Enzo will like Cecilia," he observed. "She's just his type. But we'll be late if we don't leave, and he won't like that."

He waited at the door while she and Nell finished getting ready, but he stopped Cecilia when she reached for her coat. His hand rested on her shoulder. "That won't do at all. Nell, get her one of yours. It'll be too big, but better than what she has."

Embarrassed, she left her jacket hanging where it was. Franky stepped closer and she could smell the spicy scent of his cologne, mixed with the oil of his pomade.

"You'll soon forget how to blush," he said in a low, teasing tone. "Are you sure you want to work at the Orpheus?"

Cecilia lifted her shoulders and looked him in the eye. "Of course I do."

He grinned. "That's my girl."

Nell came out with a jacket and Franky chivalrously helped them into their coats.

"It's a cold one out there tonight," he said, buttoning the top button of Nell's coat and straightening her fur collar. He did the same for Cecilia and the act seemed too intimate for such a new acquaintance. She glanced at Nell in confusion, but Nell had already gone to the door. She didn't seem the least bit bothered by Franky's attention, and Cecilia shrugged off her uncertainty. Surely she was just nervous. Soon there would be more men than Franky to worry about.

Two of Franky's men waited for them in the car. The driver tapped his fingers impatiently on the wheel. He tipped his hat to Nell as they settled in. The backseat was snug, but Nell was a buffer between Cecilia and Franky. Cecilia didn't mind having Nell pressed up against her. Nell's softness reminded her of that afternoon, and she licked her lips. Nell smiled at her as if she knew what Cecilia was thinking. She turned her head, watching the snowflakes melt as they hit the pavement.

"She said she wouldn't be gone long." Nell's raised voice startled Cecilia from her thoughts.

Franky looked annoyed. "I told you Lina was flighty," he replied, his tone equally sharp. "Enzo said she's sacked. He has no time for it. If she comes back, you know she can beg for her job back."

"He should have waited." Nell crossed her arms, pouting. "I'll be giving him a piece of my mind."

Franky chuckled. "He won't listen."

The car drew up in front of the Orpheus, gliding slowly to a stop at the curb. The man in the front seat got out and opened up the back door. Snow drifted in.

"Sir?" The man held the door still and Franky got out. Nell followed him in a huff, and Cecilia slid across the seat, nervously trailing Nell. The man nodded to her and she gave him a tentative smile. He closed the door and followed them in.

❖

Cecilia could hear the strains of music over the animated chatter in the entryway, filled as it was with men and women. Franky divested her of her coat, and Nell urged her through the arched doorway and into the ballroom. Two bars, each staffed by uniformed bartenders, took up the back corners, the dark wood glimmering under the brief flashes of light reflected from spotlights onto the shining chrome accents.

As they edged along the side of the expansive dance floor, between chairs and tables, she caught her first glimpse of the band through the dancing couples—a full orchestra in black tie.

"Close your mouth, darling," Nell purred in her ear, her hot breath brushing Cecilia's cheek. Her hand skimmed over Cecilia's back.

Cecilia's cheeks burned, but she hoped the powder Nell had applied would hide the worst of her embarrassment. Nell pulled her down to a chair at an empty table. She felt like a little girl trying to be an adult, completely out of her depth. All around her were the rich and sophisticated; women in beautiful sequined gowns glided by effortlessly on the arms of their handsome, tuxedoed escorts, champagne glasses glittering, and their poise seemed impenetrable.

"That'll be you," Nell said, nodding toward the woman Cecilia had thought the most elegant. She wore a slim-fitting gown in pale blue, and when she turned, the detailed stitching glittered in the light. Her hair was styled in a short blond bob and diamonds shone in her ears and at her neck.

Nell waved a man over to their table. He wore his tuxedo as comfortably as a second skin on his strong form, one hand in his trouser pocket, looking as if he could have stepped from a magazine advertisement. What had seemed to be slicked-back hair turned out to be longer hair pulled back into a short ponytail, to her surprise. Cecilia watched as he gallantly kissed Nell's hand, flashing her a grin.

"And who is your friend?"

"Enzo, meet Cecilia Mills. Cecilia, Enzo is the manager here."

Cecilia put out her hand and Enzo bowed over it, though he didn't kiss her hand as he'd done to Nell. "How do you do." She tried to project an air of confidence, but she soon realized he'd seen right through her.

"Come dance with me," Enzo said abruptly, pulling her to her feet. She glanced at Nell, receiving an encouraging smile. Enzo led her out onto the dance floor, taking her into his arms just as a song ended. The band started up a slower tune and Enzo led her through the steps. She stumbled once, but by midsong she had begun to relax. She could do this.

"What brings you to the Orpheus?" he asked, his blue-eyed gaze calm as he took her through her paces.

"I need work," she answered honestly. He gave a chuckle at that and she frowned.

"How refreshing," he said, turning her easily around the dance floor. "Most girls want to meet a man, or they tell me they want to be famous, or rich, or both."

"I don't need to be famous," she replied. The song came to an end, but Enzo didn't relinquish his hold.

"One more," he said. "You'll come here Tuesday through Saturday from seven until closing. I pay my girls out every week, based on how many tickets you collect from your men." He spun her into a graceful twirl and when she came back to his arms, he continued. "Between dances, you need to encourage your men to buy drinks—for themselves, for you, I don't care. I pay bonuses to the girls who sell the most liquor."

She followed his lead as he matched the rhythm of the song, and she was glad for all the dances back home that had given her the skill she needed.

"You'll do," he said as the band finished with a flourish. "Nell can show you the rest, I'm sure. But don't call yourself Cecilia. It's too prim." He pondered her, and she grew warm under his attention. "CeeCee, I think. Short, memorable. No more Cecilia." He escorted her back to the table, then departed.

"You did well out there," Nell confided. "Enzo approves."

"He doesn't like my name," she replied. "I'm supposed to be CeeCee now."

"CeeCee." Nell tried out the name. "I like it. It suits you." She laid her hand over Cecilia's and gave it a squeeze. Cecilia withdrew her hand as Franky approached, a drink in hand. He was followed by another man, somewhat heavyset in a dark suit, who carried two glasses of bubbly champagne cocktails. Franky took the drinks one by one and handed them off to Nell and Cecilia before settling into a chair. He slung his arm over the back of Nell's chair. The other man stood nearby, idly smoking, keeping an eye on the crowd. His gaze kept darting back to Cecilia, and she gave him an awkward smile. He finished his cigarette and came over to her as the band began to tune their instruments for the next set.

"May I have this dance?" He held out a fleshy hand and she glanced at Nell, who gave a slight nod, before taking it. She rose, leaving her half-finished champagne behind.

"Of course."

As they walked onto the dance floor, he slid a ticket into her hand.

"You'll need that later," he noted. She tucked it into the small purse that hung from her wrist.

"You haven't introduced yourself," she said as they came together. She rested her hand on his shoulder. "I'm CeeCee."

"Sandro," he said.

"Have you known Franky long?" she asked, wondering how she could draw him out of his shell. He seemed content to lead her around the dance floor.

"Years."

"And Nell?"

"Not as long," he replied.

She fell silent after that. She envied Nell her easy charm. As they turned on the dance floor, she could just see Nell through the crowd, on the arm of an older man. She was laughing at something he'd said, leaning into him.

When the song ended, Sandro left her at the edge of the dance floor. She stood watching the couples, feeling ill at ease without a partner or a purpose. She decided to go back to the oasis of the table.

"Leaving already?" A man hooked her elbow, tugging her around. "I always have to dance with the newest girls." His Cheshire-cat grin seemed genuine.

"And who might you be?" she asked, looking up at him from under her lashes in what she hoped was a flirtatious manner.

"Erven Vogt," he said, obviously expecting her to recognize his name. She bit her lip. "You haven't heard of me?"

"I haven't lived in Chicago very long," she explained, though she supposed that was stretching the truth.

"Then you're forgiven," he said grandly. "My father was a brewer, though now he makes alcohol for industry." He winked. "Most people know me thanks to him."

"Are you a brewer?" she asked.

"Not with the Volstead Act." He chuckled. "But that doesn't matter, I'd never have enough time to work." Erven chuckled.

"Your father doesn't mind?" She could hardly imagine her mother countenancing such a thing.

"Someone has to spend the money he makes," Erven replied. He spun her suddenly, and when he drew her back toward him, she staggered into his chest. He pulled her closer.

"Sorry," she said as she trod on his toes.

"Forgiven, my dear," he said easily. "You're such a delightful change from all the others—cynical and heartless, all of them. Tell me your name and where you live and I'll fill your apartment with flowers."

She told him her name, but hesitated. She couldn't tell him where she lived. He'd never want to spend time with her if he learned of the filthy tenement she lived in.

"Sweet, yet coy," he said approvingly. He slid a ticket into her hand. "I'll see you later, my dear."

He relinquished her to a waiting man, but not before kissing her hand, and she thought she might do well here after all.

CHAPTER SIX

Tony needs you tonight." Sal caught Sheridan as he was leaving the warehouse, pulling on his jacket and wrapping a gray woolen scarf around his neck. It had seen better years, but it would do.

"A delivery?" Sheridan asked. If they were headed to the Orpheus, he might see that gorgeous redhead again. He certainly wouldn't complain. It was time for another delivery, as Thursdays were the start of the busy period.

"A little more than that," Sal replied. He patted Sheridan's shoulder in an almost fatherly manner. "Do well tonight and you'll move up in the world."

Sheridan grinned. "When have I ever failed?"

Sal chuckled. "Not yet, but they always expect the Irish to fail. Anyway, you need to change first," he said. "No wearing that where you're going." He waved a hand at Sheridan's workman's clothes. "A suit, not too fancy."

"I have one, but back home."

"Tony will meet you here in two hours," Sal replied. "Plenty of time." He turned and went into his office.

Sheridan leaned on the door frame. "What should I expect?"

"Just do what Tony tells you." Sal settled behind the desk, lighting a cigar. "Now go. You have work to do."

Sheridan retreated, walking swiftly from the warehouse. Instead of walking, he caught a cab, covering the blocks between the warehouse and home, though the driver wouldn't take him directly to his house.

"I don't go there," he'd said.

Sheridan walked the rest of the way, fuming. He nearly ran over a young woman and muttered an apology as he took the stairs to his small room two at a time but forgot about her entirely by the time he'd stripped off his clothes and pulled on his suit. He washed with the icy remains of the morning's water, removing the day's grime. The small mirror that hung above the washbasin showed his pale face and little else. He waited impatiently for the day he could afford to move from this sparse room and into a proper apartment.

He would love to burn his old clothes and buy another suit and a handful of shirts. Maybe he would, if Sal deemed him too good to work in the warehouse. Even just to see the look on Angelo's face when he heard of the promotion—oh, how he'd love that. It would be better revenge than the beating.

He made it back to the warehouse with little time to spare. He didn't see Tony, only a black Chevrolet idling nearby. A horn sounded and the driver leaned out.

"Paddy!" Tony made a rude gesture and Sheridan grinned. He slid into the passenger seat.

"No truck?"

Tony chuckled. "No deliveries tonight," he said, talking around his cigar. He revved the engine and shifted into gear.

They didn't go far. A few blocks away, they entered a small family diner, its neat rows of tables decked in red-and-white checked tablecloths. The low buzz of conversation died away and the diners shot wary glances their way.

Sheridan paused on the threshold, but Tony continued on, ignoring the looks and whispers. He trailed Tony as the man pushed open the swinging door, striding into a cramped kitchen that smelled of frying beef.

The chef, an overweight man in greasy dark trousers and a splattered white shirt and apron, stared at them in alarm. He held a large spoon and it dripped tomato sauce onto the floor as he gaped. Sheridan eyed him, wondering if this was who they'd come to see.

"Where's Cristiano?" Tony barked, the laid-back demeanor he'd shown in the car disappearing. The chef pointed to a closed door, his hand shaking.

Tony didn't bother to knock. An older man, around Sal's age, glanced up from his ledgers. The tiny office stank of cigar smoke, and one wall held shelves of ledgers, loose papers, and a small iron safe.

"I haven't got it," Cristiano said. "And you can tell Capone himself that I won't pay him anymore. What does he do for me, eh? He doesn't eat here, doesn't bring me business, but charges me money." He threw up his hands.

Tony started to laugh, but there was nothing amusing in the sound. It made the hairs rise on the back of Sheridan's neck.

Cristiano got to his feet. "You can try," he said, "but you don't scare me." He waited on his side of the desk, hands at his sides.

"Close the door," Tony said.

Sheridan pushed the door shut and leaned against it.

In an instant, Tony was around the desk. He seized Cristiano's swinging fist and slammed it into the glass top of the desk, which shattered. Cristiano swore and backed away, his hand dripping blood. Tony grasped him by the collar and he struggled to get away, but Tony was half his age and strong. A punch to the jaw had Cristiano on his knees, and Tony pressed the man's head into the ledgers and broken glass.

"Had enough?" Tony asked. Cristiano struggled and Tony hauled him up. "Come here," he said to Sheridan. "He's all yours."

Sheridan didn't hesitate. He'd seen the look in Tony's eye—the expectation, the knowledge that he could become one of them if only he proved himself tonight. As he swung his fist into Cristiano's soft, unprotected belly, Sheridan knew he'd made it.

❖

The heat in the crowded ballroom conspired with the champagne, and Cecilia's vision shimmered and blurred. She focused on the glass in front of her, tracing the stem with a fingertip. She didn't know what time it was, only that it was late. Her purse held at least a dozen dance tickets, and her feet ached to prove it.

Erven had claimed several dances throughout the evening and now he lounged in a chair next to her, idly smoking a cigarette. Aside from a slight loosening of his tie, he looked as impeccable as when the evening began.

"You'll be here tomorrow night, won't you?" he asked her. She glanced up, his face blurred through the haze of her exhaustion.

"Every night, I'm sure."

Every night, dancing with men, making small talk, drinking. It hardly seemed like a job at all. Except—she fiddled with a sequin at the neck of her borrowed dress—she needed more clothes. There was no way around it. She couldn't keep borrowing from Nell.

"I'll come to the Orpheus just for you," Erven replied. He hooked his free hand over the back of her chair and she felt the lightest touch of his fingers on her back. She let him touch her, but when his touch increased in pressure, she shifted and sat forward.

The last flourish of the orchestra covered her discomfort as the crowd broke out in applause. She clapped along with them, searching the mass of people for Nell's familiar bright hair. Soon she spotted Nell weaving through the crowd.

Nell bent and kissed her on the cheek before sinking into a chair. "How did it go, CeeCee, darling?" she asked. She took a deep sip of Cecilia's champagne.

"Wonderful," Cecilia replied, thinking of the dance tickets tucked in her purse and the drinks she'd been bought, and better still, the drinks she'd encouraged men to buy.

Nell smiled languidly and laid her hand over Cecilia's. Her red nail polish was a bright slash of color against Cecilia's pale skin. "Good," she said. "And in a few minutes, when the customers clear out, we'll go see Enzo and you can get paid." She stroked Cecilia's wrist.

Cecilia stifled a shudder of desire. Why couldn't Erven's touch have done the same? He was a good-looking man, and wealthy, but he didn't provoke any feelings in her beyond a pleasant fondness.

Franky strode over to the table and Nell moved her hand away, taking up the glass of champagne. "Ready to go?" He shook hands with Erven.

"Soon," Nell replied, finishing the wine.

"I'll say good night," Erven said. He gave them an elegant bow and departed.

"Go see Enzo, then I'll meet you out front," Franky said. He left them at the table.

The last trickle of people exited the ballroom and it was as if the evening had never been, except for the glassware on the tables and the candles burned low in their holders.

"Let's go." Nell took Cecilia's hand and tugged her up. They followed the other dancers to the back of the ballroom where they clustered around Enzo. Cecilia waited her turn, unwilling to push forward through the other girls.

"You did well," Enzo said when she came to the front of the line, holding her tickets.

"Thank you." She watched him count the tickets and consult a leather-bound book before he peeled off a couple of bills from his roll.

"See you tomorrow." He favored Nell with a smile. "Good night, ladies."

Nell hooked her arm through Cecilia's as they walked through the empty ballroom.

"You should come home with me," she said, leaning close. "Franky's away and we could have some privacy." The slight squeeze she gave Cecilia's arm put an emphasis on the last word.

Cecilia flushed at Nell's not-so-subtle hint. She wanted to accept, but she hadn't been home for hours. Her mother must wonder what had happened.

"I don't know," she said. "I should really get home."

Nell frowned. "We could drive you," she suggested.

"No, that's all right." She didn't want Nell to see where she lived: the filthy tenement, the rats, the cold. She wouldn't help a girl from a tenement—they were of completely different classes. She would be horrified to see where Cecilia came from.

Nell pushed through the crowd in the lobby to the coat check, handing the girl their tickets. A man looked to object to their preferential treatment, but she gave him a challenging look. He opened his mouth, but suddenly Franky was beside them.

"What's taking so long?" he asked irritably. Nell smiled at him and Cecilia saw the complainer melt away into the crowd. It always amazed her what Franky's mere presence could do. He helped them on with their coats and shepherded them to the door.

"You're always in such a rush," Nell teased. His stern face softened for a moment, but then he frowned. Cecilia said nothing.

"My night's not over," he replied. "I'll drop you two at the apartment."

Cecilia wanted to say something, but she didn't dare. She couldn't object to Franky, not when she owed so much to Nell's indulgence. And Franky himself…he frightened her. His cold gaze, his calculating eyes, made her squirm. He was powerful. It was easy to see, and she never wanted to be on the other end of that power.

Once in the car, Nell chatted with Franky about her evening until Franky glanced at Cecilia.

"What about you? You're quiet as a mouse."

Cecilia swallowed. She preferred being quiet around him, unnoticed. "I enjoyed myself." She enjoyed the money she'd made even more. It would pay for two weeks' rent for her and her mother, and she could buy a few cheap dresses to tide her over.

"Enzo is impressed," Nell added. "She's a regular now."

"Good." Franky lit a cigarette. The car rolled to a stop.

"You're not going to see us up?" Nell asked with a pretty pout.

"Things to do," Franky replied. "I'll see you girls tomorrow."

Nell kissed him good night before they exited the car. It pulled away from the curb, gliding down the quiet street. Nell took Cecilia's hand.

"Come on, it's cold out here." She pulled Cecilia into the bright lobby. The night doorman tipped his cap and they rode the elevator up to Nell's apartment. Nell dug in her purse for the key.

"I should go home," Cecilia said, even as she stepped over the threshold.

"In the morning," Nell said. "You'll never get a cab at this hour."

Cecilia let herself be drawn past the brocade sofa and into the bedroom. Nell's things had been tidied and the pots of makeup on her vanity were neatly arranged. The clothes she'd left strewn about had been gathered and hung in the wardrobe. A lamp burned low on the night table, the light making the crisp white sheets seem to glow where the bedcovers had been turned down.

She swallowed, her fingers smoothing the front of her dress. She wanted an evening like their first afternoon. As if divining her thoughts, Nell came up behind her, sliding a warm hand down her arm. Her lips ghosted over Cecilia's neck, raising goose bumps.

"We have all night," Nell murmured in her ear. Cecilia turned in Nell's embrace. Her world shrank to the dimly lit bedroom and she gave herself over to the moment.

Sheridan flexed his fingers and winced.

"You did well," Tony said, lighting his cigar. He sat back in his chair and blew a smoke ring toward the low ceiling of the saloon. It was a tiny place, barely a hole-in-the-wall on the edge of the Levee district. Though it was late, the tables were full. Close to them, a slim prostitute plied her trade on an increasingly inebriated john.

Sheridan sipped his whiskey. "You don't just work for Sal, do you?"

Tony chuckled. "I don't answer to Sal."

"Then why take me with you tonight? I'm a mick, not one of your own." He tipped his glass and swallowed, feeling the burn of the whiskey. It curled comfortably in his stomach, warming him on that cold night.

"Sometimes an outsider is the best choice," Tony remarked. "Someone with no other loyalties."

"How do you know I'm not from the North Side?"

Tony looked amused, the corner of his mouth quirking up. "I asked around. Anyway, you'll be back to the warehouse until the boss decides."

"Capone?"

"Nah, not that high up." Tony waved a hand and the bartender came to fill their glasses. "Leave the bottle."

Sheridan tried to think which of Capone's lieutenants Tony might answer to.

"Franky Greco makes all the decisions for anyone involved with the Orpheus," Tony continued. Sheridan drew in a breath and forced himself to relax, though the fury that pulsed through him was as fiery as the whiskey. "I'll put in a word. He needs more men like you."

Sheridan took a drink. He was on his way up, there was no doubt. "Another heavy?"

"An enforcer," Tony said, "but you'll probably end up with more than just bruised knuckles." He raised his glass. "To the Orpheus."

Sheridan echoed his toast and downed the whiskey. Tony poured him another. He sipped this one with more caution, remembering the night with Angelo.

"How'd you get working for Franky?" he asked Tony, who had leaned back in his chair to snag one of the passing girls. She slid onto his knee without protest, snuggling into his side. He kissed her affectionately.

"Paddy, meet Marie, my favorite girl." She dipped her head and her dark curls spilled over her forehead. She was pretty, with a generous bosom and lips, and Sheridan envied Tony his good fortune.

"How do you do."

Tony ignored his earlier question and Sheridan sat back, glass in hand. He watched Tony with Marie until their affections bored him, and then he downed the rest of his drink. Tony whispered in Marie's ear and she rose, leaving them alone.

"Isn't she gorgeous?" he remarked, his eyes following her until she vanished into the back of the saloon. He turned his attention to the table and poured another drink.

"I started for Colosimo, God rest his soul, when I was a boy," he said. "Washed dishes in his café."

"You knew him?" Sheridan remembered the tales of the man, the head of the Chicago Outfit, the South Side gang. He'd been in prison when Colosimo had been gunned down.

"Knew him, but not well," Tony replied. "When I was old enough, he made sure I had a job. Bashing heads in, mostly." He grinned. "One of the best jobs for a nineteen-year-old to do, you know."

"So you moved up from there?"

"Bit of everything, but I can still bash heads with the best of them. Even taught Franky some." He broke off as Marie approached the table, hand in hand with a slender red-haired girl, pale but for patches of pink on her high cheekbones.

Sheridan glanced at Tony.

Marie urged the girl forward and she came to stand in front of him, blocking his view of Tony. Her perfume was heady, too strong for a delicate girl like her, as if one of the others had hurriedly doused her.

"What's your name?" he asked, holding out a hand. She slid cold fingers into his and gracefully perched on his knee.

"I'm Perla," she said. She leaned against him so her breasts pressed against him, rising in her bodice until they nearly spilled over the neckline of her blouse. His hands found her waist and he felt a flare of lust as she shifted in his lap. She gave him a sultry smile and murmured in his ear. "I have a room upstairs."

He let his lips brush her bared shoulder, feeling her shiver. He lifted her to her feet and rose.

"On me, Paddy," Tony said, raising his glass.

CHAPTER SEVEN

The cabbie dropped Cecilia at the edge of the stockyards.

"That's as far as I'll go," he said. This routine was becoming familiar after two weeks at the Orpheus. Cecilia dug the money from her purse and alighted in the filthy street. The wind blew cold between the buildings and she shivered as the breeze curled its fingers around her stocking-clad legs. The nylon was delicate and she'd loved the feel of it on her legs when Nell had given the stockings to her earlier, but now she wished she had a thicker pair to keep out the chill.

She scurried along the rough sidewalk, picking her way around the garbage left for pickup. The quiet and the darkness unnerved her and she wished she could have stayed over at Nell's again. She would have, but Franky had stayed in, and there was little option but to make her good-byes. Nell gave her a chaste kiss on the cheek as she left.

The clatter of a garbage can made her start in surprise, but there was no danger, only a pair of thin cats pawing through the refuse. One glanced up at her as she passed, its eyes glowing in the faint moonlight. She was relieved when she finally reached her house, though the stench in the neighborhood seemed worse than ever. The stairs creaked as she climbed, and she kept close to the wall, as the rail was loose. She let herself into the room, groping in the dark until she reached the table, finding the matches.

The match flared, illuminating the grease paper and the kerosene lamp. She lit the lamp, but turned it down low. Her mother was a lump under the quilts, and she shifted and turned.

"I didn't mean to wake you," Cecilia whispered. Her mother tried to speak, but her words turned into a fit of coughing. Cecilia brought the lamp over beside the bed. "I thought you said you were getting better."

Her mother's cheeks were flushed and her eyes bright, though the hand that reached from the covers to clasp her own was bone thin and cool.

"I'll be fine," her mother said, her voice thin and reedy.

"I'm going to fetch a doctor." Cecilia stood.

"No—no doctors," her mother protested. "Too expensive."

"In the morning then," Cecilia replied, "if you're not any better. We can afford it now." She thought of the money in her purse, and the money she'd been putting in the tin. They had enough for several weeks' rent, and food. They could spare some for a doctor. If she had to, she'd sell one of her dresses, cheap though they were. She had half a dozen now, though none were as lovely as the gown Nell had lent her on the first night. They sufficed, but almost any dress looked good under the half-light of the Orpheus.

"Morning, then," her mother agreed. Cecilia stripped off her clothes and got into her nightgown before turning out the lamp. She crawled into bed.

"In the morning."

Cecilia woke to the sound of the kettle being set on the stove. The air in the room was brisk and she tucked her head under the covers until her face felt warm. When she emerged, her mother was washing her face and combing out her long graying hair. Compared to the night before, she seemed well.

"Oh, you're awake." Her mother smiled. "Come sit up at the table. I've made porridge and the water's on for tea."

Cecilia slid over the side of the bed and reached for her shoes. She didn't want to feel the cold floorboards under her toes.

"Are you feeling better?" she asked as she pulled on her socks and laced up her shoes.

"Much." Her mother gave her a comforting smile. Cecilia felt as if a weight had lifted from her chest. She watched her mother wrap a shawl over her shoulders and put on her coat.

"Are you well enough for work, Ma?" she asked, coming over to stand in front of the stove. It gave off a feeble heat.

"Of course I am. You can't be the only one supporting us. Soon we'll have enough money to move someplace nicer."

"In the new year," Cecilia replied. "I don't think I'll have enough before then."

"It's not too much longer. We can manage. Now, eat your breakfast and I'll see you tonight."

"Yes, Ma." She kissed her mother's cheek and watched her leave. If only she could make just a bit more money, then her mother wouldn't have to work at all. The kettle began to whistle and she sighed. She wanted a place like Nell's, with real heat, comfortable furniture, and, above all, no mice.

❖

In the daylight, the outside of the Orpheus looked worn. The inside looked worse, tawdry and cheap. A crew of middle-aged black janitors methodically swept and mopped the dance floor, illuminated by house lights that gave a sallow tinge to the great ballroom.

Lang spared them only a glance as he followed one of Franky's men back into the bowels of the hall. Franky had an office there and Lang knew—unofficially, of course—that he directed most of his bootlegging operation from within those four walls.

Franky was on the phone when Lang arrived, but he waved him inside. Lang stood, waiting. Finally Franky finished with his call and motioned to him to take a seat.

"What a surprise," he said genially, though Lang knew it was nothing of the sort. Franky was too well-connected. He'd likely known when Lang had left the station. "So, what can I do for you, Detective?"

Lang glanced at the man who hovered in the doorway, his wide shoulders blocking any view of the hall.

"Go on, Gio, get some lunch."

The man withdrew, closing the door behind him. Lang settled in the chair in front of Franky's desk, leaning back into the leather, hearing it creak. He lit a cigarette and took a deep drag before he spoke.

"We found a body you might be interested in," he said. Franky didn't move, merely smiled. "She's been in the morgue for a while now, and Navarra figured you should know before she's put in a pauper's grave."

"How long?"

Lang shrugged. "A while. We weren't sure who she was at first." The lie slipped off his tongue as easily as the truth. The beat cop hadn't known, nor had the coroner. But he'd known.

"A lot of people go missing," Franky remarked. "Drink?"

"Sure." Lang took the proffered glass. "You always have the best stuff."

Franky smiled at that. "So, the body…?"

"It's Lina."

Franky's expression didn't change. Lang took a sip of his brandy, letting the moment drag out.

"Since she worked here," Lang continued, "we were wondering if you knew of any relatives of hers. We can't keep her forever."

"No idea," Franky replied curtly. "I won't miss that little whore."

"None at all?" Lang pressed. "I know she spent time with Nell, so maybe she'd know."

"Just bury her," Franky retorted. He dug a roll of bills from his pocket and tossed it to Lang. "That should cover it."

"Will you tell Nell?" Lang inquired, pocketing the cash, keeping his expression solemn to hide his distaste. There was enough to bury the poor girl and then some.

"She doesn't need to know," Franky said flatly.

"But they were friends."

"Friends." Franky snorted.

"When did you last see Lina?" Lang inquired.

"I can't recall."

"But you didn't like her."

"No, not especially," Franky replied. "But that's no secret."

"Only if someone knows the real reason you didn't like her," Lang noted. "But how many people do?"

"What do you mean by that?"

Oh, Franky was playing it innocent. He might have laughed if it hadn't been guaranteed to offend Franky further. He bit back a smirk. "It's just that she and Nell spent a lot of time together," he replied.

"You wouldn't be hinting at something, would you, Detective?" Franky growled. "Basing investigations upon unsubstantiated speculation is a way to get yourself demoted."

"True." Lang let that threat pass. He knew the truth, for whatever it was worth. He could risk his career, but the sacrifice would be worthless. Nothing would change. "You don't happen to know how she might have ended up in the river, do you?" It was a question he already knew the answer to.

"No clue." Franky shrugged. His gaze hardened when Lang didn't reply. "Just get her buried, Detective, with as little fuss as possible."

"And Nell?"

"It's better she doesn't know. I always knew that girl would come to a bad end. She didn't know what was good for her. Telling Nell would only make things difficult." He stared at Lang. "You know what I mean."

Lang stared back. "No, I can't say that I do."

"You're going to push things over a dead whore?" Franky asked. "I thought better of you, Detective. Let me lay it out nice and clear for you. If you tell Nell about this matter, I'll make sure your perverted queer ass becomes public knowledge to the entire police force." He sneered. "And then I'll hand you over to some of my men for playtime."

Lang took a sip of his brandy and schooled his features to impassivity. He regretted ever letting slip to Nell that he didn't like women—she must have inadvertently let on to Franky about his tastes. Franky was in earnest this time, his contempt apparent. "Do you want to know when she's buried?"

"Not particularly. Will the force be investigating further?" The challenge lay between them.

"No. We don't have the resources to investigate every death in the city, and certainly not one of a woman of low moral character." The words tasted bitter in his mouth, though they were the truth. He hadn't been able to find enough evidence to justify continuing the case. He drained his glass and rose.

Franky chuckled. "A shame about the funding," he remarked. "I appreciate you bringing this to my attention."

Lang turned to leave.

"If I find out you've told Nell," Franky said from behind him, "I'll be very disappointed."

"Understood." Lang didn't stop. Franky's reaction hadn't surprised him in the least.

"Don't be a stranger," Franky added. "You haven't been to the Orpheus much lately. You should come by tonight. I'll cover your tab."

Lang glanced back. "Generous of you."

Franky smiled. "Always the best for my friends on the force, Detective."

❖

Cecilia pulled the clinging red dress carefully down over her head and past her hips. The sateen clung to her body, and she knew it made her look nearly naked underneath, though she wore stockings, her usual underwear, and a slip. She twisted to do up the zipper at the back, managing awkwardly as she bent over, clutching the fabric in her hands to hoist it closer to her neck.

She peered into the small chipped mirror hung on a nail over the washbasin. Even though it was still light outside, the room was dim and she could hardly see her reflection. The lamp sat on the table but she didn't want to use it. It would be a waste of kerosene and she knew they couldn't afford it. She brushed out her hair and pulled on her red cloche. Once she was at Nell's, she could finish her preparations for the evening.

She buckled up her patent-leather Mary Janes and pulled her jacket on over the red dress. Her mother hadn't yet come home from the factory, but she couldn't linger. Locking the door behind her, she hurried down the steps and out into the chill.

A hand seized her arm and she nearly fell.

"Rent's due tomorrow," the landlord warned, his fingers biting into her arm. He grinned at her, revealing blackened teeth. His breath stank and she recoiled.

"You'll have it," she retorted, and he let her go.

"I'd take off some if you showed me your dress," he said, eyeing the red sateen that peeked out from beneath her jacket. She shuddered.

"I have to go."

She strode down the street, dodging a group of youths that kicked around a battered rubber ball. She heard the catcalls as she passed, and she quickened her pace until she was trotting down the sidewalk.

When the tenements began to make way for the nicer, larger, and better-kept buildings, she slowed, feeling her heart thumping in her chest. Her breath rasped in her ears and she knew her face would be as red as her dress, but at least she was *away*. If only she could leave those streets behind forever.

A silver Rolls Royce sidled to the curb and pulled up next to her. She hardly noticed until she heard someone call her name.

"CeeCee!" Erven leaned over the passenger seat. "What on earth are you doing out here? This is no place for you." He stopped the car and opened the passenger door. She stared at him. Her mouth went dry.

"Get in!" He waved a hand and she stepped off the sidewalk and into the car, settling onto the wide leather seat. She glanced over at Erven as he gunned the engine and the car sped down the street. He slowed for a traffic light. She'd never seen him outside the Orpheus, or dressed as casually as he was, with a suit but no tie. His crisp cotton shirt was open at the collar.

"Where are you headed?" he asked as the car idled at the red light.

"I'm going to see Nell," she said. "I don't want you to go out of your way."

"It's no trouble at all," Erven replied. He looked over at her, his hand coming up from the gearshift to touch her cheek. "Especially when you look so lovely."

Cecilia felt her face grow warm. It wasn't anything she hadn't heard before, but it was different here, in the early dusk, driving down a public street. She wasn't at work, drinking and dancing in the sensuous half-darkness of the Orpheus. Real life and the nightclub had seemed so far apart until now.

Erven turned right at the next intersection and pulled up behind a black Packard idling at the curb.

"Will you save me a dance tonight?" he asked, his large hand coming down to cover her small hands resting on her lap.

"Of course," she said immediately. Erven was one of her best clients—he was a skilled dancer, and he didn't attempt to take liberties like some of the other men. She could trust him.

"Good." He leaned closer and kissed her cheek, his mouth lingering so she could feel his breath hot on her cheek. He squeezed her hands and released her. "I'll look for you."

"Thanks for the ride." She slid from the car and hurried toward the apartment building. The doorman nodded at her and she took the elevator to Nell's floor. When she knocked, it took Nell longer than usual to answer. Her head was wrapped in a towel and she still wore a white terrycloth robe. She looked frazzled, and it was unlike her.

"You're early," she said by way of greeting, drawing the door open so Cecilia could enter.

"I ran into Erven and he gave me a ride," she replied, but Nell didn't seem to be listening as she went into the bedroom.

Cecilia unbuttoned her coat and left it lying on the arm of the settee. Nell sat at the vanity, jars of makeup spread out before her. Cecilia's breath caught in her throat as she glimpsed the bruise that shadowed Nell's cheekbone.

"What happened?"

Nell pressed her lips together, her hand closing over the powder puff she held. Their gazes met in the mirror and Cecilia saw the sheen of tears.

"It was nothing," Nell replied. Her gaze skittered away, taking in the open wardrobe.

"Truly?" Cecilia came forward, sliding onto the wide stool next to Nell. Nell's arm came around her and they clung to each other.

"I made him angry," Nell said finally. "I kept asking questions and I shouldn't have."

"About what?" Cecilia frowned.

"My friend Lina has been gone a long time, and I think—" Her voice sounded like it would break. She took a breath. "I know he's keeping her from me. There haven't been any letters from her, even though she promised to write."

"He's taking your mail?"

"He must be. She'd have written by now."

"But why would he? Didn't he like her?" She couldn't understand why Franky would concern himself so closely with Nell's friends.

"He's jealous of her," Nell said. "He thought we spent too much time together."

As the meaning of the words sunk in, Cecilia felt jealousy prickling in her heart.

"You love her," she said, her voice low, as if to say it aloud would only make things worse.

Nell tightened her embrace. "That doesn't mean I don't love you," she said, "but yes, I do. We'd broken things off before she left—she said she couldn't keep seeing me if I couldn't be only hers."

"Why couldn't you?" Cecilia knew she wanted to ask Nell the same thing on her own account, but she hadn't been able to get up the nerve.

"He's always taken care of me," Nell said softly. "I would have been dead by now in some awful flophouse if it wasn't for him."

"When did you meet him?" She could hardly imagine Nell in such straits that she could have been a prostitute.

Nell shook her head. "Those were hard times. I don't want to relive them." She pulled out of their embrace, taking a deep breath and composing her features.

Cecilia tried not to feel hurt, but when Nell stroked her cheek, she knew it had shown on her face.

"Talking about it brings me back there," Nell explained. "I just can't."

"I understand."

Nell straightened, reaching for the foundation powder. "Once I get this done, I'll do your hair up," she said. Her smile widened but seemed brittle.

Cecilia rose and walked to the window, looking out over the darkening street. The jealousy still lingered, but it wasn't as sharp as it had been. She wasn't sure who she felt more jealous of, Lina or Franky. Each of them held a piece of Nell's heart, a piece that wasn't hers.

CHAPTER EIGHT

Lang hated crowds, the crush of bodies, the heat, the perfume, and the noise, so he lingered on the street outside the Orpheus for as long as he could. Only when the crush slowed to a trickle did he make his way inside, checking his coat at the counter. He adjusted the jacket on his one fancy suit, knowing that anyone who looked close enough could see that he was carrying. He never went anywhere without his standard police-issue revolver, even on his night off.

Tonight even a gun wouldn't protect him from what he was about to do. Nell was in there, dancing, having fun, and she had no idea. He had to tell her, though Franky's warning still rang in his ears. Nell treated him as a human being, not as a deviant or a pervert. For that alone she deserved to know the truth. They were two of a kind, him and Nell.

He left the lobby and headed into the darkened ballroom. At first he didn't see her, but as the crowd parted, she was there, dancing with Franky to the band's slow, romantic tune. Her black dress glittered and her red hair was in a stylish up-do. She laughed at something Franky said and Lang imagined he could hear her laughter over the music.

He meandered along the edge of the room, his gaze flitting back every few moments to check on Nell. When Franky led her back to their table and left, he slid through the crowd to her side. The table wasn't empty—Erven Vogt sat there with a dark-haired young woman. She looked familiar, but he couldn't place her.

Erven gave him a nod, but when Nell saw him, she grinned and jumped out of her seat to give him a hug. He held her close for a moment, inhaling the jasmine scent of her perfume.

"It's been so long, Detective," she said. She loved calling him by his title. When he'd made rank, they'd celebrated with champagne. "Sit down. Have a drink."

He took the chair next to her. "I felt a bit lonely, so what better place to be?" He gave her a wink.

"A very good choice," Nell agreed. "I've missed you. Oh, and you remember Erven, of course. And you've met my friend CeeCee."

CeeCee smiled at him. Of course Nell wouldn't want to let on how they'd met. "I don't think he remembers me," she said, partly to Nell, and partly to him, "but we did meet once or twice, at the café."

Lang pretended to give her a once-over. "You've done well for yourself," he replied. "I nearly didn't recognize you."

Franky returned to the table, trailed by a couple of men. Lang recognized Tony Rossi, one of Franky's men, but not the other.

"So you did make it." Franky clapped him on the shoulder, his expression pleasant and genial as always, though his grip was firm.

"Just taking your advice," Lang replied. Franky gave him an approving nod. The men settled at the table and a waiter brought a round of drinks, champagne for the ladies and whiskey for the men. Tony, Franky, and Erven were affable, but Tony's friend sat back, nursing his whiskey.

Tony interrupted Franky midsentence. "The girls don't wanna listen to us jaw," he said, taking a swig of his whiskey. "Paddy, why don't you and the detective take 'em for a spin on the dance floor?"

Tony's companion rose and held out a hand to CeeCee. Lang copied him, holding out his hand for Nell. This might be his only chance. Nell took his hand and they moved onto the dance floor as the band struck up a lively tune.

"Of course they're talking business," Nell said with a pout. "But at least Tony's sensible. He knows I'd get bored."

"And your friend too," Lang observed.

"She's lovely, isn't she?"

"Very pretty," he agreed, watching her dance with the Paddy. She seemed at ease, though a bit shy.

"I know she's not your type," Nell teased. "I haven't met any nice young men to introduce you to lately." He chuckled, beginning to move them to the other side of the ballroom, away from Franky.

"Definitely not. Maybe the one she's with, though," he replied. She threw her head back and laughed.

"I don't think he plays on your team, Lang," she said. "He came round with Tony a while back and he looked me over good."

"A pity," Lang said. "Maybe CeeCee is his type too. Though that young man working the bar with Tomas is delicious."

"I'll tell Tomas you said so," Nell said. Her next words were hushed. "CeeCee's mine, though."

Lang tightened his grip on her hand and moved so they were hidden from Franky, behind one of the columns. "Is that a good idea?" he asked. He didn't want to have to pull CeeCee's body from the river in a few months.

"No," she said, "but I adore her, and Lina's been gone so long."

Her words gave him the entry he needed. "There's something I need to tell you," he said, still reluctant. "But, Nell, you have to promise me that you won't react."

She frowned up at him. "What do you mean?"

"He threatened me, but I couldn't not tell you. Promise me." He squeezed her hand in emphasis. She nodded, and Lang cleared his throat. "I found Lina."

Her eyes widened and she went to speak, but he went on, forestalling her. "She's in the morgue, Nell. We pulled her from the river a while ago. She'll be buried soon."

Even in the muted light of the dance floor he could see her pale. She swallowed and blinked hard. He held her as she trembled, and they turned slowly to the music. He wanted to shake her, to break through the shock.

"I shouldn't have told you. You can't do anything, you know that. He won't allow it."

"I don't care what he'll allow," she said vehemently.

"Keep your voice down," he warned. "And what about her, about CeeCee?"

"He was always jealous of Lina," she said, allowing him to lead her into the mass of couples on the dance floor.

"And he'll be jealous of her too, in time. You know I can't do anything. He's too powerful."

"She'll be fine. I'll keep her safe."

"It'd be safer to send her away."

Nell nodded and straightened her shoulders. Her eyes glittered, but the tears didn't fall.

"I can't let her go, Lang. And Franky...I'll do something," she said. Her mouth was a thin line and the sorrow he'd expected was muted by fury in her voice. "He'll regret it."

CHAPTER NINE

New Year's Eve 1925

Sheridan accepted Tony's invitation to the New Year's bash at the Orpheus without hesitation. He'd joked with Tony about the dames, but women were the least of his concerns. He wanted in. He hadn't managed to crack Franky's inner circle, no matter how many times he'd been to the Orpheus in the past few months. He was unremarkable, neither rich nor powerful enough to gain attention.

He and Tony wove through the bustling crowd, sliding in past a muscled doorman in an immaculate tux who gave Tony a nod even as he held back a pair of men determined to push their way in.

"Biggest party of the year, Paddy!" Tony exclaimed. Sheridan grinned.

"Sheridan!" A man clapped him on the shoulder and he turned to see Dooley at his side, resplendent in a tailored black tuxedo with a green silk tie and matching vest. They shook hands and Tony gave Sheridan a wave as he continued into the ballroom.

"You've done well," Dooley said with approval. "An invite to the Orpheus tonight is like gold at the end of the rainbow, my friend."

"I wasn't going to be a warehouse rat for long," Sheridan replied.

Dooley chuckled. "Of course not. Anyway, I hardly recognized you like this—all fancy."

Sheridan adjusted his cufflinks. He didn't wear a tuxedo—he couldn't afford one—but he had on his nicest black suit. "It'll do well enough."

"And you've come with Tony Rossi," Dooley observed.

"It's still not enough," Sheridan replied, his voice low. Dooley nodded.

"You'll never be satisfied," he said. "Now come have a drink with me and we'll toast the new year. I know here I'll get a proper whiskey." The crowd was three or four deep around the bar, but Dooley managed to worm his way up to the front. He emerged holding two brimming glasses.

"How'd you manage that?" Sheridan asked, taking a sip. The whiskey burned his throat as he swallowed.

"Money, my friend. Lots of it, and consistently. That fellow tending bar is a pal of mine." He grinned. "To us." He drank down half the glass in a huge swallow, then sighed in contentment. "Get me a girl and I'll be in heaven."

Sheridan followed him toward the ballroom. He didn't have a preference, but he'd take what he could get. Beside him, Dooley strained to see over the crowd.

"Can you see a gorgeous little blonde, about five foot nothing and curvy?" he asked Sheridan.

"Short hair? Long? What's she wearing?" Sheridan craned his neck to see over the people in front of them.

"Short hair, curls," Dooley answered. "She's my best gal, little Scarlett."

A glint of red hair under a spotlight caught his eye, and he saw Nell at the edge of the dance floor, talking to her friend CeeCee. Next to them stood a girl that fit Dooley's description. He nudged Dooley.

"That her?" He indicated the three women.

Dooley chortled with delight. "That's her. Let me introduce you."

Getting to them proved to be a challenge as Dooley was stopped several times by dancers looking for a client. He waved them off, promising to look for them later.

"Done the rounds, have you?" Sheridan quipped.

"Wouldn't you?" Dooley gave him a wink.

"Haven't had the chance," he replied. He didn't have the money to spend at the Orpheus night in and night out, even if he wanted to. He'd only recently moved to a better, albeit tiny, apartment, and out of the tenement near the stockyards.

"Scarlett!" Dooley exclaimed. The young woman embraced him with a charming giggle.

Nell looked on with an amused smile. Her friend CeeCee laughed before her attention was pulled away by Erven Vogt. Sheridan didn't care for the man, the way he flashed his wealth about and looked down on everyone else. The couple headed out to the dance floor.

"Good evening." Sheridan gave Nell a brief courtly bow.

"How do you do." She gave him a measured look in return, moving aside as Dooley took Scarlett out into the crowded dance floor, following Erven and CeeCee.

"May I have this dance?" Sheridan asked, holding out a hand. This could be his only opportunity, and he wasn't going to pass it up. She gave his hand a light squeeze and let him lead her into the crush.

"I wondered when you might finally ask me for a dance," she said, giving him a flirtatious smile as she pressed closer. He could hardly believe his luck.

"Your friend doesn't make it easy," he replied.

"Franky?"

"Quite."

"And you're more sensible than most," she observed. "But it makes for a lonely time for me. You seem to be the only one man enough to chance it tonight."

Sheridan chuckled. "He can't do anything to me." Nothing worse than what he'd done already. And if dancing with Nell was the way to hurt Franky, he'd do it gladly.

Nell watched him as they moved about the dance floor, and he watched her in return, his gaze roaming over her bare shoulders, across her cleavage, and to her elegant and poised face. Her lips were richly painted and her gray eyes seemed smoky thanks to her dramatic eye makeup.

"So you're one of Tony's pals," she noted. "But you're definitely not Italian. That's odd for Tony, you know."

"I suppose I made an impression."

"How did you manage it?" She seemed truly curious.

"I made my mark," he said, and recounted his experience with Angelo. "And now I work with Tony."

Nell nodded, more to herself than him. "I have a favor to ask of you, Mr. Sheridan," she said, her voice low, husky like it had been when he first saw her in the back rooms of the Orpheus.

"What can I do?" He imagined her asking him to take her away. He would save her from Franky; it would be the perfect way to provoke Franky Greco into a rage and put him off his guard.

"I need you to pay court to CeeCee."

He stopped dead and Nell had to nudge him.

"What for? Vogt seems to have that well in hand."

"It's complicated," Nell replied. "But I need you to because you're not one of Franky's friends."

"That still doesn't make sense." He'd danced with CeeCee a couple of times and the dances were pleasant enough, but he hadn't considered more, not when she spent most of her time with Vogt.

"I can't tell you," Nell said, her hand tightening on his shoulder.

"You'll have to." Messing with the girl of one of Franky's friends wouldn't help his cause.

"If I tell you, will you help me? You can't say a word."

"I won't say anything," Sheridan assured her. "But I won't decide until I know why."

Nell gave a cautious glance around, barely moving her head. She must have been satisfied that they were well hidden in the crowd, because she leaned forward. "I love her."

"So?"

She glared at him and raised a brow. And waited. The pieces began to fall into place.

"And you want me to do this because…?"

"It'll take Franky's attention off her." Nell forced a smile as if they were talking of something amusing and inconsequential. "He has a jealous streak, a dangerous one. I don't want him to hurt her."

Sheridan considered her statement as he moved automatically through the final steps of the dance.

"I want a favor in return," he said as the music ended with a flourish.

"What?"

"I don't know yet," he said, "but I want your word."

Her brow furrowed. "If it's in my power, you have it."

"I'll let you know." He let go of her hand. "You'd best go." He could see Franky at the edge of the dance floor.

"Soon?" she asked. He nodded and stepped away, averting his attention before Franky noticed them. He saw her turn as Franky reached her, giving him a brilliant smile and taking his arm. He watched them go. This could be his chance.

❖

Cecilia lingered at the edge of the dance floor, only half listening to Erven. She wanted the evening to end, for Franky to drop her and Nell at her apartment. Erven paused in his speech and she smiled at him. He took it as encouragement and clasped her hand.

"Shall we dance this one?" He handed their empty glasses off to a passing waiter.

"Of course."

They joined the crowd of couples, barely able to do more than stand in place. She glanced around, wondering where Nell might be. "I've never seen it so crowded," she said by way of excuse.

"My father used to tell me about the First Ward ball," Erven said with a grin. "I think tonight is as close to that revelry as we'll ever get."

"When was that?" She'd never heard of the ball.

"Years ago," he answered with a wink. "Before you were born, I'll bet."

She began to reply, but someone nudged her in the back and she stumbled forward. The crowd had drawn in ever closer and she felt a surge of claustrophobia. Erven steadied her.

"I think we should give up on dancing," she said, raising her voice to be heard over the music.

"Indeed." Erven began to move through the crowd, his height breaking a path through the couples. Once they reached their usual table, she breathed a sigh of relief.

Franky's man Tony sat at the table alone, apparently keeping watch, for he rose as she settled into a chair. "I'll be back shortly," he said, disappearing into the crowd.

"Sensible, keeping him here," Erven remarked. "Else our table would be taken over by the rabble. Another drink, CeeCee?"

"Please." She watched him go before turning her gaze back to the dance floor. Where was Nell? She didn't want it to come midnight without having seen her.

"Can I join you?"

Tony's friend stood there, and he rested a hand on the back of a chair. She'd seen him more regularly in the last few weeks, always with Tony, though he never said much to her. His attention had usually been fixed on his glass of whiskey. Or Nell. He seemed to have a fondness for her, though most men did. She gave him a nod, and he settled into the chair next to her, pulling out a silver cigarette case. He flipped it open, offering her one. She almost declined but then decided, why not? It might help her pass the time until Nell came back.

"Thank you. Are you enjoying yourself?" she asked as he lit her cigarette. She inhaled cautiously, the scent of the smoke sharp in her mouth.

"About as much fun as you," he said, his mouth quirking up at the corner. Not quite a smile, not quite a smirk. "She's with Franky."

Cecilia schooled her expression. His dark gaze rested on her, seeming to judge her reaction. "I'm sure I'll see her before midnight."

He shrugged. "Maybe. But you'd rather be with her than with Vogt." He rested his elbows on the table and leaned forward so his words wouldn't carry.

"Erven's very nice," she replied, focusing on her hands on the tablecloth, willing them to stay relaxed, unclenched. She picked up her cigarette from the ashtray.

Sheridan chuckled. "That's not a very glowing endorsement," he observed.

"And what business is it of yours?" she asked sharply.

"Probably nothing. But still, I can't have been the only one who's noticed. It's dangerous. Do you think Franky would allow it for long?"

Suddenly the overly warm ballroom seemed very cold. She couldn't think of what to say to him. Her words caught in her throat, like the smoke from her cigarette. She stubbed it out.

"Excuse me." She left him there, weaving through the tables and the crowd until she reached the ladies' lounge. She ignored the chatter of two women retouching their makeup at the mirror, and sank into a chair, praying for few moments of privacy.

She'd hardly thought of Franky at all beyond a vague uneasiness easily pushed aside. She'd never felt for anyone the way she felt for Nell—every night they were together took her breath away, and she could hardly imagine life without her. And she knew she couldn't leave. She needed the job, and most of all, she needed Nell. She pulled up her legs and rested her head on her arms, propped on her bent knees.

"CeeCee?"

Nell's voice startled her, and she sat up and smoothed her dark, sequined dress. Nell looked relieved to have found her, though it seemed strange she could be relieved over such a little thing—after all, she hadn't been gone long. Sheridan's words echoed in her mind.

"I felt a bit dizzy," she replied. A flimsy excuse, but she didn't want Nell to worry. "I think I had too much champagne."

"Are you feeling better now?" Nell clasped her hand. "I wanted to find you before the countdown. But Sheridan will take you home—I can't chance angering Franky tonight."

"Sheridan?" Why him, of all people? Why not Erven? She said as much to Nell.

"Sheridan's safer," Nell said. She pulled Cecilia closer, and Cecilia was thankful the room had emptied out. Nell stroked her cheek.

"Safer?" Cecilia echoed.

"Trust me on this," Nell said, giving her a too-brief kiss. Her usually animated face was solemn.

"Of course I trust you," Cecilia replied. "But why are you concerned now?"

"I can't tell you yet," Nell said, giving her another kiss. "I just need you to trust me, and know that I adore you."

Cecilia caught Nell's hand as she began to walk away. "Has something happened?"

"I promised Franky I'd spend more time with him." Nell gave her hand a squeeze before she let go. "It doesn't mean I love you any less." She slipped out the door and Cecilia stared blankly at the empty room. She tried to think of when Franky had ever said or done anything to show his distaste for her, but she couldn't bring up even one unpleasant time.

But how had he been with Nell? She hadn't seen any bruises since that night, but Nell had begun to withdraw. She wanted to confront Franky, even imagined shouting at him and taking Nell aside, but she knew it was a fantasy. Franky ruled the Orpheus with an iron fist in a velvet glove. Sometimes she was sure he removed the glove. She shuddered.

Sheridan it was.

❖

Nell found him by the bar when he least wanted to be found. Angelo prowled about the ballroom with a couple of his friends, drinking heavily, and Sheridan knew he'd be in for a beating if he was caught alone. He nursed a whiskey and considered what favor he'd ask of Nell.

It would be easy enough to spend time with CeeCee. She was a lovely girl, delicate and pretty, though not with the same kind of brash confidence that Nell seemed to exude. It didn't mean she did poorly with the men looking for a companion; her small stature and quiet elegance attracted more than a few. Men liked women who looked as if they might break, but did he?

"Have you decided on your favor?" Nell asked as she sidled up to him, giving the bartender her order. She hardly looked at him and as he glanced up from his whiskey, he saw Franky waiting for her a few paces away. Fury simmered just below the surface and he took another sip of whiskey to keep his calm. That bastard.

"I haven't decided, but you needn't worry."

Nell's hand brushed his as she reached for her drink, noticeable to him, but Franky would miss the casual touch. "Thank you," she said, mostly to the bartender, though she inclined her head to him. He saw her relief. "She knows."

"All right." Sheridan knocked back the dregs of his drink and pretended not to notice her leave, though he turned just in time to see Franky rest his hand possessively on the small of Nell's back. He led her into the ballroom, and Sheridan saw her give Franky a tender smile. He could believe she meant it. She was good. He pushed off from the bar and went to find CeeCee.

After dodging Angelo yet again, though the man was roaring drunk enough to almost lose his footing on the few steps leading up from the dance floor to the lobby, Sheridan found CeeCee just outside the ladies' lounge. She conversed with another of the dancers but paused to give him a tremulous smile. He took that as an invitation and joined them.

"Good evening, my dear," he said smoothly. The other woman, a buxom blonde, took the hint and left them, going in search of her own partner.

"Hello again," CeeCee said, hooking her arm through his. It felt surprisingly easy. He set his hand over hers. This would be the way into Franky's circle of friends.

"It's almost midnight," he said. The waiters were beginning to pass out glasses of champagne and he took a glass, handing it to CeeCee, then grabbed one for himself. He led them into the ballroom. "Do you want to find your friend?"

"I don't know that she'll want to see me," CeeCee said with a frown. Her gaze drifted toward Nell, and her expression grew sad. She and Franky were onstage, sharing a laugh. Another man joined them, the pair bracketing Nell. He knew Erven Vogt mostly by reputation and tales from Tony; they'd never spoken beyond pleasantries. He was nearly as criminal as Franky, though his image was squeaky clean.

"I could tell you tales about her boyfriend," Sheridan said, pitching his voice low so it wouldn't carry to those couples standing nearby. It worked to take her attention from Nell. CeeCee's eyes widened.

"What?" she whispered.

"Later, perhaps," he said. There were too many people, too many ears to carry the tale back to Franky Greco.

A great cheer went up from the dance floor where couples had crowded near the stage. There was a drumroll and the spotlight picked out the bandleader, who held up a hand.

"Ladies and gentlemen!" he bellowed into the microphone. "We're nearly there, at 1926! Now, I want you to count with me—" He drew out an ostentatious pocket watch.

The crowd buzzed with anticipation.

"All right, here we go!" The bandleader began to count down and the crowd joined in. When the count reached one, there was a great cheer and the jingle of glasses clinking. Confetti and balloons cascaded from the rafters, let go from a cache opened by a pulley system.

"Happy New Year, CeeCee."

They clinked their glasses and Sheridan took a long sip, though she barely touched hers.

"And a kiss for the new year!" the bandleader shouted, pulling a dancer up beside him on the stage. He bent her back over his arm and kissed her deeply. Sheridan chuckled and handed his empty glass off to a waiter.

"We'd best do this properly," he said. He stroked CeeCee's cheek and she looked up at him, her lips parted in surprise. He kissed her gently at first, until he felt her respond, then he deepened the kiss. She tasted of champagne and her mouth was soft. When they broke apart, he wanted to kiss her again, and not because Nell had asked him for a favor.

CeeCee rested against him, her head on his shoulder. He held her, caressing her bare arm. Around them the celebrations went on, but the moment seemed to stretch.

"Sheridan!"

He heard Dooley's voice, then he was clapped on the back. Dooley swayed where he stood, his face ruddy from drink and his hair mussed from running his hand through it too many times. His glasses were still on straight, but that was a wonder. He was trailed by Scarlett, and she looked peeved, and quite sober in comparison to Dooley.

"All right?" Sheridan asked, catching him by the arm as he

staggered. CeeCee stepped back and he saw her and Scarlett exchange a commiserating glance.

"Fine, fine." Dooley waved away the concern. "You've found yourself a lovely dame, you lucky bastard," he slurred, eyeing CeeCee appreciatively.

"And you're neglecting yours, my friend," Sheridan replied. He'd bet a day's wages that Scarlett would leave him before the end of the night for someone more capable—and less drunk.

Dooley stumbled and Sheridan walked him over to a table, depositing him in an empty chair. Scarlett sighed and plopped down into the seat next to him, propping her chin on her hand. Dooley said something but it was incomprehensible. He crossed his arms on the table, rested his head, and began to snore.

"Leave him there to sleep it off," Sheridan remarked to Scarlett.

"So much for a night to remember," she quipped, rolling her eyes.

Sheridan glanced at CeeCee and found her several steps distant, her back to him. Her gaze centered on Franky's table, where he sat with Nell, Erven Vogt, and several others. Franky put his arm around Nell. Coming up behind her, Sheridan heard CeeCee sigh.

"It's not fair," she muttered.

"Shall we join them?" he asked. It would give him an opportunity to size up Franky face-to-face.

CeeCee's shoulders slumped and she shook her head. "No. I don't think I could stand seeing him all over her. I'd rather just go."

"I'll take you home." Nell couldn't say that he hadn't indulged her favor completely. CeeCee probably lived in some posh little pad, maybe one that a fellow like Erven paid for. That's what dancers were always angling for: a rich man to set them up nicely.

"Stay," CeeCee replied. "I can make my own way home."

"It's late, and it's no trouble." Franky could wait, for now.

"You're only here as a favor to Nell, and as far as I'm concerned, it only extends to being in public with me. I can take a cab."

"Where do you live? We could split the fare." Sheridan took out his cigarette case—it was new and he was fond of it, as it showed he was moving up in the world—and lit a cigarette.

"None of your business." CeeCee glanced toward Nell again and her mouth compressed into a thin line. Franky was kissing Nell— and it was more than a tender press of lips. Sheridan raised a brow. Marking his territory, Sheridan thought, noting the fleeting looks of disappointment from several men nearby.

"All right, let's go." CeeCee turned away from the scene. He took her arm and they collected their coats from a tired-looking coat-check girl with smudged makeup and a pale face. Sheridan left her a tip, and she perked up enough to give him a smile.

He helped CeeCee on with her coat, then settled his hand at the small of her back, leading her out into the cold night. A line of cabs sat at the curb. Attending such a lavish gathering had its advantages. He took CeeCee to the front of the line and handed her up to the backseat of the Checker cab. He stepped up after her.

"Where to?" The driver asked.

"Well?" Sheridan asked her.

"West Forty-Ninth at South Morgan," she said wearily, slumping back against the cold leather seat, stuffing her hands into the pockets of her woolen jacket.

"'Fraid I don't go that way," the driver said with a snort. "I'll take you as far as West Pershing though."

Sheridan leaned forward, hooking the collar of the man's jacket and twisting it in his fist. He slammed the man back against the seat.

"You'll take us all the way there," he said, "or you won't have a way to make a living when I break your legs."

The driver struggled to breathe and Sheridan let up the pressure for a quick moment.

"All right," the driver gasped. "All right." Sheridan released him and sat back. The driver straightened his collar, muttering to himself.

"What was that?" Sheridan leaned forward again. The driver gulped.

"Nothing, sir," he said. He started up the car and with a shudder, they trundled forward.

CeeCee was silent during the ride, her face turned toward the window. The driver didn't bother with conversation either, which made for an interminable trip. Sheridan hadn't shown any surprise when CeeCee had named one of the worst tenement areas of the city, but now as they reached the edge of the district, he wondered why a girl with so many high-ranking friends would choose to live in such a place.

The cab shuddered to a stop in the middle of the refuse-strewn street.

"We're here," the driver said unnecessarily.

Sheridan dug a couple bills from his pocket. "Happy New Year." He helped CeeCee from the cab and watched as it drove away, leaving them standing in the empty street. "Which one's yours?" he asked, glancing at the dilapidated buildings.

CeeCee pointed to one of the worst. "I'll be fine from here." She avoided looking at him, starting across the street. He caught up to her easily.

"I'll see you up," he said, tucking her hand into the crook of his elbow, resting his hand over hers. "You think I haven't seen a tenement before? I used to live a few streets over."

That got her attention.

"We're not so different, you and I, except maybe you've not been in as much trouble as I have." He chuckled as he said the words. He doubted she'd ever spent time in jail, or juvie hall. She looked too soft for that. But Nell—he'd bet she'd done time somewhere.

"Where do you live now?" CeeCee asked, her demeanor softening. They ascended the creaking stairs to the front door and he pushed it open, letting her duck under his arm and inside.

"A little place just north of the river," he said. "You should come see it sometime."

She smiled at that. "One of these days." She took a key from her purse. On the third floor she stopped in front of a sagging door. "Thank you for seeing me home."

"You're not in yet," he remarked. He waited as she turned the key and pushed the door open. The room was dark, but she walked in and soon he saw the flicker of light as she lit a lamp. He turned to go, but stopped when he heard her cry.

"Ma!"

CHAPTER TEN

L ang shouldn't have come. Navarra was carousing with Franky
Greco, a young and lithe dancer by his side, hanging on his every
word. Or, more likely, hanging on for a chance at a good night's pay.

He turned back to the bar and gestured for another whiskey. It was
so easy for them—they could fondle and flirt as openly as they pleased,
and he was forced to skulk and hide, resorting to quick encounters in
darkened bars and the occasional alleyway.

A pity. The bartender's assistant was delicious, though, in his
starched vest and bow tie, even though the cloth had started to wilt with
the late hour. He caught the young man's eye, and even in the dim light
he could see the flush on his cheeks. A possibility? He didn't want to
spend the night alone, and the man had seemed receptive last time.

When the young man retreated into the back with an order from
the bartender for more champagne, Lang tossed back his whiskey and
followed. The glare of the lights bouncing off the whitewashed walls
nearly blinded him, he'd been so used to the darkness of the ballroom.
When his vision cleared, the young man stood nearby, smoking a
cigarette. His foot rested on a case of Veuve Clicquot. He gave Lang a
rakish grin.

"I thought I might see you," he said, sidling closer and laying a
hand on Lang's lapel. "What can I do for you?"

Lang smiled. They both knew the answer to that question. "What's
your name?"

"Gabe."

Lang felt Gabe's lean fingers slide down his lapel and brush over
his crotch, a quick tease before he took his hand. Gabe led him down
the hallway, pausing at a plain closed door. Lang was hard already; he
could imagine those fingers on his zipper and then on his cock.

Gabe gave him a mischievous half smirk as he opened the door. The aroma of bleach and cleaning chemicals wafted out, but Lang didn't care.

"Broom closet," Gabe said, tugging him inside. He stumbled in the near darkness, catching himself on a wooden shelf that creaked under his weight.

Gabe pressed himself full against Lang's back and his fingers fumbled with the zipper of Lang's trousers, finally pulling it down and sliding his fingers inside. Lang groaned. Those fingers were calloused and warm against him, wrapping around his cock, stroking him. He could feel Gabe's erection pressing against him and he wanted nothing more than to have their roles reversed so he could bend Gabe over the wooden crates in the corner and have his way with him.

But he didn't. He braced himself against a shelf and groaned as Gabe stroked him, making soft noises in his ear as he ground himself against Lang's ass.

"Do you like that?" Gabe murmured. Lang bit out a yes, and he heard Gabe chuckle. Gabe slithered around in front of him and dropped to his knees.

Lang saw stars as Gabe's hot mouth engulfed him, sucking him in deep. It had been so long. He clutched at Gabe's short, curly hair, forcing him into a rhythm that made him gasp. He wasn't going to last long, but at that moment, he didn't care.

"I'm going to—" He gasped, and Gabe held his hips, taking him in fully, till the tip of his nose touched his belly. He arched his back and closed his eyes, shooting deep into Gabe's mouth. He vaguely heard the creak of the door, and the light snapped on. He opened his eyes, just in time to be blinded by a photographer's flash lamp.

❖

"She'll be here for some time," the doctor said kindly, his tired, lined face compassionate. The compassion almost made the news worse.

"But she'll get better?" Cecilia hated how desperate she sounded. Without her mother…She didn't even want to think about life if her mother died.

"I've rarely seen a case as progressed as hers. You're very lucky you didn't catch it yourself."

She knew he meant well. The worn, sterile white walls seemed to press in on her, the smell of chemicals and stale air burning her nostrils. She hadn't slept and it was nearly dawn. Her feet hurt in her dancing shoes, and the dress she'd worn to the Orpheus seemed garish in the midst of such bleak surroundings. How could anyone get well in such a place?

She felt a hand on the small of her back. Sheridan had waited with her and now he stepped up beside her to face the doctor.

"Thank you," she said to the doctor. Her mother rested in an isolation ward. She wanted to stay with her, but a nurse had told her brusquely that no one was allowed. She'd stood at the window, watching the bed with her mother's frail form until the doctor had come.

"Go home and rest. When you come back later, you can see her then." The doctor glanced at Sheridan as if he was responsible for her.

"Let's go," Sheridan said. "You're dead on your feet." His arm encircled her and she let herself lean on him as he led her down the hallway and down the flights of stairs, out into the cold morning air. A breeze gusted around the corner of the building, and whatever warmth she'd retained vanished. She clenched her teeth tight so they wouldn't chatter.

"We'll go to my place," Sheridan said, flagging down a passing cab. "It's closer."

She had no energy to argue. He bundled her into the cab and she slumped against the seat and closed her eyes. If only she'd pressed the matter more, made her mother see the doctor. It shouldn't have come to this.

❖

Cecilia woke when the cab came to a lurching stop.

"CeeCee, come on." Sheridan's voice was surprisingly gentle for a man who'd strong-armed their cabbie earlier in the night, but now he treated her as if she were spun glass. He took her hand and helped her out of the cab, paying the fare while she stood groggily on the sidewalk. The street was completely unfamiliar, but she saw it only briefly.

Sheridan took her into a brick apartment building and up several flights of stairs. He unlocked a wooden door, like every other in the hall, and they went inside.

"You'll have to excuse me," he said. "I wasn't expecting company."

She nodded. All she wanted was sleep—someplace warm she could curl up, and a blanket.

Sheridan's apartment was smaller than she'd expected, hardly more than a single room. There was a stained radiator under the window, and it clanked and shuddered. She could see the shadow of a fire escape. One wall was taken over with a large cabinet that ran its length, and a small sofa and table were shoved against the other wall. A door opened into a small bathroom.

"Where do you sleep?"

He gave her an amused smile as he walked over to the cabinets. He tugged on a handle she hadn't noticed and an entire section of the cabinet began to descend, revealing a bed.

"Go get washed up," he said.

Once in the bathroom, she stared at herself in the small mirror. Her makeup—what remained of it—was smudged beyond repair and she looked pale as death. She shuddered.

Sheridan opened the door and she gave a start. He held out a shirt of striped white cotton. It looked like one of his. She tried to refuse it.

"You don't want to sleep in that dress," he said. "Just put it on." She took the shirt and he closed the door.

She stripped off her dress and put on the nightshirt, leaving on her stockings and underthings for warmth. The shirt smelled faintly of laundry soap and cologne and it fell to her knees. It would do. She washed her face and dried it on a rough towel. The tile floor was cold on her feet and the water made her feel colder still. Would she ever get warm?

When she emerged from the bathroom, Sheridan had pulled the curtain over the window, shutting out most of the faint sunlight, though the room still wasn't very dark. He stood watching the street through a crack in the curtain, his back to her. The covers on the bed had been nicely pulled back on one side and the pillow plumped. She clutched her folded dress to her chest, curling her toes against the wooden floor.

"Where will you sleep?" she asked. The sofa was too small to stretch out on; it was barely long enough for two people to sit on comfortably. Sheridan turned from the window, tugging the curtain closed. His tie hung loose and his shirt had been unbuttoned at the collar, showing the hollow of his throat and a sparse shadow of hair.

In this low light, brighter than the gloom of the Orpheus, she got her first good look at him. The toes of his shoes were slightly scuffed and she could see now that the cloth of his suit was not as fine as it had seemed. His hair fell over his forehead; he'd run his hand through it and mussed the carefully combed style. His dark blue eyes watched her patiently as she took him in.

"We'll have to share," he said. She looked at the bed again, then at him. The bed was a double, but it didn't seem big enough for two people to have much space. She gave him a level glance and decided he wasn't likely to bother her. There were shadows under his eyes and he looked nearly as tired as she was.

"All right." She set her dress on the sofa and sat on the bed. Sheridan went into the bathroom, closing the door behind him with a sharp snap. The bed creaked slightly, then settled. Cecilia drew up her feet and tucked under the covers, laying her head on the pillow and drawing the sheets up around her chin. Her feet felt like ice and she curled up on her side, hoping for some warmth to return. She stared at the door, at the drab respectability of the small room. Another suit of brown serge hung on the hook to the left of the door, and a handful of clean shirts hung next to it. A second pair of shoes sat below the clothes, and a worn woolen jacket lay slumped on the floor where it must have fallen.

She closed her eyes and tried to will herself to sleep, but the place was too different. She wanted her own bed. How had she ended up here? She wanted to be home with her mother; even if it was in a tenement, at least it was theirs. Her room would be empty now, the mice free to roam over the table and in the sheets. She shivered again. If Franky hadn't been with Nell, she could have been curled up in bed next to her, in her gentle arms, cocooned in soft, perfumed sheets. Here she was alone, in a stranger's room, and her mother was dying.

Cecilia choked back a sob and pressed her lips together. She wouldn't cry. She couldn't. Once she started, she knew she'd never stop.

The bathroom door opened and she heard Sheridan's footsteps, and the rustle of cloth as he dumped his clothes on the sofa. The bed dipped and creaked as he sat on the other side, and she dared not move.

He lay back and pulled up the covers, and she felt the tug as he adjusted the sheets. His arm brushed her back, then pulled away. She could hear his breathing. Her fingers clutched tightly at the sheets. She wished with all her might to be back home, but it didn't work.

The sobs choked her throat and she tried to swallow, tried to stifle her misery. Her shoulders shook and the tears squeezed out from under her lashes, wetting the pillow under her cheek.

She felt the mattress dip and shift as Sheridan turned over, and she knew he was facing her. The bed creaked again as he leaned up on one elbow. She wouldn't cry; she just wouldn't. She felt his hand on her hair, a gentle caress, much like the ones her mother used to give.

The dam broke and she sobbed aloud, clutching at her pillow in agony. She felt his hands turning her over, and then she was drawn to his bare chest. He drew the covers around them and held her as she cried, stroking her hair and murmuring soothing, incomprehensible words. She thought she heard him call her darling, but she couldn't be sure.

The cold began to give way to the warmth of his body, and when her sorrow had run its course, she slept.

❖

When a key scraped in the lock, Lang wearily lifted his head. If he found that little bastard... After the flash and disorientation, he'd found himself locked in the broom closet. Alone. He squinted into the sudden spill of light from the hallway. A dark figure stood in the door and Lang groped for his gun.

"You won't need it," the man said, and the voice was familiar. He heard the man chuckle. "Come on then, Detective, let's go."

Lang staggered to his feet. When he reached the door, his vision had cleared and he found himself next to Franky's man, Tony Rossi.

"Where's that little bastard?" he growled. Tony laughed.

"At home asleep by now," Tony said, taking a cigar from his pocket. He stuck it in his mouth but didn't bother to light it. "I don't know what you did, Detective, but the boss isn't very happy with you."

"Why couldn't he just say so?" Lang muttered, more to himself than to Tony.

Tony snorted. "Given his mood, the janitor's closet is better. But if you piss him off any more, he said to tell you he'll make sure your little playtime is splashed all over the papers."

Lang punched the wall in fury.

CHAPTER ELEVEN

Sheridan woke with the scent of perfume in his nostrils and a soft form curled against his. He blinked away some of the fatigue and sat up in bed. Whatever springs there'd been in the old Murphy bed protested, waking his companion.

Though he'd slept with the young and lovely Perla only a few days before, waking up next to CeeCee was head and shoulders above anything he'd experienced in Perla's arms. He hadn't even seduced CeeCee, but already he liked her. As she shifted in bed, he pushed the covers back and got up. He never lingered once he woke, not even if a lovely girl was in his bed. He had to face the day.

He parted the curtains, brightening the drab room as he glanced outside. The sun shone brightly, reflecting off the snowy streets. A new year. He hadn't thought it would end up this way.

"What time is it?"

He glanced at CeeCee, who sat up in bed and drew the covers around her shoulders. Her dark hair was a chaotic mess and her face was devoid of makeup, but a word popped into his head. Beautiful.

"Midafternoon, I think." He remembered to answer her question before taking more time to ogle her, though a delicate flush had already spread over her cheeks.

"That's late."

"It was a long night." He found his cigarettes on top of the bureau and lit one to give his hands something to do.

"It was." She looked pensive, though the barest hint of the flush still clung to her cheekbones. "I should go back to the hospital and see if they'll let me see Ma."

"We'd best get you home first, so you can change." He nodded at the dress folded on the sofa. "That's not suited."

CeeCee let the blankets fall from her shoulders and she got out of bed. He admired the way his pajama shirt looked on her, though he wished she hadn't kept on her stockings. She looked tiny, dainty even, in the oversized shirt, no bigger than the fairies his mother used to tell him about.

"Excuse me." She grabbed her dress, flitting into the bathroom and shutting the door. He shrugged, taking a drag on his cigarette before he stubbed it out. He might as well get dressed. If he lingered he'd want to take her back to bed and relieve his tension.

It was nearly impossible to find a cab, so they walked most of the way to the back of the stockyards, with the exception of a short distance when the driver of a rickety old truck allowed them to perch on the running board. CeeCee clung to him and he was a bit disappointed when the truck shuddered to a stop and they had to keep walking.

CeeCee kept her hands shoved into the pockets of her coat, and she didn't look at him as they trudged through the snow and muck. As they reached the edge of the stockyards, she glanced at him. "You don't need to escort me," she said.

"It's no trouble." It wasn't really. Tony had told him Franky always allowed New Year's Day as a holiday for his organization, so there wasn't much for him to do unless he wanted to spend the day in a diner somewhere—if they were open. Still, he was glad when they reached the run-down tenement where CeeCee lived. He rubbed his chilled hands. He could use a cup of coffee, if she had any.

CeeCee knocked the snow off of her shoes and preceded him into the building. The inside wasn't much warmer and he could see his breath. They ascended the stairs and he was caught off guard when CeeCee suddenly stopped.

In place of the doorknob and lock to her room sat a locking bar and a padlock.

"You're behind on your rent," called a voice from below. Sheridan glanced down. A barrel of a man with greasy, lank hair and an untidy suit climbed the stairs, shoving past them to stand before the door. "Until you pay up, I can't let you in."

CeeCee found her voice. "You have no right!"

"I have every right," he said with a sneer. He looked CeeCee over and Sheridan saw the man lick his lips. "If you can afford that dress, you can afford your rent."

Sheridan caught CeeCee's glance. He knew she'd paid out almost her night's worth of tips for the men who took her mother to hospital, and she'd need the rest to pay the hospital bill.

"How much does she owe?" he asked the man.

"Who are you?" the man challenged. He turned back to CeeCee. "If you want in, I want money in advance for the next month. You and your ma are too unreliable."

"I don't have that much," CeeCee retorted, "and you know it."

The landlord chuckled. "Then that's just too bad."

Sheridan had heard enough. Before he could even consider his actions, he'd grasped the man by the shoulders and slammed his bulk into the wall next to CeeCee's door. The landlord grunted and brought his arms up to knock Sheridan's hands aside. Instead of fumbling to retain his grip, Sheridan let go, targeting the man's midsection with a sharp right hook. When the man bent forward, Sheridan had him by the throat. He squeezed. One thing about prison and being one of Franky Greco's thugs—it had done wonders for his strength.

The man struggled but Sheridan didn't ease up. When he began to turn blue, Sheridan relented just enough for the man to gasp.

"Give me the key," Sheridan commanded. The landlord gurgled out something that might have been a slur, and Sheridan tightened his grip once more. He glanced over at CeeCee. She was wide-eyed but didn't look as if she'd interfere. Good.

"If you think the cops are going to come when your body is found in the alley later today, you'd be wrong," Sheridan said flatly. "My boss"—he hated calling Franky that, but it was the truth, after a fashion—"has them in his pocket."

The man fumbled in his jacket pocket but his hand fell limply to the side. As he collapsed, Sheridan stepped back to avoid being caught by his bulk. He fished for the key and drew it out, handing it to CeeCee. Her hand was like ice.

"Go on in, make some coffee. I'll be in once I take care of him." The landlord was just beginning to come around. She gave him a jerky nod and unlocked the padlock, pushing the door open. He hauled the man to a sitting position, propping him against the wall. The landlord blinked and gasped for air.

"Now," Sheridan said, his tone companionable. "You and I need to have a talk."

"Have you always done that?"

He didn't answer her at first and Cecilia wondered if she'd been too nosy.

"Done what?" Sheridan sat casually at the table, his hand loose around his coffee cup, looking as if he belonged there.

Cecilia sat down across from him, warming her hands on her own chipped teacup. The room was beginning to get warmer now that he'd stoked the fire in the small stove. She'd changed into one of her everyday dresses, a plain dark woolen dress she'd chosen more for warmth than looks. She felt dull and ugly now that she was out of her evening dress.

"Do you always rough people up when you can't get your way?"

His level stare seemed empty, then he shifted in his seat. "It's what I do," he replied. "It's what I've had to do."

"But why?" Her own parents had held no truck with violence, and until she'd come to Chicago, the worst she'd seen was a drunken brawl after a social dance in town. He seemed to stifle a smile, or maybe a smirk, but she could tell he was amused by her question.

"You're in love with the girlfriend of the notorious Franky Greco and you don't know why?" He drained his cup and stood. "Ask the lovely Miss Prescott to explain it to you."

No, she didn't know. She knew there were gangs; she read the papers sometimes, but she'd never seen any of the men come to blows. She glanced up. Sheridan stood near the door, shifting his feet impatiently.

"I will ask her," she replied. "But I don't see why you couldn't just tell me."

He strode the few steps till he was next to her again. His finger raised her chin and she stared up at him, into his dark blue eyes.

"It's power," he said bluntly. "It's how men like me survive. Now get your coat and I'll take you to see your mother."

CHAPTER TWELVE

It took over a week of escorting CeeCee to the Orpheus, and spending more money than he had planned, before Sheridan managed to corner Nell. She bestowed an amused smile on him and gave him her hand when he asked her to dance. CeeCee had been monopolized all evening by Vogt, and this was his chance.

"You've been avoiding me," he remarked as they strolled onto the dance floor. The ballroom had begun to feel like a second home—one with rats scurrying in the shadows.

"Have I? You've been so busy." She wouldn't give him an inch. So be it.

"I want the favor you promised me," he replied evenly.

She sighed. "Ask."

He waited until the music grew to a crescendo and they were a couple of feet away from the other couples. "I want to know where to find Franky this week." He'd have a few days to plan his optimal ambush and then it would all be over.

Nell's brow crinkled as she frowned. "Why on earth would you need to know that—are you wanting a better job?"

"I always want a better job." Let her think that. Franky would have no warning.

"He's usually at the Orpheus," she replied. Her gaze slid over the crowd and he knew she was searching for their subject.

"When does he arrive?"

"Midday. Whenever." She shrugged. "He leaves me and I don't always bother asking where he's going. Why don't you just show up? He likes men with initiative."

"Where else does he go?" Sheridan persisted. The dance

wouldn't last forever and more than one dance would lead to unwanted speculation.

"Good God, follow him and find out," Nell snapped in exasperation. "He's often at Colosimo's café, but it's the Orpheus he loves."

The song ended and she dropped his hand.

"We're even," she said.

"No, we aren't. I could have had that from anyone, and you know it. But I won't press—not yet. You still owe me."

"No, I don't."

"You do, unless you want me to stop spending time with CeeCee. She'll do fine with Vogt but you know as well as I do that it'll keep her close enough to you for Franky's jealousy to kick in."

"Fine." Nell gritted her teeth. "But don't come asking for anything else tonight." She pushed away and left the dance floor. He watched her stalk up to the bar.

"I told you to stay away from her," Tony said when Sheridan returned to the corner where the man sat, nursing a large whiskey. "Piss her off and you'll have Greco down your throat."

"I know."

"She is gorgeous, I'll give you that," Tony allowed. "Will you be taking that little brunette home again? I was going to head over and see Marie, and I know Perla's been asking for you."

"That sounds like just the thing," Sheridan replied. "Let Vogt take her home tonight."

❖

Lang tugged the collar of his coat up so it shielded his neck from the biting cold, and stuffed his hands deep into his pockets. It was silly anyway—no one within several blocks of the Orpheus would dare try anything without Franky's blessing. It was probably the safest street in all of Chicago's South Side.

Franky. It had been two weeks, but Lang still wanted to punch walls. Actually, he wanted to punch Franky, a good right-handed roundhouse, but then his colleagues would drag his waterlogged body from the river. He didn't want to end up like Lina, no matter how much he wished for Franky's demise. He spent as little time as possible at the Orpheus under Franky's gaze. He sometimes wondered how Nell and her little CeeCee were getting on, but he didn't want to be always looking over his shoulder. He would have preferred if Franky had forgotten about him altogether.

Bad enough that his boss Navarra had taken his instructions from Franky to heart. Navarra had essentially demoted him to beat cop on Franky's say-so, pulling him off Lina's case and filing it under unsolved. Lang knew it had been done purposely, to coincide with one of the coldest weeks of this year so far.

Unable to feel his toes, he ducked into the small diner across from the dance hall. He settled stiffly at the counter and the pretty blond waitress snapped her gum as she poured him a cup of steaming coffee.

"What'll you have?" she drawled, a hand on her hip.

"Soup," he said, wrapping his hands around the mug. He downed it before she returned with his bowl of minestrone.

"Another?" She refilled his cup and this time he added cream and sugar from the pitcher and bowl in front of him. His toes began to ache and he started to feel warm, so he unbuttoned his coat and hung it over the stool next to him.

Lang turned to glance out the window and his gaze was caught by a man sitting alone at one of the small booths, nursing a cup of coffee. A half-eaten piece of pie sat on the table in front of the man, its creamy innards spilling onto the porcelain. He might have thought nothing of the man, but his gaze was intently fixed on the street, and he seemed familiar. He knew he'd seen the man at the Orpheus but couldn't recall his name.

Pity it wasn't Gabe. He'd seen Gabe the last time he'd been at the Orpheus and had received an anxious, wanting glance in return. The want had nearly floored him. So it hadn't been just a ruse; he wanted to see that young man again, somewhere far away from Franky.

Lang turned back to his soup. He didn't need to think about Gabe, not now. That man's name would come to him. He ate greedily but neatly, barely tasting the soup. After that cold morning, he would have eaten nearly anything. He heard a creak and half-turned to see the man—Sheridan, he remembered now, the name popping into his head—rise from his seat and tuck a bill under his plate.

It shouldn't have bothered him—the movement was innocuous—but it did. Lang dug in his pocket for money to pay the waitress and then he put on his coat and followed Sheridan out the door.

❖

It was time.

Midafternoon—the quietest time at the Orpheus, barring first thing in the morning. Franky would be inside, counting his money or his booze, or whatever it was that he did in the afternoons. Then he'd come out the back, walk to his car, and drive away.

Except this time, he wouldn't be driving anywhere. Not if Sheridan could help it.

The gun was heavy in his coat pocket, but it was primed and ready. He'd waited for this moment for years—from the time he'd seen Franky as a boy, laughing as the house burned and Sheridan's mother screamed. Revenge kept him alive through juvenile hall, his initiation into the North Side gang, and prison, and soon all the suffering would be worth it.

Sheridan strolled down the sidewalk, crossing the street at the corner. At the far edge of the dance hall, he paused. The street was almost empty—quiet for a weekday—but the bitter cold kept all but the most hardy indoors. It'd be perfect. Franky wouldn't expect it.

With one last glance at the empty street, he moved down the back side of the building, pressing into the shallow alcove of an access door. He knew this alley well from his many deliveries with Tony and knew there were several such doors. A pity they were kept locked—a violation of fire rules, but security for the gang.

He checked his watch. Soon.

The second alcove he ducked into was the closest to the main delivery door, and he ducked out of sight just as a black Packard came into view, its engine seeming loud in the confined space of the alley. It wouldn't be long now. He was sure of it. He'd watched the building for several days, and the routine was always the same.

Sheridan pulled the gun from his pocket, holding it down by his leg and out of sight. He had a slightly obstructed view of the metal delivery door, but he could see well enough. As soon as Franky opened the door, he would be dead, and over twenty years of waiting vengeance would be satisfied.

The door scraped roughly against the built-up ice on the concrete stair, a sound like nails on a chalkboard. Sheridan slowly raised the gun.

A body tackled him, sending him tumbling back into the darkened alcove. Sheridan cursed and tried to get to his feet, but the other man pulled him down, holding fast to his arms. He kicked out, but the man dodged the kick, retaliating by knocking Sheridan's head into the door frame. His vision darkened around the edges and he saw stars.

The sound of the engine grew louder and the Packard passed them by without stopping, its lone occupant apparently oblivious to his near escape.

The man let him go and Sheridan staggered to his feet, looking for the gun in the snowy muck.

"Don't even bother." The man's voice was weary. "What the hell were you thinking?"

Sheridan's vision still swam but he managed to focus on the man in the plain trench coat and fedora.

"Who the hell are you?" he growled.

"Detective Lang, Chicago PD."

"Christ." The last thing he'd expected had been a cop. One of Franky's thugs, perhaps, but not a policeman. "I suppose I'm under arrest?"

Lang shrugged and knocked snow from his coat. "What good would that do? Most of you thugs get out as fast as you're put in, anyway. But why take a shot at Greco? You'd be a dead man."

"Like you care." Sheridan's vision began to clear. "He's no saint."

Lang became solemn. He seemed to be considering something. "What shall I do with you?" he muttered to himself.

"You stopped me. Be satisfied with that." Sheridan spotted the barrel of the gun protruding from a gray patch of snow. He snagged the weapon and slipped it back into his pocket. He'd need to clean it. Lang moved out of the alcove.

"Be smarter next time. You don't win if you end up dead too."

CHAPTER THIRTEEN

E rven dipped her as the music came to a close, his lips setting on her cleavage. Cecilia could feel the heat and damp of his breath against her skin, but her head swam from the movement and the champagne she'd consumed over the course of the evening. When she didn't move at the start of the next song, Erven led her to the edge of the dance floor, looking down at her with concern.

"Are you all right, darling?" he asked.

She let her forehead rest against his tuxedo-clad shoulder and took a deep breath. No, she wasn't all right, but she had to act like she was. That's what this job was, an act. Erven's wealth was a godsend; she could spend the entire evening with him and make more than she did when she'd danced with a dozen or more men a night. Enzo loved her for it and always had a smile for her on payday. She forced a smile and lifted her head.

"I'll go freshen up," she said, releasing her hold on him. "I won't be long."

"I'll be waiting."

She took a circuitous route through the ballroom, weaving her way through the gaps in the crowd. A couple in leopard-print costumes posed for an admiring circle of observers, and the man lifted his female companion to his shoulder, drawing gasps from the women watching. They'd end up onstage in a few hours, entertaining the masses while they drank and had their midnight supper. The woman laughed as the man pretended to drop her before scooping her into his arms. They dipped into a bow to scattered applause.

Cecilia continued on. Near the bar, she saw Sheridan standing with his friend Tony. He caught her glance and made to start toward her, but she smiled and shook her head and he stayed where he was.

Once inside the dressing room, the cacophony of the ballroom lessened, dampened to a dull roar when she closed the door. She braced her hands on the sink and looked up at the mirror. Her lips were pale where her lipstick had worn away, and even under the makeup she could see the dark circles under her eyes. Only a few more hours and she could go home to crawl into her cold and empty bed. Another payment was due to the hospital tomorrow and the last few nights' wages would cover the cost. She could do it. She had to.

The noise from the ballroom intruded and she glanced at the door.

Nell stood there, looking beautiful as a Grecian goddess in her dark royal-blue gown. She pushed the door shut. "Erven said you weren't feeling well." She came to the sink and ran a gentle hand down Cecilia's back. Cecilia closed her eyes. She'd missed that touch, the scent of Nell's perfume, the heat of her body. She pushed away from the sink.

"I'll be fine." She didn't want pity.

"I could tell Enzo. I'm sure he'd let you go early." Nell followed her to the overstuffed settee in the corner, sitting close enough that their legs touched from hip to knee.

"No, don't." She needed every dollar.

"Are you sure?" Nell stroked her cheek before taking her hand. Her fingers were warm and Cecilia craved more of that warmth. She had to stop herself from leaning closer. "I'm sorry we haven't spent much time together, but don't you ever think I haven't noticed you. You're going to work yourself to death." When Cecilia stayed silent, Nell added, "I worry about you."

"I'll manage," Cecilia replied. She wanted to tell her about her mother, about the hospital, but she didn't dare. Nell would never want her if she knew. She deserved more than a girl from the tenements. "I always do."

Nell pressed a soft kiss to her lips. "I can't take you home with me tonight, but soon. I miss you."

"When?" One kiss wasn't enough. Cecilia leaned in and captured Nell's lips with her own and they sank into an embrace on the settee. Her free hand slid down over Nell's hip and Nell cupped the back of her neck, drawing her closer. If only they had more time.

They broke apart, gasping for breath.

The door opened and they looked up in surprise. Scarlett stood there, her mouth open. Cecilia turned her head into Nell's shoulder.

"Don't you ever knock?" Nell snapped.

Scarlett continued to gape and finally she began to stutter a reply. "I...didn't expect anyone."

Cecilia chanced a look. Scarlett closed her mouth, and her expression changed. She seemed speculative, a small smile on her lips. She felt Nell's fingers tighten on her arm.

"Get out."

"I'm going, I'm going," Scarlett muttered. She closed the door with a crash.

Cecilia let out a breath.

"Soon," Nell said and Cecilia had to think of what she'd asked just moments ago. "But tonight, CeeCee, go home. I'll make sure Enzo doesn't short you any money. I promise."

"I'll have to go say good night to Erven," Cecilia said. He wouldn't let her go with just an easy good night.

"Stay here," Nell said, "and I'll take care of it." She untangled herself and rose from the settee. She leaned over and kissed Cecilia's forehead in an almost maternal way. "Don't move."

Cecilia closed her eyes. She heard the rush of noise as the door opened and then the muted music as it closed. She could go home.

She woke when the door opened and blinked in confusion. It wasn't Nell, but Sheridan who stood there, his eyes shadowed by his fedora. Her heart sank. She'd hoped to see Nell one more time tonight, for a few more minutes to tide her over until the next evening.

"Nell told me where you were," Sheridan said by way of explanation. "She couldn't come back. Franky wanted her." There was something in his tone when he said that, an emotion that she couldn't place.

"You don't need to do anything," she said, rising shakily to her feet. "I can get home on my own."

He came forward and she noticed he held her jacket in his hand.

"That might be so, but I don't mind." He helped her into her coat, buttoning it up to her chin so that the wool felt scratchy on her neck. He hooked the strap of her purse over her shoulder. She'd completely forgotten it. It had been left at the table. "Nell tells me your wages are inside."

Cecilia closed her eyes in relief. "Thank you." She opened her eyes. "Don't you want to stay?"

"Not much for me to stay for," he remarked. "But it's still too early for bed. Have you eaten?"

Had she? She couldn't remember. She might have had a bite of something before coming to the Orpheus, but she certainly hadn't had anything since.

"Not really."

He took her hand and rested it on his arm. He wore his coat already and a muffler hung around his neck. "Then we'll go for a bite to eat," he said. He squeezed her fingers. "You look like you need it."

❖

"She's worried about you," Sheridan remarked. He lit a cigarette and leaned back in his chair, an empty plate in front of him. Cecilia picked at her own food; the roast beef and potatoes sat in a swiftly congealing pool of gravy.

"She hardly notices me," she bit out, trying to control the surge of anger. If Nell really cared, she'd be the one here right now, not Sheridan. "She has Franky."

Sheridan crossed his arms. The cigarette hung from his lips as he talked. "It's more likely that he has her. You know that, don't you? Not just anyone can gainsay Franky Greco—not even Nell."

Cecilia mashed a potato with her fork, pressing it into the dark gravy. "Sometimes I hate him," she muttered, glancing up nervously. It wasn't something she should have said aloud. If there were no Franky... She could hardly imagine what it would be like to be with Nell and not to have to worry about him.

"I'm sure you're not the only one," Sheridan replied, keeping his voice low. The diner had few customers and they were seated several tables away, but their conversation shouldn't be overheard.

"So what did she promise you?" Cecilia asked abruptly.

"Does it matter?"

"Yes. I know she asked you to spend time with me, back on New Year's Eve, but you don't have to keep doing it."

"I could have let Vogt take you home," Sheridan replied, "except that you wouldn't have made it home. He changes women like he changes his shirts, and never the same one twice."

"So you're here for my virtue?"

"No, I wouldn't go that far. But do you think you'd make the money you do without his interest?" He stubbed out his cigarette in the ashtray. "If you keep stringing him along, you'll make more. I know your mother's still in the hospital. It can't be easy to afford that."

Cecilia tightened her grip on her purse. She hadn't let it leave her lap as they sat there eating. Her wages were inside and she needed every penny. A core of fear had lodged itself inside her and every time she went to see her mother, she left wondering if it would be the last time. She'd do whatever she could to help her mother get well.

"Is she any better?" Sheridan asked, his voice kindly. Cecilia shook her head. To avoid speaking, she put a piece of roast beef in her mouth and chewed. She set down her fork as she swallowed. She couldn't eat any more. It was such a waste, but the food tasted like sawdust. She wanted to go home, where she'd be alone and could let herself give in to the tears.

"Had enough?" Sheridan rose and held out a hand. She took it and the warmth and strength of his grip was the most reassuring thing she had felt all night.

They left the diner and still he held her hand. When he raised his arm to hail a cab, she stepped close, tucking herself against his strong form. She felt safe there. She changed her mind.

"I don't want to go home," she whispered and saw his fleeting smile. Home was cold, but Sheridan wasn't. He wouldn't ever be. They climbed into the cab and she settled beside him.

Since the start of the year, he'd been the only one she could lean on, the only one who'd given her any support. It wasn't fair to Nell, she knew, but there were times when her growing fondness for Sheridan was beginning to outshine what she felt for Nell. Ever since the night she'd seen the bruise on Nell's cheek, Nell hardly existed in her world. A gulf separated them, and that gulf was named Franky Greco.

Sheridan squeezed her hand and she realized the cab had come to a halt. She opened the door and stepped out onto the curb, her shoes sliding in the wet. Sheridan steadied her, and he didn't let go once they were inside but kept his hand on the small of her back as they went upstairs to his small apartment. Once inside, she sank down on the sofa, all her energy draining from her. Sheridan hung his coat on its peg and set his fedora on the small shelf above. He unbuttoned his suit jacket and shrugged out of it, hanging it next to his jacket. In his shirtsleeves and vest, he approached the sofa, but he didn't sit next to her. Instead he sank to one knee and took up her right foot, unbuttoning her shoe and sliding it off.

He gently chafed her cold toes until they began to warm, and

Cecilia felt the heat creep into her cheeks. He did the same with her other foot, and when he was done, he rested her feet on his knee.

"Why are you so nice to me?" she asked. The question slipped out before she could stop herself. She had wondered, but asking now made her sound ungrateful. "It's not that—"

"Someone needs to be."

The rest of what she'd been about to say caught in her throat. He watched her as if waiting for her to object. When she didn't, his fingers curled around her ankles. She'd seen him rough people up, but those hands that had dispensed violence were now as gentle as could be.

His touch crept up her stockinged calves and her eyes fluttered closed. When he stopped, his hands resting at the bend of her knees, she gave an involuntary whimper. Her eyes flew open. She lifted her head from the back of the sofa and leaned forward, catching his hand and tugging him toward her.

His mouth met hers and she clung to him, sliding awkwardly off the sofa and onto his lap. They sprawled to the floor and Cecilia gave a startled cry at the chilled wood against her thin stockings. Sheridan began to chuckle. He lifted her off him and rose, catching her hand to pull her to her feet.

"I have a better idea," he said and hooked one arm behind her knees and the other behind her back, lifting her easily. He settled on the sofa with her in his lap. "Not so cold this way."

Cecilia rested her head against his chest. She could hear his heart beating and though they were as close as they'd ever been, she felt safe. Safe, but thoughts of Nell flickered across her mind. She loved Nell, didn't she? But Nell had pushed her into Sheridan's arms and she didn't want to deny him, or herself. She raised her head and his lips came down on hers.

She'd only really kissed him properly once before, and New Year's Eve had passed in such a blur that she hadn't really remembered what it was like. But now she knew, and though it was different than with Nell—harder, somehow—she knew she wanted him just as much.

Cecilia fumbled at his collar, loosening his tie and finally managing to pull it off. She dropped it to the floor and started on his buttons, feeling the light dusting of hair on his chest. Sheridan caught her hand, and instead of scolding her for going too fast, he brought it to his lips, kissing her palm. The delicate gesture made her breath catch in her throat. He trailed his lips over the inside of her wrist. She shivered, and he lifted his head to gaze at her.

"Have you ever been with a man?" he asked. He must have seen the answer in her eyes. Her stomach fluttered with nerves, more than when she'd first been with Nell. Men weren't gentle. She'd learned that from the other girls at the Orpheus, had listened in on their bawdy conversations, but when Sheridan continued to trail kisses up her arm, some of her apprehension faded. He hooked a finger into the neckline of her dress, tugging the fabric aside to bare her shoulder. His mouth was warm on her skin.

Cecilia let her head fall back as he kissed and nibbled up the line of her shoulder, nipping her where her neck and shoulder joined before tracing a path up to her ear with the tip of his tongue. He held her securely as he lavished attention on her, bracing her against his arm when she relaxed into his touch. When he unbuttoned the back of her dress and tugged it down farther still, and her slip and bra with it, she arched into his touch as he cupped her breast. His thumb brushed over a nipple and she let out a moan, her fingers bunching the fabric of his shirt.

Nell had done these things too, but his hands felt different on her skin, the roughness of his calloused fingers a far cry from Nell's smooth and silky fingertips. Nell had let her nails scrape delicately over Cecilia's nipples before sucking them, but Sheridan let his teeth do that work, teasing her nipple erect before sucking hard. She squirmed on his lap, wanting more. She tugged at his vest, feeling the buttons slide free of the heavy cloth. She went back to work on his shirt as he moved to suck at her other breast but lost patience and tore the shirt free. She vaguely heard a button hit the floor. Sheridan laughed softly.

"Impatient," he murmured against her breast. He straightened and shrugged off his shirt, and she spread her hands on his chest.

"Better."

"Not yet," he quipped. He pulled her dress up and over her head and let it fall to the floor to keep his shirt company. Only her delicate stockings and underwear stood between them. She wasn't naked, but she felt exposed. Sheridan slid his hand up her leg and under her fallen slip, cupping her between her legs and stroking her through the thin lace of her underwear.

Cecilia let out a small cry, tilting her hips to press against his hand, closing her eyes to focus on the delicious sensation. She felt him shift and lower her so her head rested against the arm of the sofa. The fabric was cool on her bare back. His hands left her, but he made short work of her slip and stockings. Finally, she felt his hands on her hips, his fingers dipping beneath the lace of her underwear, finding the hollows of her hipbones. She opened her eyes as his hot breath brushed her stomach. He kissed her there, just above her belly button, and she ran her fingers through his dark hair.

"Please," she whispered. He lingered at the lacy edge of her underwear.

"So beautiful," he said, dragging the fabric down, too slowly for her taste, caressing every revealed finger's breadth of flesh. When his mouth found her center, she let out a stuttering gasp, her legs parting for him.

Sheridan patiently teased and tasted her until she was whimpering with need, and when he slid two fingers into her while he flicked her clitoris with his tongue, she came apart. His fingers left her and she let her breathing slow as he stood and stripped off his trousers. She couldn't help but stare, and her nervousness returned. He settled beside her on the sofa and lifted her into his lap so that she straddled his legs.

"Don't be frightened of me," he said. She could feel him between her legs, hard and pressing against her wetness.

"I'm not." She lifted herself slightly and took him in her hand, hearing his breath catch as she touched him, stroking him, feeling the strange dichotomy of his soft skin and the eager hardness. His hand came around hers and he guided her strokes, tightening her grip and encouraging her to stroke from root to tip. She indulged him, and when he let her go, she lowered herself onto him.

The penetration took her breath away. Goose bumps rose on her skin and she clung to him as he rocked his hips. "Don't stop," she murmured in his ear.

"I won't." His voice was hoarse and he quickened the pace, grasping her hips, directing their rhythm. She arched her back and took him deep, hearing him groan. The sofa's springs creaked as they moved, and she felt the desire building in her again and knew she was close.

Sheridan's hand left her hip and she felt his thumb press against her clitoris. She cried out, tightening around him, her head falling to his shoulder as she shuddered with her second climax. He thrust into her, his breath rasping in her ear, going deep with each stroke, until finally, with one last hard thrust, he came. She could feel the heat of him as he spilled inside her and could hear his heart pounding in time with hers. When she lifted her head from his shoulder, he kissed her deeply, and she didn't want to be anywhere but in his arms.

CHAPTER FOURTEEN

Sheridan woke early, the sunlight falling across his face as it streamed through a crack in the curtains. He shifted, blinking away the brightness. CeeCee slumbered on beside him, but she murmured something unintelligible when he carefully untangled his limbs from hers. He crouched at the side of the bed and stroked her hair, lulling her back to sleep before he tucked the blankets in around her. The chill in the room drove the last vestiges of sleep from him and he found his cotton pajama pants on the floor and tugged them on.

He walked to the bathroom, stretching. He splashed water on his face and wet his hair, straightening it from its sleep-flattened state, then took care of the rest of the morning's ablutions. He dug in his suit jacket for his cigarettes and settled on the sofa. CeeCee turned over in bed, dragging the blankets with her. He could just see the back of her head, and her hair was a thick tangle. He took a drag on his cigarette.

It hadn't been his plan to bring her home, or to take her to bed. He'd gone to the Orpheus to stew over his failure and watch Franky Greco from afar while he thought of a better way to kill him. Still, he couldn't say no to Nell, or to the delicate woman who now slept in his bed.

That Franky had a cop—and a detective, at that—as part of his protection was startling, but at least he hadn't ended up in the clink. He frowned and scratched the side of his nose. Lang didn't even have to book him to do his job; he could have just handed him over to Franky, and that would have been the end.

Really the end. Sheridan knew he'd escaped certain death, whether from a bullet to the back of the head, or by concrete boots at the bottom of Lake Michigan. He stubbed out his smoldering cigarette and lit another. There had to be another way to get to Franky. Nell still owed him a favor, but he had to see her when Franky wasn't around. He glanced at CeeCee. She had an in.

Sheridan smiled. CeeCee and Nell wouldn't even know, not until Franky was dead.

❖

Cecilia held on to Sheridan's arm and was loath to let go as he walked her to the hospital and dropped her at the front door.

"Will I see you tonight?" he asked, bending to kiss her cheek. "Or maybe earlier?"

She leaned into his embrace. "I'm going to see Nell this afternoon, later, but I'll be at the Orpheus as usual tonight."

"I'll see you then," he said, kissing her once more. She watched him go, then turned and entered the hospital. The acrid smell of bleach and other cleaning products hit her as she opened the door and she breathed shallowly as she skirted the orderly mopping the floor. Once on the ward upstairs, she lingered outside the plate-glass window of the isolation ward.

"Miss Mills?" A young nurse, her uniform crisply starched, touched her elbow. She knew the girl's name, but couldn't think of it.

"How is my mother?"

The young woman led her down the hallway away from the ward, until they'd reached a pair of chairs set into a small alcove. The nurse settled into one and Cecilia took the other.

"There's been no change," the nurse said gravely. "The treatments seem to be having little effect. She eats, but not much." She paused, and Cecilia waited, hoping for a scrap of good news. When the nurse stayed silent, Cecilia spoke.

"But she's not getting any worse?"

"If only she would eat more." The nurse looked at her with sad eyes. "We have to coax almost every bite."

"I need to see her," Cecilia replied. When the nurse began to object, Cecilia cut her off. "I understand that she's still infectious, but if I didn't catch it before, I doubt I would now. I might be able to convince her to eat."

"All right." The nurse stood. "The doctor's not here, so he won't know."

Cecilia remembered him, a cantankerous old man who seemed to think he ran the hospital. Perhaps he did; the nurses were terrified of him, and the other doctors intimidated.

The nurse took her back to the ward and Cecilia went to her mother's beside. Her mother lay on her back, propped at an angle with pillows to help her breathe. Her eyes were closed and her chest rose and fell in a regular movement. Cecilia perched on the edge of the bed and took her mother's thin hand. She gave it a gentle squeeze. The flesh seemed weak and fragile and she worried she'd hurt her.

"Ma?" Her voice cracked, and she tried again. "Ma?"

Her mother's eyelids fluttered and finally opened, squinting in the light that came from the window.

"Cecilia, oh, my darling girl."

Her mother began to tremble, and tears spilled down her cheeks. Cecilia reached up to brush them away, biting her lip to keep from crying.

"The nurse tells me that you need to eat more," she managed to say, trying to keep her tone cheerful to hide her agony. Her mother was wraithlike, almost as pale as the sheets, but for some color in her cheeks and the blue of her eyes.

"I try." She wheezed and coughed into her handkerchief.

"Please try harder," Cecilia begged. "Please, Ma? For me? I know you can get better. You need to help me decide on a nicer place to live, remember?"

Her mother brightened, just a little. "Like home," she said. "Trees, a little stream…" She smiled to herself, closing her eyes. "A lovely hearth, a quilt on my lap…" Her voice trailed off and her breathing evened out again.

Cecilia bowed her head, clutching her mother's hand. She wouldn't let the tears come, not now.

"Miss." The nurse touched her arm. "You should go. The doctor will be here soon and there'll be hell to pay if he sees you here."

Cecilia leaned forward and kissed her mother's cheek. "Good-bye, Ma. Sleep well," she whispered. She rose and followed the nurse back to the public area, glancing behind her to catch one last glimpse of her mother.

❖

Sheridan paused outside Nell's apartment building. He knew he didn't have long; CeeCee would come to see Nell and he wanted to be gone by then. No need to give his game away—he could have CeeCee and his revenge too.

The doorman gave him a once-over but reluctantly called up to Nell's suite. He listened, then frowned as he set down the receiver.

"Go on up," he said, obviously disapproving. "Third floor."

The elevator attendant gave Sheridan quick glances from the corner of his eye, but Sheridan stood relaxed, his feet shoulder-width apart, and his hands casually in his trouser pockets. The boy brought the elevator to a halt and opened the folding metal gate. "Number 303," he said. Sheridan tipped his hat.

"Obliged." He strolled down the hallway and knocked at Nell's door. He glanced back at the elevator boy, who abruptly closed the gate and descended. His patience began to fray and he'd just begun to knock again when the door opened.

Nell regarded him with a mixture of annoyance and distaste. She turned her back on him and he took a moment to admire the curve of her hips, accentuated by the satin dressing gown she wore. Her red hair was drawn up in a bun at the back. She wasn't made up and he was surprised at how pale she was, like a washed-out version of the Nell everyone knew.

"Did I interrupt something?" he inquired. He followed her into the living room. She didn't sit on the gaudy brocade sofa, so he remained standing.

"Only my usual preparations," she said with a long-suffering sigh.

"This won't take long, if you tell me what I need to know," he said. He removed his fedora and set it on the coffee table, running a hand through his hair.

"And what is it you want, exactly?" Nell opened a brass box on the fireplace mantel, withdrawing a cigarette. Sheridan drew out his lighter and moved forward, stepping up to light her cigarette. She allowed it, looking at him from under her lashes.

"Tell me about Franky Greco," he said, putting his lighter back in his pocket. Nell glided away from him, her gown rustling against her legs.

"What do you want to know? I told you where he hangs out already." She turned to face the window. The smoke from her cigarette drifted in a thin plume toward the ceiling.

"How long have you known him?" Sheridan knew he couldn't start in like he had before, not without knowing how much Nell was involved. Somehow she was no casual fling for Franky, no simple prostitute.

She shrugged. "Franky got me here," she said, her tone defiant.

"You owe him."

She had been about to say something more, but paused. To cover her hesitation, she took a drag of her cigarette. "Maybe," she said finally.

Sheridan helped himself to a cigarette. Interesting. He'd expected a more vehement reply, but then, she'd begun to defy Franky when she'd asked him to look after CeeCee. He needed her defiance.

"Franky likes to be in control," Sheridan observed. He sat on the arm of the sofa. "He loves to be the one to decide who lives and who dies." He saw the flames, smelled the smoke, and heard the screams as his family burned to death, but it was only a flash of memory.

"You talk like you know him."

When he didn't answer, she turned away from the window and stubbed out her cigarette in the ashtray on the coffee table.

"It doesn't take much to know that about him," Sheridan replied.

Nell gave a short laugh. "No, it wouldn't. But you haven't really told me anything."

"Tell me where I could meet him, alone."

"What do you want from him? A promotion? Money?"

"Maybe." If only it could be so easy. "I need to speak with him privately."

Nell sighed. "I told you that he spends time at Colosimo's when he's not at the Orpheus."

"Alone?"

"How would I know? I don't spend all my time with him."

"I bet he'd love to know what you get up to when he's not around."

Nell glared at him.

"Not that I'd tell," he continued. "At least, not if you can tell me where I could truly find him alone."

"He drives alone," she said. "Most of the time."

"I'll have to thumb a ride," he remarked. "Where does he live when he's not with you?"

"He has a house near Hyde Park."

"And I suppose he takes Lake Shore Drive?"

"Maybe. I don't know."

The phone rang and Nell went to answer it. A smile flickered on her lips as she listened to the speaker on the other end. "Send her up."

"CeeCee?" Sheridan inquired. He rose and picked up his fedora.

"Yes," Nell replied, her lips quirking in amusement. "Don't you want to wait for her?"

"Not particularly." Having CeeCee find him here would drag her into his revenge. The less she knew, the better.

"You'd best go out the back stairs," Nell said. She led him through the small kitchen to a door, opening it to reveal a darkened staircase. "It'll let you out into the alley." He moved past her and she caught his arm. "I don't know what you're doing, but if you seriously think you can get one over on Franky, you're sadly mistaken."

"Thanks for the warning."

She flicked on the light.

Cecilia fidgeted in the elevator. It crawled toward the third floor and she wanted to clamber out and urge it to go faster. The elevator boy said nothing but she could tell he was trying not to stare.

Nell let her in and Cecilia wanted to sink into her embrace and forget everything. Instead she stood just inside the door, her coat still on, unmoving.

"CeeCee?" Nell touched her cheek and she took a breath and closed her eyes. She wanted to confide all her troubles, but she couldn't.

"It's been a long day." She slowly unbuttoned her coat and shrugged it off. Nell took it from her.

"What is it?" Nell led her into the living room, tossing her coat on a chair. She could smell cigarette smoke and the faint hint of cologne.

"Is someone else here?" She didn't want it to be Franky; she couldn't stand to have to face him. Not today.

"There's no one," Nell said. "Cecilia, tell me."

Cecilia sank onto the sofa and clasped Nell's hand when she sat down beside her, grasping it as a drowning man might grasp at a life preserver. Nell didn't flinch.

"I don't know where to start." How could she explain about her mother, without Nell becoming disgusted with her? She didn't want a girl who went home to a dingy room in one of the worst areas of the city. She should have someone better, someone rich, like her.

"Just tell me," Nell urged. Cecilia glanced up from their entwined fingers. Nell was pale, her face absent its usual makeup. She seemed tired and there were shadows under her eyes. Cecilia stalled. Nell looked as if she didn't need anything else to worry about.

"It's nothing."

"Don't worry about me," Nell said, as if she'd read her thoughts on her face.

"I'm broke," Cecilia blurted out in a quick rush, so quickly the words seemed to swim together.

Nell frowned, her thin brows crinkling. "But you've been earning money at the Orpheus. Enzo told me how well you've been doing."

"It's not enough." Cecilia swallowed down the sudden surge of grief. Her mother wasn't ever going to get better.

"Were you robbed?" Nell seemed to still be puzzled. Cecilia shook her head. She tried to speak and her words came out in a croak. She tried again.

"My mother's in the hospital," she said. Her voice cracked on the last word and she turned her head away.

"Why didn't you tell me before?" Nell chided her gently, gathering her into an embrace.

First Sheridan, now Nell. She hated that she couldn't control her tears. She wiped at her eyes.

"How much do you need?" Nell stroked her back and Cecilia relaxed into Nell's warmth and softness. Nell's perfume, Chanel No. 5, enveloped her. Here, she felt safe, but guilt assailed her. She'd felt safe in Sheridan's arms too.

"I need enough for rent, or I'll get kicked out," she said, resting her head on Nell's shoulder. Sheridan had threatened her landlord, but what about when he wasn't around?

"Would fifty dollars help?" Nell asked. Cecilia nodded. "Well then, that's easy." Nell brushed the tears from Cecilia's cheeks, her touch lingering.

"I'll pay you back," she promised.

"Don't worry about it." Nell shifted on the sofa and rose. "Come into the bathroom and you can get cleaned up. You can't go to the Orpheus and charm the men with tear tracks on your cheeks."

"I'd rather charm you," Cecilia replied as they walked into the bedroom on their way to the bathroom. They never made it. Nell took Cecilia into her embrace once more and they stumbled toward the bed, lips meeting in hungry kisses. Cecilia fumbled for the slick satin tie of Nell's robe, finally pulling it free. The robe fell open and she slid her hand underneath the satin to cup Nell's breast, thumbing over her nipple.

Nell sprawled back on the bed, pulling Cecilia down with her. She tugged at the hem of Cecilia's dress, dragging it up her legs and torso. Cecilia sat up and pulled the dress over her head, tossing it aside. She sank down beside Nell, whose hand was already finding its way up under her slip, teasing at the flesh left bare at the top of her stockings. Cecilia pushed the satin away from Nell's body, baring her from head to toe. She bent her head and took one of Nell's nipples in her mouth, flicking her tongue against the hardening nub. When Nell arched against her with a gasp, she felt the satisfaction of knowing that she could make Nell respond so easily. She sucked harder, dragging her teeth over the sensitive flesh, as Sheridan had done to her.

"Touch me," Nell gasped, and Cecilia moved her hand downward, over her sternum and the soft skin of her belly, down over her curls. Her fingers slid into Nell's damp warmth, and she wanted to bring Nell to climax; Nell was her savior, her beautiful angel. She stroked Nell and slipped two fingers into her, going deeper as Nell pushed onto her hand.

Cecilia slid in another finger and felt Nell tighten around her. She kept her thumb on Nell's clit, pressing in tight circles as she knew Nell liked. Nell gave a sobbing cry of need and Cecilia straightened her fingers and thrust deep, then curled the tips to stroke the most sensitive spot. Nell moaned and Cecilia felt a small gush of wetness dampen her hand, her own breath coming faster with arousal. She pressed her thighs together, wishing for Nell's touch, even as she teased Nell to a second, smaller climax.

She rested against Nell's side, hearing her heart beat and feeling her chest rise and fall with her slowing breaths. She shifted her leg over Nell's, getting closer still, putting a delicious pressure on her needy flesh.

"Let me," Nell said, rolling Cecilia on her back and lying over her, Nell's robe draping them like a satin curtain. It brushed Cecilia's legs as she spread them to allow Nell to strip off her stockings and underwear.

Nell pushed up Cecilia's slip and bent down, pressing a kiss to her hipbone before trailing her tongue down just above her sex.

"I adore you," she murmured as she spread Cecilia with her fingers and flicked her tongue over her clit.

Cecilia shivered with pleasure. "Please," she begged. Nell took her clit in her mouth and Cecilia nearly came apart, her eyes tightly shut. She could hardly bear the sensation, the sucking of Nell's mouth, the flick of her tongue, the occasional scrape of her teeth against the delicate flesh. She moaned.

A man cleared his throat and her eyes snapped open.

CHAPTER FIFTEEN

Detective Lang stared into his cup of coffee, his hands wrapped around the white porcelain. The late afternoon chatter ebbed and flowed around him, but all he heard was a faint buzz.

He'd acted from instinct when he'd seen the thug—Sheridan—with the gun, his years of police training taking over. He'd followed him into the alleyway but only tackled him when his intentions became clear.

What if he'd let Sheridan have his crack at Franky Greco? He couldn't even imagine life without Franky, without the cold oversight the man had on his part of the city, the tight hold he had on Navarra, and the fiefdom he ruled, first under Torrio, and now under Capone.

Lang pushed away the coffee cup and left some cash for the waitress. He needed more than coffee. At the back of the diner was a room half the size, packed with tables and a small bar. A couple of shots of whatever rotgut they were selling would help clear his head. The waitress winked at him as he walked through, but he ignored her. She was cute in a brassy, overdone sort of way, but really not his type.

The back room wasn't yet full, but it reeked of smoke and stale beer. Nothing fancy, just a place for the locals to come for a drink.

"Vodka," he told the bartender, who grabbed a bottle from the rack and spilled a few fingers' worth into a tumbler, setting it on the bar. Lang settled onto a stool. Better to be here staring into a glass of vodka, he thought. The fumes were beginning to tickle his nose. He lifted the glass and took a gulp, closing his eyes and trying not to grimace at the sharp burn. He'd gotten used to the top-shelf booze at the Orpheus. This stuff could clean a dirty carburetor. His eyes watered and he blinked.

"I'm pretty sure they make that stuff in the bathtub," someone next to him remarked.

Lang opened his eyes. Gabe leaned on the bar next to him, holding a mug of beer. "They probably do," he agreed, taking another swig. It didn't burn so badly this time. He tapped the empty glass and the bartender gave him a refill.

"I'm sorry about before," Gabe said, and Lang took a good hard look at him. He was dressed in worn clothes and his jacket had seen better days, but slowly the anger and desire filtered through his alcohol-sodden brain.

Lang's punch sent Gabe staggering back, his beer mug shattering on the floor. The bartender leapt over the counter, catching Lang's arm as he began to take a second swing at Gabe.

"You bastard," he growled, trying to shake off the bartender. "Let me go!"

"No brawling in here, not even for cops," the bartender sneered. "Pay up and get out."

"It's my fault, Marv," Gabe said to the bartender. He pulled a couple of bills from his pocket and held them out. "Let him go—we'll leave."

Marv let go of his arm and Lang straightened his jacket in a quick, jerky motion. He glared daggers at Gabe, who seemed not to notice.

"Let me buy you a drink somewhere else," Gabe offered. Lang shook his head.

"Why shouldn't I just hit you again, you little shit?" he growled.

"Outside, then," Gabe said and left Lang to follow in his wake.

The crisp evening air went straight to his head. Gabe turned back after he'd gone a few paces from the diner.

"I didn't want to set you up," he said.

Lang barely managed to hold his temper in check. "A little late for that."

"Greco has a way of being persuasive," Gabe said. He stuffed his hands into his pockets. "Come on, I'll buy you a drink."

"Not trying to set me up again, are you?"

"No, not this time. I like you, Detective, though I doubt you'll believe me."

"What did Greco do to you?"

Gabe shuddered. "I'd rather not talk about it, if you don't mind."

"He hurt you?"

Gabe was silent.

"All right." Maybe Gabe would have some information he could use against Franky later. His anger still simmered, but he pushed it back. He'd do a lot to get back at Franky now. "Where to?"

"Come with me."

Gabe took him to an apartment building a few steps away and Lang followed him up the stairs. He glanced about cautiously, but the street was quiet, and no one would see them enter together.

The apartment had two bedrooms. One was tidy, but plain; the other had its bedsheets askew and clothes littered the floor. Gabe pulled the door shut on the mess and took off his coat, tossing it on the sofa.

"You share this place?"

"Can't afford my own—my roommate is a salesman. He's gone a lot, at least." Gabe walked into the tiny kitchen and opened a cabinet, pulling out two glasses. "What'll you have?"

"Whatever you've got," Lang replied. Gabe took the glasses into his bedroom and Lang followed him.

"Have to keep this under lock and key," Gabe said, setting the glasses on the nightstand and unlocking the cupboard below. "My roommate would drink it all if I didn't. I bought this bottle off one of the bootleggers I know. Real Canadian rye."

"Haven't had that in five years. Sure you want to drink it?"

"I only give it to the special ones," Gabe said. He cracked open the seal on the bottle and Lang raised a brow. Gabe caught his look. "There haven't been any." He poured a generous portion of rye into the glasses before capping the bottle.

Gabe put the bottle on the nightstand. "You going to stay?"

Lang took off his fedora and Gabe took it from him. He unbuttoned his trench coat and shrugged it off. Gabe deposited them in the living room, with his jacket. Lang picked up one of the glasses.

"Are you sure about this?" Lang wasn't sure if he was asking Gabe, or himself.

"You wouldn't be here if I wasn't," Gabe replied, picking up the remaining glass and taking a slow, savoring sip of the rye. Lang held the glass to his nose, then took a sip. The rye had a smooth taste and he wanted to down the entire glass.

"Come here," Gabe said, sprawling back onto the bed and patting the cover beside him. Lang took a gulp of the rye and sat, setting his glass back on the nightstand. Gabe handed him the other glass, and Lang put it beside his own.

"Do you always seduce coppers?" Lang asked, sprawling beside Gabe.

The young man chuckled. "Only you." He leaned in and brushed his lips over Lang's.

Lang placed a hand on Gabe's chest. "This has to be kept between us," he warned.

"I promise," Gabe said, rising up on his elbow and closing the distance between them.

Cecilia turned her face away, pushing down the hem of her slip to cover her nakedness, her heart in her throat, the fear curling in her belly.

Nell rose, drawing her satin dressing gown together with unhurried ease, her movements slow, her head held high. "Don't you ever knock?"

"You didn't hear me. Anyway, the door wasn't locked. I got worried."

That voice wasn't Franky's. Cecilia glanced over. It was one of Franky's men, and he looked startled, almost sheepish as he stood in the doorway.

"What does Franky want, and why couldn't he just have called?" Nell sounded irritable, though as Cecilia watched her pace to the vanity and pick up her powder compact, she could tell Nell was nervous.

"He won't be coming by to pick you and Miss Mills up. Some of Mr. Vogt's Canadian investors have come and he'll be busy all night."

"I see." Nell nonchalantly powdered her nose. Cecilia sat up, straightening her slip as best she could. In another hour, maybe less, Franky would know what they'd been doing, and that would be the end. She couldn't stifle the fear.

"Tony, could I speak to you a moment in private?" Nell glided back to the bed and rested her hand on Cecilia's shoulder. Cecilia glanced up and Nell gave her a comforting look before she turned toward Tony. "We need to chat. CeeCee, darling, your dress for tonight is hanging in the closet."

With that, Nell swept from the room and Tony followed. Cecilia rose from the bed as she heard their voices in the living room, murmurs leaking through the closed door. She crept to the door and turned the knob slowly, opening it just a crack. Nell's next words came through loud and clear.

"If you tell him, I'll make sure your life is a living hell," she said, her voice colder than Cecilia had ever heard it before.

"And how would you do that?" Tony inquired. He seemed to not be concerned, and Cecilia bit her lip. He'd tell; she knew he would.

"Just because I'm with Franky doesn't mean that I can't have my fun," Nell replied. "Just as your being married doesn't stop you from using prostitutes."

Tony scoffed at her words. "You can't blackmail me," he said. "My wife knows, unlike Greco, who would love to know."

"I don't care what your wife knows."

Cecilia cracked the door open another inch and peered through the gap. Nell stood by the sofa, but she couldn't see Tony. "But I know that if I ask her to, your Marie would turn you away."

"That doesn't scare me," Tony retorted, but his words sounded like pure bravado.

"Try me, and find out. I know you love her. Let me have mine and you can have yours."

"You wouldn't."

"I would. Marie owes me," Nell said. "Now go. Tell Franky you delivered the message, but nothing else. And buy something pretty for Marie."

Cecilia saw Nell take a roll of bills from the drawer of the coffee table and her eyes widened as Nell peeled off several.

"You'd best be careful," Tony said, mollified by the cash. "Greco's not blind."

"I know."

Cecilia heard the front door close and she released a breath. They were safe, for now. She drew open the door and came face-to-face with Nell.

"Everything will be fine."

Cecilia moved forward into Nell's embrace, the warmth and solidity comforting her. Nell stroked her back in slow, wide circles. When they parted, she kissed Cecilia's forehead and pressed the rest of the roll of bills into her palm, closing her fingers over the money.

"I can't take this." It was too much. Way too much.

"You need it," Nell said simply. "And there's more where that came from. Being Franky's girl has some perks."

Even without counting the bills, Cecilia knew the cash would pay for several more weeks of hospital bills. She felt some of the tension she'd been carrying ease.

"Now come back to bed." Nell drew her into the bedroom. "I've locked and bolted the door and we have a few hours until we need to be ready."

"But what about—" Cecilia began.

"He won't say anything."

❖

Sheridan bided his time, nursing a beer at the back bar of the Orpheus, watching Franky Greco's table. Men came and went and for a while Nell and CeeCee sat there, the two women conversing while Franky made a point of manhandling Nell to mark his territory.

Finally, just after midnight, Franky sat there alone, and Sheridan picked up his pint of beer and ambled over.

Franky gave him a nod and Sheridan sat in one of the empty chairs.

"Tony tells me you've been doing well," Franky remarked.

"I'm glad." Sheridan wondered if Franky remembered him from twenty years ago, but in all this time, there'd been no sign of it. Surely he'd have disposed of him long ago if he had.

"Tony doesn't recommend just anyone," Franky noted, lighting a cigarette. "He tells me you started at Sal's thanks to Dooley."

"I did."

"How do you know Dooley?" Franky watched him intently.

"Met him back in juvie," Sheridan replied. "I suppose you could say he's a childhood friend."

Franky chuckled. "I met lots of my friends in juvie too. Dooley's a good accountant, when he's not drunk. He tells me you did some time."

"Robbery," Sheridan confirmed. So far this was easy—all his bona fides were being checked, and with Tony's backing, he was sure to have an in to the higher ranks of Franky's organization.

"You weren't very careful, then."

"We weren't prepared," Sheridan agreed, taking a swallow of his beer.

Franky's gaze drifted over the crowd and Sheridan saw him linger on where Nell and CeeCee stood with Erven Vogt and another man. Erven had his arm around CeeCee and Sheridan clenched a fist under the table. If he could, he'd break that arm just for touching her.

"She's a pretty little thing, isn't she?" Franky said. "Are you fond of her?"

Sheridan wondered how to answer, not wanting to betray any vulnerability. "More than most."

"Nell found her working in some café," Franky said. "She always finds the prettiest girls for the Orpheus, and I think she had Vogt in mind when she brought CeeCee here."

"He likes her." Sheridan kept his calm, though he could tell Franky was baiting him, trying to get him to react.

"You'll get your turn when he's done." Franky chuckled. "But enough of that. I'm glad you came over, Paddy. One of my boys went and got himself killed out in Atlantic City and I need to replace him. Tony says you'd be up for it."

"Of course." Sheridan stifled a smile. This was exactly the chance he needed.

"Giovanni worked here most nights, keeping the place secure. I'll talk to Enzo and let him know you'll be taking Gio's place. He needs another bruiser to keep out the riffraff."

"I appreciate the opportunity," Sheridan replied. He didn't have to fake his gratitude. Now that he was officially inside the Orpheus, he could plan a foolproof attack.

Franky smiled and pushed back the hair that had fallen over his forehead. Sheridan caught a glimpse of the white scar across his forehead as the mirror ball flashed over them. "Don't let me down," Franky said.

"I won't." This time he wouldn't hit Franky with a two-by-four. He'd do it properly.

CHAPTER SIXTEEN

The ward was quiet for midafternoon and the click of Cecilia's shoes seemed loud against the low murmurs and occasional coughs she heard. The nurses were absent, and when she came to the isolation ward, she saw that it was half-empty. Her mother lay in a bed near the window, away from the other two patients.

She opened the door and slipped in on tiptoe. Standing at her mother's bedside, she could see how the illness had ravaged her over the month since the nurse had allowed her to sneak in; once robust, her mother was a pale shadow of her former self, with hardly more color than the bedsheets.

Cecilia settled on the stool next to the bed and took her mother's hand. Her fingers were cold and Cecilia could feel her frail bones through the papery skin. Her mother squeezed her hand, so gently she could barely feel the pressure. Her eyes opened, though she seemed to struggle to keep them from drooping closed again.

"Hi, Ma," Cecilia said, trying to manage a smile. The corners of her mother's mouth turned up. Her mother squeezed her hand again, then turned her head away to cough, leaving a pale redness on the white pillow. When she turned back, her lips were flecked with red.

"You're here," her mother whispered. Cecilia nodded. "Good." She smiled wearily, her eyes falling closed for a long moment before opening again.

"Do you want some water?" Cecilia asked, at a loss. She couldn't make her mother better, and the doctors had been able to do little more than keep her comfortable.

Her mother shifted in bed and her mouth opened and closed, though no words came. Her free hand twisted in the sheets and she moaned. To Cecilia it sounded like agony.

"Ma?" Her chest tightened and she wanted to cry, but she couldn't.
She had to stay strong.

Her mother gasped and twisted in the sheets, and Cecilia stared in
horror at the pain on her face, a skeletal grimace. Her head turned and
Cecilia saw the sorrow in her mother's eyes, the urgency. She tried to
speak, gripping Cecilia's hand hard, then fell back on the pillow.

She gave one final gasp and lay still.

Cecilia slumped to the bed, holding her mother's hand to her
cheek. It couldn't be. But it was. The tears came, but they were silent,
soaking the bed linen in a hot rush. She felt the touch of a hand on her
hair and heard a voice, but it seemed far away, much removed from her
present anguish. She heard footsteps, coming, then going. Hands tried
to move her but she clung to her mother's hand and to the bed until they
gave up.

She was alone. No more would she come home to her mother's
comfort, her quiet assurance. No one knew her.

She must have cried herself to sleep, because she woke to a
familiar voice and hands lifting her up. She struggled, but the hands
held her fast.

"CeeCee." It was Sheridan. "It's all right." He lifted her into his
arms and took her out of the room and into another much smaller room,
empty except for them.

"No, it isn't," she managed to reply before the racking sobs came.
He settled into a chair and held her, her face buried in the dark serge of
his suit jacket. She felt him stroke her back, but mostly he just held her,
his embrace tight and secure.

When her sobs came to a stuttering halt, she lifted her head from
his chest and looked at him through eyes blurred with tears. He pulled a
linen handkerchief from his pocket and dabbed at her cheeks.

"What am I going to do?" She could barely speak, but she choked
out the words.

"We'll figure it out," Sheridan replied.

❖

He didn't know what to do, so he took her home. She went
quietly; her earlier torrent of sobbing seemed to have exhausted her.
She slumped on the sofa, staring into space.

Sheridan changed his clothes, stripping out of his tear-sodden shirt and into a fresh one, with a new dark tie that went with the black suit he wore. As one of the security at the Orpheus, he was expected to blend in. He glanced at the clock. He had to leave soon. A look at CeeCee confirmed that she wouldn't be able to work. He'd never seen anyone so forlorn, though he was sure he might have looked the same way when they'd pulled his mother's body from the ruined apartment.

He settled on the sofa beside CeeCee and took her hand. She turned her head to look at him.

"I'll tell Enzo you're ill," he said.

"And Nell too."

"The real reason, or should I just tell her you're sick?"

"You can tell her," CeeCee said, leaning her head on his shoulder and closing her eyes. "She knows."

"I'll put the bed down for you," he said, "and you can sleep. I won't be back until late."

She made a small noise, to show she was listening. He squeezed her hand gently and eased her head off his shoulder, rising to his feet. She opened her eyes.

"Are you hungry?" he asked.

"No."

"I'll bring you something later, then." He bent to kiss her and she gave him a half-hearted response. He set up the Murphy bed for her, then grabbed his jacket and fedora. He glanced back once as he left, but she hadn't moved.

❖

Enzo took the news with his usual irritation, muttering, "She'd better not make it a habit."

Sheridan didn't bother to find Nell. When she realized CeeCee wasn't here, she'd seek him out. In the meantime, he had work to do. He relieved the daytime man who covered the back of the Orpheus and took up his rounds. He would have preferred to be up front with all the excitement if CeeCee were here, but he wanted this opportunity to properly canvass the back offices.

Behind the stage, a warren of rooms served as dressing rooms for the band and the dancers. They might provide cover, but access was through a single hallway, so he discounted the area. If he managed to take out Franky, he'd never go through that hall. Too easy to get cornered. But now he strolled through, giving a wink to Dooley's girl, Scarlett. She blew him a kiss and he chuckled. Dooley had tried to make it up to her but had failed miserably. Lately he'd seen her on the arm of one of Vogt's friends.

Once out of the dressing rooms, he took a right, following the hallway back behind the bar. The night's supply of liquor was stacked in crates along the wall, making the space snug, though not as claustrophobic as the dressing rooms. He passed the janitor's closet along the way, where an older black man was putting away the supplies.

He took the stairs at the end of the hall, up into the office Franky maintained as a sort of private bordello. Leather sofas framed a large room with its own small bar. The place was empty, but it was early yet. After midnight it would fill with thugs wanting a bit of privacy for their conversations or their lady friends.

Several doors opened off the larger room and each led into a much smaller lounge. Entertainment areas, Franky had called them, when he'd outlined Sheridan's duties. A brothel by another name.

But there was one door still shut, and Sheridan had only once seen into the room that was Franky's office and sanctuary. He lived like a king at the Orpheus, stepping on lush carpets, lounging in his chair behind an elegant mahogany desk.

"It's reinforced." Franky had patted the wall. "Bulletproof."

"No windows?" he'd asked.

"No need for them." Franky hadn't elaborated, but Sheridan took that to mean Franky had another way out. He had to, or else the palace would become a death trap.

Sheridan didn't bother knocking. If Franky was in there, he wouldn't want to be disturbed. He nodded to the bartender setting up for the evening, then retreated down the other set of stairs. This route brought him out near the giant storeroom and the back door. He knew it well from his deliveries with Tony—it had been his first glimpse of Franky, and of Nell.

He cracked open the back door and breathed in the cool night air. The alley was empty and he took a careful glance into the darkness before closing the door. Time to retrace his steps and begin again. He lingered at the door to the ballroom, hearing the low chatter of its patrons, the discordant noises as the band tuned their instruments. He'd take a turn through the ballroom later, when it was busy.

He imagined catching Franky unawares as he came out of his

office, shooting him and letting him lie on the lush carpet, his blood soaking into the floor, spreading in a red halo. If only it were that easy. He wanted revenge, not suicide.

The girls for the first show came scurrying out of the dressing rooms, their sequined bodysuits brilliant in the bright lights. He'd never understood the point of putting on a show so early. The ballroom was nearly empty and the dancers stood idle, gossiping. A few couples wandered in, finding seats near the stage.

To the strains of the piano and the small ragtime band, the dancers appeared onstage. He didn't bother watching; he'd seen the show before and it didn't interest him. He gave the ballroom another once-over, then retreated into the back halls.

On his way through the hall behind the bar, he nearly ran into one of the bartenders' assistants, Gabe. The kid hefted two cases of champagne and Sheridan neatly sidestepped him before continuing upstairs. A couple of girls lounged on the leather sofas and the door to Franky's office was open. He sat inside, a cigarette smoldering in the ashtray and a ledger laid out on the desk before him. He glanced up and beckoned Sheridan in.

"All good?" he asked, pushing the ledger aside.

"As always," Sheridan replied, standing casually in the doorway. "Quiet down there if you don't count the dancing girls."

Franky chuckled. "Some of them will get good, but I need some way to weed out the chaff. Anyway, any mugs in this early deserve what they get."

"There are a few that might make the cut," he replied, even though he didn't really know. They all looked the same in their ridiculous sequins.

"Speaking of cuts," Franky said, leaning back in his chair. "You've made the cut here. Of course, I've never doubted Tony. He has an eye for quality."

"I'm glad to hear it."

"Tony didn't know where you were from—he figured you were a local, but I know I would have known you if you were."

Sheridan had been expecting the question, but far before now. He had his answer prepared. "Born here," he began, "but spent most of my growing up in New York with relatives. Came back, got in a mix up with O'Banion's boys, and then was buried in the clink for a few years."

"Robbery, right?"

"Yeah. Not the smartest thing I've ever done, but they needed someone to take the fall. My lawyer was an idiot."

"O'Banion didn't spring for a better one?" Franky ground out his cigarette and lit another. "Come, sit down. It'll be a long night."

Sheridan settled in the leather chair in front of Franky's desk.

"Someone had to take the fall." He gave a negligent shrug, as if he had accepted his fate. He'd hated prison.

"Who was on the caper with you?" Franky asked. He watched Sheridan closely. He wanted names, more bona fides. Sheridan straightened. He had them.

"Arthur, McCarthy, and Nails," he said easily. Arthur and Nails were dead, and McCarthy had left town. "It was McCarthy's fault—the idiot took down a couple of guys he shouldn't have. That's why one of us had to go down."

"Careless," Franky remarked. "But I'm not surprised."

"I learned a lot in the still," Sheridan said with a dry laugh. "Mostly how I wanted to stay clear."

"Easy enough to do." Franky seemed relaxed now, as if his suspicions had finally been quieted.

Sheridan lit a cigarette. "Glad to hear it."

"We wouldn't want your girl pining for you, now would we?"

"I'd like to avoid that," Sheridan said. "Even if she is more Vogt's girl than mine. She's had enough hardship lately, what with her mother dying."

"Poor girl." Franky said the right words, but his tone was unsympathetic. "You'd best get back to work. It'll be busy soon. I'll need you out front later tonight."

"Of course."

Sheridan left Franky's office. He rolled his shoulders as he came down the stairs. One obstacle cleared.

❖

Nell cornered him after the second show, pulling him aside in the hallway near the dressing rooms. She didn't even say hello. "Where's CeeCee?"

"She's not well." He answered her in the same short tone. She bristled.

"Is she sick?" Her tone softened at the end and she paused on the word.

"No. Her mother died."

Nell looked stricken, or at least, as stricken as she could manage. Over the last month he'd seen almost every emotion pass over her features and knew most of them were false. She could fool anyone.

"I already let Enzo know," he said. "At least he was understanding, though I don't know how long that will last. She's distraught. I doubt she'll be able to work tomorrow, or even the rest of this week."

"I'll talk to him," Nell assured Sheridan. "Is she at home? She should be with someone."

"I took her to my place. Hers isn't fit." He paused. "You've never seen where she lives, have you?"

"Why do you ask?" Her surprise looked genuine.

"She's been in dire straits." He didn't want to give away all CeeCee's secrets, but Nell should have known. She probably thought everyone lived in the same splendor as she.

"She never said. She asked for money and I gave it, but she never said."

"She'll be fine, I'm sure." He felt the need to mark his territory, show Nell she wasn't the only one who wanted CeeCee. "I'll take care of her."

Nell moved toward the dressing rooms but paused at the door. "How's your new job?" she asked.

"Fine."

"I encouraged Franky to move you up. Via Tony, of course."

"That's kind of you."

"We're even now." She disappeared through the door. He supposed they were. She'd gotten him into Franky's organization. Her, and Tony. He suspected it was more Tony's doing than hers. Guys like Franky didn't take their women seriously. He recalled their first meeting, when he'd been hauling cases of liquor. She thought she had a hold on Franky Greco, but his reaction afterward had shown the lie to his indulgent words. He didn't care about her, except for what she could bring him. To her misfortune. She wouldn't be young and pretty forever.

CHAPTER SEVENTEEN

Detective Lang took his whiskey from the bartender and gave Gabe a quick glance as he stacked empty bottles in a crate. He didn't look up and Lang turned his attention back to the stage. He kept away from Gabe now when they were under Franky's roof. The guilt he'd feel if Gabe ended up the way Lina had—he wouldn't be able to stand it. He took his drink with him as he slipped into the crowd. Nights like tonight, when the Orpheus seethed with guests, the high class rubbing elbows with thugs, made it easy to become anonymous.

He stayed clear of Nell, catching glimpses of her across the ballroom, dancing with Franky. He let his gaze wander to the stage, where a pair of dancers dressed in leopard-skin costumes did some sort of ludicrous pantomime. What was Enzo thinking? He looked away and his gaze caught on a man standing near the stage, his dark hair slicked back, his expression carefully blank, at least until their gazes met.

Recognition widened the man's eyes and he began to move through the crowd until he stood next to Lang. He held a half-full glass of beer and as he turned to glance across the ballroom, his profile revealed his identity.

"What are you doing here?" Lang tried to keep his voice low, yet loud enough to be heard over the music.

Sheridan smirked. "I'm always here."

"You have some nerve." Lang wasn't sure if he should be impressed at Sheridan's daring, or at his disregard for his own life. This man had tried to kill Franky Greco, yet he stood in the Orpheus, calm as anything.

"I work here," Sheridan said.

Lang took a sip of his whiskey to hide his surprise. "And Franky doesn't know about—before?"

"Not unless you told him," Sheridan said.

Lang shook his head. He'd considered it, but he couldn't do it. At times he hoped someone would take out Franky Greco, as Capone's boys had taken out O'Banion in his flower shop, and Colosimo in the café. "I didn't see the point of it," Lang replied.

"You don't like him much, do you?"

Lang grimaced.

"Come have a drink with me," Sheridan said. "Domenic has the late nights, and I'm done. Let's get out of here."

"Why should I?"

"I have a proposition for you," Sheridan said. "And it's one I think you'll like." He set his pint glass on a nearby table. Lang downed the rest of his whiskey. Curiosity killed the cat, but he'd take the chance.

Lang kept half a step behind Sheridan as they made their way to a nearby speakeasy. It was a small place, the back room of a restaurant that he rarely visited. He kept a close eye on Sheridan—the man had tried to off Greco, after all. It occurred to him that Sheridan might want to dispose of him, but once they entered the bar, he began to relax. Offing him in the middle of a speakeasy, with witnesses, would hardly keep things hushed. As it was, he'd made inquiries about Sheridan after the incident. The man was a textbook thug: brought up in the tenements, according to his juvenile record, and in and out of prison ever since. If he'd had more influence and connections, he might not have spent as much time behind bars.

Sheridan chatted easily with the bartender; it appeared he knew the man well as they bantered back and forth. Lang stiffened. Maybe Sheridan *would* off him, if he had connections here. They might hush up the hit out of loyalty.

"What'll you have?" The bartender's attention came to him.

He snapped out, "Whiskey."

The bartender seemed to look at him with more respect, and Sheridan grinned. "Good taste," he remarked, taking his own whiskey and laying a couple dollars on the bar. Lang dug in his pocket. "On me," Sheridan said.

They took a table far from the bar and an empty table lay between them and the next nearest customers.

"Sláinte." Sheridan took a sip of the whiskey and made a face. "Not the best stuff."

Lang sipped his whiskey. It made his eyes water. He coughed.

"Easy." Sheridan chuckled.

"What did you want to talk about?" Lang cleared his throat. "You know I haven't said anything."

"That's why I wanted to talk to you," Sheridan replied. "I figured since you didn't rat on me, you might want to help me out the next time."

Lang was speechless. Of all the things he'd expected, this hadn't been one of them. He'd expected a bribe, a bit of cash to grease his palm and keep him quiet. Or threats. Not this.

Sheridan waited, a small smile playing on his lips. Lang thought of Franky's retribution if they failed, but then he thought of Gabe. If Franky were dead, no one need ever know of his predilections. And he could see Gabe without having to worry about either of them being shot. He stared down into his drink.

"I don't know."

"Does he bribe you? Is that it?"

"Not me. But my boss…" Lang shook his head. Franky went free because Navarra had closed Lina's file. Money and connections talked, not justice.

"Typical."

Lang wondered how many other women Franky had murdered, how many times he'd gotten off scot-free. If he helped Sheridan…He thought of Gabe, who still hadn't told him what Franky had done to him. "What's your plan?"

"I need to be able to get at him where he's not expecting it," Sheridan said, his voice low, barely more than a whisper. "I need backup. I don't want to turn this into a suicide mission. I have things I want to do with my life."

"Female things?" Lang couldn't help the quip. He'd heard of how Sheridan had taken an interest in Nell's lover, CeeCee. Sensible on Nell's part, to get her out from under Franky's nose.

"Maybe."

"So what's in it for me?" Lang asked.

"What do you want?"

"Money." With enough cash, he could get the hell away from here and take Gabe with him. He'd heard San Francisco was good. It would be far enough from the mob, from attempts at revenge. Far enough for no one to know who they were. "Twenty thousand."

Sheridan gave a low whistle. "I'm not Rockefeller," he said.

"If I help you, and I'm found out, I'm a dead man," Lang pointed out. "I should ask for more. It'll follow me my whole life."

"If we have a chance to rob him, you can have his roll," Sheridan replied. He finished off his whiskey and signaled the bartender for another. Once the bartender had come and gone, they resumed their conversation.

"If I could track his movements, I could take him out," Sheridan said.

"What's stopping you?"

"Manpower." He grimaced. "I can't work and track him outside the Orpheus at the same time."

"I thought you thugs always had pals," Lang replied.

"None that I trust that much." Sheridan shot Lang a questioning glance.

"I'm not using police power to do it," Lang retorted. "That'd be like signing my own death warrant, courtesy of my boss. And anyway, I can tell you that Greco's not as stupid as O'Banion. He won't stick to a pattern."

"What about his house?"

"Possibly. He lives near Capone, but he's smart enough to have guards."

Sheridan cursed under his breath. "What about inside the Orpheus?"

Lang let out a bark of laughter. "I thought you said you weren't suicidal."

"Even his guards get bored when he spends so much time in his office," Sheridan said.

"But without cash, I'm not doing anything," Lang reminded him.

"You'll get it."

"This won't go any further until I do."

"Half up front?"

"That's fair." Lang tossed back the dregs of his whiskey and rose. "I'll be seeing you."

"When I'm ready, I'll find you."

Lang gave Sheridan a nod and wove between the tables, letting himself out through the back door. The night air was chill and the wind had picked up, blowing fiercely down the street, but he could smell the start of spring.

❖

Cecilia woke in Sheridan's bed, her eyes scratchy and sore. Weak sunlight filtered through the crack in the blinds and she sat up. Sheridan lay beside her on his back. He snored lightly. His shoulders were bare and she wondered how he could possibly be warm. Already she was shivering, the draft from the window curling around her body.

As the events of the previous day filtered back into her conscious mind, a lethargy overtook her. Her mother wouldn't be there to welcome her home, give her a cup of tea and a kiss. She'd never do that ever again. The tenement room would be empty, barren of the loving presence she'd always known. She'd try not to remember the last few months or even the last year of her mother's life: the factory work, the long hours that sapped her energy, and finally the lingering consumption. Back at the farm, her mother had been a vibrant woman, always up with the dawn, busy with all that needed doing.

Cecilia wished she could turn the clock back. She'd appreciate those days more now, if she had the chance to do them over. She'd savor every moment.

She shuddered, the cold having sunk into her while she'd sought happier times. Her teeth chattered, and though she slid back under the covers, she couldn't get warm. Her toes were numb, her arms and legs goose pimpled, and her entire torso felt as if it had been dunked in an ice bath. She curled up next to Sheridan, hoping to siphon some of his warmth without waking him. He'd come in late, so very late, and he needed sleep.

He shifted against her and rolled over, his head resting on the pillow next to hers, his breath ghosting warmly over her face. She stared at him and saw his eyelids flicker, then open. Without a word, he drew her closer, his hand sliding over her hip until she was against him, her head tucked into his shoulder.

If she kept her eyes closed, could she pretend everything was still the way it had been? She wished it could be true. Sheridan's warmth slowly seeped into her. He stroked her back and she did close her eyes.

The room was bright when she next woke, the curtain pulled aside to let in the late-morning sun. Cecilia lay in bed alone and a quick glance of the room told her it was empty. The door to the bathroom stood ajar, the light off. She heard steps from the floor above, and water running. She pushed back the covers and rose, padding into the bathroom and pulling her slip over her head, dropping it on the floor. She ran the water in the claw-foot tub, and as she waited for the tub to fill, she stared at her face in the small mirror.

Her dark hair was flat, almost lifeless, and her eyes were red around the edges. The imprint from the pillow lay across her cheek and she rubbed at it before turning back to the tub. The pipes clanked as she turned off the taps and she stepped carefully over the side of the tub, the heat of the water almost too much. She lowered herself until she was submerged up to her neck. As she rested her head back, she closed her eyes. If only she could stay here forever, she could hide away and pretend nothing was wrong.

Her mind wouldn't let her be so frivolous. She had to arrange for a funeral, and the burial, but how? Since they'd moved from the farm, they hadn't joined a church. And even if they had, she didn't know how she would pay for it all. Her brow furrowed. Maybe an undertaker would take payments.

A knock on the door frame startled her and she sat up in the bath, water streaming down her shoulders. Sheridan stood in the entry, a paper bag in his hand. His gaze dipped down over her shoulders and breasts, and Cecilia grew warm under his scrutiny.

"I'm glad I didn't miss this," he said, giving her a wink. "I've never had a lady in my bathtub before." His tone was lightly teasing and inspired her to return his comment in kind.

"I've never had a bath in a man's tub before," she said. "Especially not when he's ogling me."

"Are you complaining?" Sheridan set the bag down on the bureau before he entered the bathroom, coming to crouch by the side of the tub. He dangled his fingers in the water, flicking them up and splashing her face.

Cecilia giggled and splashed him back, and he rose, water soaking his shirt. She looked at him and what she'd done. He chuckled, peeling off his jacket and hanging it on the hook behind the door. He took off his shoes and his socks and tossed them into the other room, and then stripped off his trousers and shirt, hanging them with the jacket.

"If that's the way you're going to be," he said, mock-threatening, "then I'd best be prepared."

In his undershirt and boxers, he came back to the bath, scooping up water in both hands. Cecilia covered her face, just in time to have the water soak her hair. She splashed him back and he climbed into the tub, catching her in his arms. She shrieked and struggled against him and he laughed.

"Don't duck me, please," she said between giggles. He didn't let go, nor did he try to splash her again. She could feel his heart beating, a flutter against her arm. He cupped her cheek, his calloused thumb stroking her cheekbone. The moment lengthened and she didn't dare speak, didn't dare to ruin this moment, where she felt so safe and so wanted. Finally, Sheridan bent his head and kissed her, and she kissed him back, clinging to his shoulders. He let her go only long enough to drag the soaking wet undershirt over his head.

"Why'd you leave that on, anyway?" she murmured, feeling the fabric of his boxer shorts under her thighs.

"I didn't want to shock you," he answered, and she laughed aloud. "Obviously I shouldn't have worried."

With silly awkwardness, they shifted in the tub until Sheridan dragged his boxers free and dropped them over the side. The wet cotton plopped into a puddle of water and she leaned over to peer at the floor.

"We've made a mess," she observed. Puddles shone on the tiles and she was surprised how little water had left the tub, given their splashing.

"Well worth it," Sheridan replied, his lips against her neck. He settled her over him and pressed between her thighs. When he penetrated her, she shuddered and made a noise in her throat, his movements causing the heat to rise in her, the desire taking over.

She rocked against him, feeling his arms tight around her. She looked down into his face, his eyes on hers, the moisture clinging to his eyelashes, curling his dark hair over his forehead. She brought her hands up and ran them through his hair, slicking back the curls before dropping a kiss on his parted lips. He surged upward and captured her mouth when she would have drawn back, and they kissed until finally she had to break it off to gasp in a breath.

Cecilia rested her forehead on his shoulder, her heart pounding. His breath rasped in her ear as he thrust into her, and she gave a low moan when his fingers brushed between her legs, pressing against her clitoris. Every muscle in her body tensed and she could feel the tingling begin in her abdomen. It spread downward, centering where he touched her. She cried out, the ecstasy taking over.

Sheridan thrust hard and his hand gripped her back, his spread palm pressing her forward. He groaned as she became boneless against him, sagging into the water.

He held her until the water began to take on a chill. Cecilia lifted herself off him reluctantly.

"I never did get to wash my hair," she said, impudently flicking water at him. Sheridan chuckled and rose, stepping out of the tub.

"You still can," he said, pulling the plug. He turned on the taps and she leaned back. His hand cupped the back of her neck, holding her in place as he angled her under the flowing water. She sat up and reached for the shampoo and they repeated the process. Then Sheridan grabbed a towel, quickly rubbing himself dry.

Cecilia stepped from the tub and grabbed the other clean towel, drying herself as quickly as he had.

"I need to get to work soon," he said, as he moved into the other room.

"I should go too," Cecilia said. She didn't want to, but Enzo wouldn't allow her to be gone that long.

"You have time yet," Sheridan replied. He took dry clothes from the bureau. By the time she emerged from the bathroom, after combing out the tangles in her hair, he was nearly finished dressing.

"I have to arrange my mother's funeral." She looked at her dress, crumpled on the floor. She'd look like a ragamuffin, wearing her wrinkled clothes. Her slip wasn't any better after being on the bathroom floor, but it couldn't be helped.

"I'll come with you."

"I'll be all right." She didn't want to completely fall apart in front of him again, and walking into the room with her mother's things there, just waiting for her to return, would be agony.

"Are you sure?"

"I'll see you at the Orpheus later," she promised.

They parted at the corner by the hospital and Cecilia went inside. At the ward, one of the nurses recognized her.

"Oh, you poor dear." She led Cecilia into a quiet corner. "We arranged for your mother to be sent to the funeral home, even though the doctor wanted her to be buried as soon as possible." The woman clasped Cecilia's hand. She gave Cecilia directions.

"Thank you." Cecilia squeezed the woman's hand and retraced her steps. Outside the funeral home, she gathered up her courage. The building was plain, appropriately solemn, and seemed quiet. She pushed open the door.

An older, thin-faced man met her inside. In a trembling, halting voice, she explained. He took her hand and led her to a chair.

"What would you like for the service?" he asked. He explained the state regulations regarding deaths from TB, but the words meant little.

"Only the most simple service," she said.

"Is there family you would like us to notify?" he asked solicitously.

"No. No one." They'd left any family far behind when they'd come to Chicago.

"We can arrange for burial as soon as tomorrow," the undertaker said. "Though I know the nurses at the hospital mentioned you might not be able to afford it." He paused, and she could tell he was trying to be tactful. "Cremation is an option, and a niche at Rose Hill is far more affordable than a plot."

"All right." She swallowed against the tears that threatened.

"It's just as suitable as a burial," he assured her. "That section of the cemetery is especially lovely. How many do you expect for the service?"

Cecilia looked down at her tightly clasped hands. "Just me."

After making the arrangements, she turned toward home. As the streets grew filthier, she dodged piles of garbage and muddy puddles. Her building looked even more forlorn, its gray weathered boards and dirty windows like most of the buildings on the street. A crumpled newspaper had caught on the banister, its headline trumpeting the arrest of some minor gangster. She went up the stairs and let herself in. There was no one about as she went to her room and unlocked the door.

The pain lanced through her and she shut her eyes tight against the tears, her hand clutching the iron doorknob as if it were the only thing in the world holding her up. A whimper escaped her and she swallowed hard. She willed her fingers to release the doorknob and opened her eyes. Her mother's nightgown lay folded on the bed, the kerosene lamp sat ready in the middle of the small table, and the kettle was on the stove, as if her mother had readied it. Except she hadn't. The stove was cold and so was the room.

Cecilia's hands shook as she pulled open the stove's heavy door, took a few pieces of kindling from the wood box, set them in a small teepee on the cold ashes. She took the matches from the table.

A heavy hand thumped against the door and she started, dropping the open matchbox. The matchsticks spread across the floor at her feet. The thump came again, and the door opened. The landlord strode in.

"There you are."

She stared at him numbly.

"Get your things," he said, his voice hard. "I've rented this room to someone who'll pay me on time."

She could hardly find words. "But I have paid—"

"Hurry up!" he barked at her. "You're not so tough when you don't have your thug with you. And don't you think of sending him to do your dirty work." His face leaned close to hers, its blackened teeth and foul breath penetrating her shock.

She scrambled away from him, dragging her mother's old carpetbag from beneath the bed. She grabbed her dresses from their hooks and stuffed them in, and then grabbed the tin from the shelf, and her mother's shawl. She looked around frantically and spotted the two teacups, her favorite and her mother's blue-and-white china cup, on the small drying rack. She tucked them inside the carpetbag gently, giving one last look around. She snatched up her dancing shoes and tried to fit them into the bag, barely managing. They stuck out the top, but that didn't matter.

The landlord took her arm and hustled her out the door, marching her down the stairs. The carpetbag bumped against her leg as she struggled to hold it. When they hit the front door, he gave her a little shove and she stumbled against the banister. The door slammed shut.

Cecilia staggered down the steps. She was homeless. Motherless. Alone. The sobs threatened to spill over but she pressed her lips together. She couldn't cry. She wouldn't. She stood in the middle of the crumbling sidewalk, wishing Sheridan had come with her after all. He'd know what to do. She remembered him scaring the landlord and a small smile quirked her lips. If only she could do the same. Her shoulders slumped. He'd be at the Orpheus by now, but she couldn't go there in her current state. She trudged down the street.

She did have someone to turn to. Nell.

CHAPTER EIGHTEEN

The doorman wouldn't let her past the lobby. He looked down his nose at her as he called up to Nell's apartment.

"Wait here," he said. "She'll be down in a minute."

Cecilia turned to look out the door toward the street. Cars moved along the road and well-off people, men in suits and women in luxurious coats, strolled down the sidewalk. They'd given her a wide berth as she'd walked to Nell's building, and she knew she looked like a street urchin. Her hands clutched the carpetbag tightly.

She heard the clang of the elevator and the murmur of the doorman. A familiar perfume reached her nose and she wanted to crumble right there on the carpet in the lobby.

"CeeCee?" Nell's voice was full of worry.

Cecilia turned but couldn't speak. Nell must have seen the agony in her eyes because she ushered Cecilia toward the elevator, shooting a glare at the doorman.

Once inside Nell's beautiful apartment, Cecilia let the carpetbag fall to the floor. Nell picked it up and Cecilia followed her through to the bedroom, where Nell set the bag by the wardrobe.

"Tell me what's happened," she commanded, taking Cecilia's hands, tugging her toward the bed. She pulled her close. "I can't bear to see you unhappy."

Cecilia rested her head on Nell's shoulder, her eyes filling with tears. She took a deep breath, trying to ease the pain in her chest. She wouldn't cry; she'd done enough of it already. With a flat voice, she recounted the past few days, skipping over the bits about her and Sheridan, telling Nell of the hospital, the death, and, now, her homelessness. Closing her eyes, she focused on Nell's warmth beside her and the soothing scent of her perfume.

Nell stroked her hair. "You'll stay here with me," she said decisively.

Cecilia blinked. "Won't Franky mind?" she ventured. She'd only ever stayed over when Franky had been out—this was Nell's apartment, but Franky had full access. He'd probably paid for it. She felt Nell stiffen.

"He has no say," she replied. "And he wouldn't object—you'd be homeless otherwise. He's mean, but not like that."

"If you're sure." Cecilia raised her head. "Still, I'll start looking for a place to rent."

Nell stroked her cheek. "Stay awhile," she said tenderly. Her hand stilled and she bent forward, brushing her lips over Cecilia's mouth.

They kissed and Cecilia felt some of her tension ease. She'd be with Nell now, curled up together in scented sheets, a shelter against the world. She sagged against Nell, relaxing into the soft pillows. Everything would be all right.

❖

Cecilia smoothed a wrinkle from her dress before she left the dressing room. She could hear the music from the end of the first show, a mix of staccato drum rhythms and low bass, Enzo's idea of an African dance. He'd gotten half a dozen of the girls into leopard-print patterned costumes, but really it was just an excuse to have them show more skin, with carefully positioned tears baring sections of midriff to the audience. She thought it was silly, but the crowd ate it up, and the dances roused them to energetic highs for several hours afterward.

The noise and music grew as she crossed the lobby. Before she could enter the ballroom, she heard her name and a tuxedo-clad arm came around her waist, amorous lips brushing the skin of her bared shoulder.

She turned in the embrace and looked up at Erven, who planted a kiss on her lips and grinned down at her.

"I missed you last night," he said, not loosening his grasp.

She could feel the buttons of his jacket pressing against her breasts. She hesitated, wondering if she should explain, but the sharp pain of loss sliced through her and she forced a smile. "It's a trick to keep you coming back," she teased. "You never know when I'll be here, so you're here every night."

Erven let out a loud guffaw. "Of course! And to make up for your absence yesterday, you need to spend the whole evening with me. I decree it." He kept an arm possessively around her waist as they went into the ballroom.

"As you wish," Cecilia agreed. With Erven, she didn't have to worry about others, or having to talk about herself. Erven was never happier than when she listened to his opinions.

"I have a table already," Erven told her, "with your lovely friend Miss Prescott, Mr. Greco, and a few others. We'll make this Saturday night worthwhile."

The performance onstage, with its drums and leopard prints, was just coming to an end as Erven pulled out a chair for her, next to Nell.

"You missed the best part," Nell told them. "Alice was tossed into the air by Alan, just as if he were Tarzan. He used to do that with Scarlett, before."

"You should dance up there," Erven said, pinning Cecilia with his gaze. "Don't you think so, Nell?"

"If she wants to," Nell said gaily. "But then she'd be busy half the night and you'd never see her. And weren't you just complaining to me last night that you were missing CeeCee terribly?"

"I don't have that much talent," Cecilia replied. "It'd take weeks of rehearsal to get me up there."

"I suppose you're right." Erven's hand slid down her back and she could feel the warmth through the thin fabric of her dress. "But I wish Enzo would throw an African masquerade one night."

"You just want to see us all half-naked," Cecilia quipped. Erven's fingers slid to the top of the low vee at the back of her dress, stroking the bare flesh. Just hours ago, Nell's hand had been there, and she'd wanted it. But Erven—he was an attractive man, and rich, and attentive, but she didn't feel anything for him beyond a friendly fondness. If only he were someone else…

Nell chortled. "I'll talk to Enzo and Franky about it," she promised. "But you men can't come dressed in tuxedos. We want to see a bit more too."

"How about a bearskin?" Erven said.

"You'll have to do better than to dress in the rug from your study!" Cecilia laughed. He'd bragged to her before about shooting a black bear and having it skinned and on his floor. "That would be cheating."

"Well then, I'll go out into the wilds of the West Side and kill myself a big cat instead," Erven replied.

"Or just go to the costume shops like the rest of us," Nell remarked, taking a sip of her champagne.

"What's the fun in that?" Erven winked at Cecilia. "Maybe CeeCee can help me choose."

"Maybe," she said with a coy smile. "But only if it actually happens. I can't see Franky allowing that sort of masquerade."

"You never know," Nell said, glancing over to where Franky stood at the bar talking to a couple of his men. One of them glanced over at the table and Cecilia saw it was Sheridan. She hurriedly looked away. She wasn't doing anything wrong, but she didn't think she'd been imagining the surprise on his face. Did he not expect her to be here? Or was it something else?

Detective Lang fought the urge to pull out his handkerchief and cover his nose like a swooning woman. He swallowed against the bile that rose in his throat and kept his hands at his sides. He knew from experience that the handkerchief wouldn't help the stench, but he wanted to do it all the same. The woman's body lay on the bed; the sheets dragged halfway across the floor. She was partly covered by a pale pink negligee, now black with rot. A gash across her head squirmed with maggots. Murder? If so, it had been a quiet one. Neighbors hadn't called until the heavy smell of death had seeped from the small apartment and disturbed their sensibilities.

He had to look away when the bugs crawled over her mouth and toward her sightless eyes. No way to tell what color they'd once been. He shuddered. He hated these jobs. Give him a gangster gunned down in cold blood over a case like this, any day.

He turned his attention to the rest of the small apartment. Room, more like—it was hardly big enough to be called an apartment, but the stern landlady downstairs had used the word. He stepped carefully over to the wardrobe in the corner, trying not to disturb the scene, pulling his handkerchief from his pocket to cover his hand. He eased open the door.

A selection of dresses hung within, their sequins catching the low light. He pulled one out, then another. Not the dresses of an average girl. More like those of a regular entertainer, probably a chorus girl. There was a flash of red as he put the dresses back and he pulled out yet another gown. It was too familiar. He glanced back at the bed. Blond curls, though matted with blood, and petite.

A knock on the open door turned his glance away. Jones looked at the body and paled. He resolutely shifted his gaze to Lang. "The landlady checked her book and confirmed the girl's name. It's Scarlett Ward. She says Miss Ward was always out late and that she didn't approve."

Lang snorted. "Without working girls, that woman wouldn't even have a business."

"Did you find anything?"

Lang shrugged. "Her name's familiar. Did the landlady say where Miss Ward worked?" He knew the answer but wanted it confirmed.

"The Orpheus," Jones replied. He risked another glance at the corpse, but it was a quick one. "Who would have done this, Detective?"

Lang could venture a guess, but he couldn't imagine why. This girl wasn't one of Nell's playthings; she'd been just one dancer of many. He needed to get over there before the news got out. "Get the boys in here to go over the place with a fine-tooth comb, but keep everyone else out," he commanded.

"What should I tell the boss?" Jones asked, already backing out the door.

"Tell him it's murder, but we don't know who or why." The who he could guess, but the why? Franky Greco always had a reason.

❖

The evening's revels were in full swing by the time he reached the Orpheus. The doorman almost didn't let him in, looking over his suit and trench coat with derision. Of course, it was Saturday night. Prime party time for the rich. When he flashed his badge, the man let him by with an apology.

"Your boss in?"

"Been here all night," the doorman replied.

"Good." Lang let the coat-check girl take his hat and coat. No need to stand out like a sore thumb. Once inside the dim ballroom, his dark suit would pass casual inspection. He wanted to talk to Nell and question the other girls in the act, and he needed to talk to Franky. Girls from the Orpheus didn't end up dead every day. It was a high-class place, not one of those dingy saloons.

He knew Navarra would likely have him sweep the whole thing

under the rug, just like Lina's death. No one really cared about a dancing girl found dead in a run-down rooming house. She was beneath the important people, and to the average law-abiding citizen, she was a step away from being a whore.

The band played a jaunty tune and the dance floor was full of couples. He glanced at his watch. Just about midnight. Early, still, to most of the crowd. The second show would have ended and the dancing girls would be entertaining men now instead of the crowd, at least until two or three o'clock. Franky and Enzo ran a tight ship.

Lang scanned the mass of couples but at first he couldn't see Nell or Franky. They could be upstairs, spending time in Franky's office. Just then the crowd parted and he saw them in its midst, Nell's red hair spilling over her shoulders as she leaned in close to Franky, whispering something in his ear. He looked pleased and Lang could only guess what she'd told him.

He lingered at the edge of the dance floor, trying to decide what to say and how to begin. Someone bumped him and he glanced over his shoulder. Sheridan. What was he doing? Their association would raise a few brows. He gave the man a nod and Sheridan moved away, circling the dance floor like a shark readying for a kill. But he couldn't be, could he? Lang followed Sheridan's gaze. He wasn't looking for Franky; he had his eye fixed on CeeCee, Nell's girl. She danced with Erven Vogt and Lang knew Sheridan would have a long wait. Vogt rarely ever gave up his companion for the evening. What that man wanted he always received. Franky wouldn't have it any other way, not with the money rolling in.

Franky.

Lang's gaze flitted back to the gangster, now slow dancing with Nell. The crowd parted and Lang could see one of Franky's hands cupping her buttocks, a possessive gesture that wouldn't be lost on the other men present. But finally, the song ended and Franky led Nell toward their usual table. Lang swiftly cut through the crowd and managed to meet them just as Franky was pulling out a chair for Nell.

"Detective," Franky said pleasantly. "What a nice surprise." For a man who'd killed Scarlett Ward, he was remarkably calm. Lang had a fleeting sense of doubt. Perhaps it hadn't been Franky.

Nell smiled at him, but it was automatic. Her attention rested on the dance floor still. On CeeCee. Her gaze followed CeeCee and Erven to the bar before she turned her attention back to the table.

"Might I have a word?" Lang inquired, returning his focus to

Franky, who easily took his measure and nodded. He'd talk to Nell later.

"Let's go upstairs," Franky said. "Darling, we'll be back shortly. Business calls." Nell rose from the table and gave Franky a kiss.

"I'll go get another drink then," she said. Franky motioned to Lang and he followed Franky back behind the stage and through the hallways. When they passed the supply closet where he'd been caught with Gabe, he purposely ignored it, though he saw Franky's mouth quirk up in amusement. They climbed the stairs to the second floor. It was empty apart from a scattering of half-empty glasses. Franky frowned.

"Needs cleaning," he muttered, and Lang didn't envy the janitor one bit. They went into Franky's office and Franky immediately went to the liquor cabinet, removing a decanter and a pair of tumblers. "Whiskey? It's the real thing." He chuckled.

"Much obliged." Lang took the glass and at Franky's invitation, settled himself in one of the leather armchairs. "Do you know a Miss Ward?" No point in beating around the bush.

Franky shrugged. "I know lots of girls." He grinned. "The Orpheus is full of them."

"Petite, blond curls. She goes by Scarlett."

"Dooley's girl," Franky said. "My accountant has surprisingly good taste."

"Had," Lang corrected. "She's dead." Franky didn't twitch a muscle, but then, Lang hadn't really expected him to. "I thought I'd tell you personally, then you could tell Enzo and let him tell the other girls."

"How did she die?"

Lang gave Franky a hard stare. "I can't say, or say when. Have to wait on the coroner, see if he can make anything of it. Poor girl wasn't found for days."

"Awful." Franky's voice was monotone; perhaps he'd already known.

"Who was she friends with, aside from your accountant? I'll need to talk to him, and to the girls."

"I haven't a clue. Enzo will know." He sipped his whiskey, leaning against the edge of the desk. "A pity I keep losing girls, but there's always more where she came from. Dooley will disagree, of course." He chuckled again. "Go see Enzo and tell him I sent you. And don't tell any of the girls, at least not until the end of the night. Tears are bad for business."

Lang tossed back his whiskey and rose. He'd talk to Enzo, and to every girl he needed to, and to hell with Franky's command. "Is Dooley here tonight?"

"He should be. Haven't seen him yet though."

"I'll find him."

❖

Cecilia felt his hand on her arm before she saw him. Sheridan tugged her out of the way of a stream of women headed to the ladies' room and back into a darker corner of the ballroom. The crowds were thick, but she didn't recognize anyone around them.

"I thought he'd never leave your side," Sheridan said tersely.

Cecilia bristled. "Erven's a lovely man," she retorted.

"Is he?" Sheridan frowned and put his arm around her. "Sorry, darling. I get a bit jealous when I see another guy spending so much time with you while I'm playing guard duty."

"It's all right." She gave him a comforting smile. "It's work."

"Come find me when you're done for the night," he said, leaning in close. She could feel his breath on her ear. "I'll take you home."

"I got kicked out."

He looked startled. "When?"

"I went back after going to the funeral home, and the landlord said I hadn't kept up on the rent. I managed to get a few things, but that was it."

"Why didn't you tell me?"

She looked away, blinking away the sudden tears and trying to still the tremor of her lower lip. His finger came under her chin, tilting it up so she looked him straight in the eye. "You'll stay with me."

"I already have a place to stay," she said. She worried at her lower lip with her teeth. "I'm staying with Nell."

CHAPTER NINETEEN

Sheridan reeled, but he kept his expression bland. After all they'd shared, all he'd done for her, she chose Nell over him.

"It'll be a crowded apartment with you, her, and Franky," he said, keeping his tone carefully casual.

"He doesn't live there," CeeCee replied.

She had no idea what she was doing to him, did she? "Are you sure?"

She nodded. "Nell has more room, and that way I won't be underfoot at your place. And you won't have to worry about me." She ducked out from under his arm, but he caught her again before she could dart away.

"I'll still worry," he told her and he wanted to take her away right then—away from the Orpheus, from the danger that was Franky, and from Nell. The woman who shared CeeCee's bed. How could it not be trouble when Nell was playing both sides? CeeCee might as well be in bed with Franky himself.

"I know." CeeCee rose onto her toes and gave him a gentle kiss, barely more than a brush of lips. "I'll see you later."

He released her and watched as she walked back toward the ladies' room. She didn't know what she was getting into. He remembered Nell coming to ask her favor and wondered how on earth she could have forgotten the danger.

Sheridan hovered in the shadows, watching people come and go. CeeCee returned to the ballroom and went straight to Franky's table, settling between Nell and Erven. Franky sat across from them—too close. CeeCee would be closer now, more likely an accidental target for violence. Being too friendly with a top gangster was dangerous. And he was the one who planned to put Franky in danger.

❖

Lang needed a drink.

After pulling Enzo aside and telling him the news, he'd had to help the man outside, where Lang waited while Enzo went from green to white and back again before finally vomiting onto the pavement. He waited until Enzo straightened and wiped his mouth with a handkerchief before asking his next question. "Do you know who she's been with in the last few weeks?" Lang inquired.

Enzo dabbed at the perspiration on his brow. "I can't keep track of where all the girls are," he explained, still looking a bit green in the light from the open door. "But she spent most of her free time with Dooley, either at the bar or upstairs later on."

"I'll talk to him," Lang assured Enzo. "Anyone else?"

Enzo shook his head. "Just any man at the Orpheus. You know how it is. Dooley couldn't afford to keep her around all the time. There are always other men, except for the lucky few girls."

"Did you notice her with anyone in particular?"

Enzo blotted his lips and threw the stained handkerchief away. "I saw her at Franky's table a week or so ago, maybe longer, chatting up Erven Vogt. His usual girl wasn't at the table then, which was odd. But then, Scarlett always did have an eye for the rich ones."

Lang patted him on the back. "I'll check into it. Let's get a drink."

"I'll need it." Enzo let Lang lead him back into the Orpheus. They stood at the back bar and Lang waved Gabe over, giving him their order.

"Give your boss the strongest whiskey you've got," he said, "and I'll have my usual."

Gabe gave Enzo a once-over, but he didn't say a word, just poured a tumbler half-full of the top-shelf brand and slid it across the bar. He poured a similar glass for Lang and shot him a wink.

Lang sipped his whiskey. Definitely the real thing. He'd be spoiled for his usual drink now.

Enzo clutched his glass. A gulp helped put some color back into his face. He took another gulp and Lang could see some of the tension ease. "What'll I tell the girls?"

"Nothing yet," Lang replied. "But see if you can't find out more. They'll answer you—most of them don't like me much." Dancing girls rarely liked him—he drank too much, rarely danced, and he spent his money on other things. It didn't seem useful to court a girl he didn't have any interest in.

Enzo took his glass with him and Lang watched him slip through the backstage door. He turned back to the bar.

"Another," he said to Gabe. "And not the fancy stuff—I'll get spoiled." Gabe poured him another glass and the first sip burned so much he nearly choked. He leaned an elbow on the bar and casually scanned the ballroom. Franky sat with Nell, Erven, and Cecilia at their usual table, looking relaxed and debonair. At first glance, one wouldn't think that he'd killed women in cold blood. His affection for Nell was obvious and his possessiveness apparent in the arm draped over the back of her chair, his hand resting on her shoulder. He and Nell shared a laugh and then Nell leaned closer to Cecilia, giving her hand a gentle pat.

The motion looked friendly, a pair of girls fond of each other, but Lang knew better. Nell should be leaving Cecilia alone; she shouldn't be touching her or smiling at her, or whispering in her ear. He had no desire to fish Cecilia's body from the river, or walk into her room to find her rotting, a rat gnawing on her dead fingers. He shuddered and downed the whiskey.

"Another."

Gabe refilled his glass without a word.

"Getting drunk? Are you sure that's safe around here?" Sheridan sidled up to the bar, nodding at Gabe. "Glass of beer."

"If the booze doesn't kill me, I'll be fine," Lang replied.

"There's worse than that." Sheridan lowered his voice so he couldn't be heard by the people around them. "CeeCee lost her place— her mother died and they kicked her out."

"So?" Lang felt a pang of sorrow for the girl's loss, but it didn't really matter to him.

"She's staying with Nell now."

This time Lang did choke on the whiskey. It burned a path down his throat and up through his sinuses. His eyes streamed and he fumbled for his handkerchief. He knew he looked like a green kid who couldn't hold his liquor, as he wiped his eyes.

"What the hell?" he managed to say through his splutters. "Is she nuts?"

After all he'd done, risking his job to tell her about Lina—had she lost her mind? CeeCee would end up in the river. A vision flashed in front of his eyes.

"I can't talk to Nell," Sheridan said. "I wouldn't be able to get away with it, not anywhere private. Franky would be on me in a second. You have to talk to her."

Lang dabbed at his eyes and put his handkerchief away. "She won't listen to me. Obviously." "I can't tell CeeCee why, and she wouldn't believe me even if I did. She's not safe there."

Lang tapped his fingers on the bar. "I'll try." Nell deserved a talking-to.

"I worry about CeeCee," Sheridan confided. He spoke the next words in almost a whisper. "If she stays where she is, she'll get caught in the crossfire."

Lang sighed. "We'll talk later. Tomorrow." He paused, considering. "Next week. Give things some time to settle."

Sheridan tossed back his drink. "See you later. I have to get back to work."

"Wait a moment—have you seen Dooley?"

"He was here earlier. I haven't seen him recently. Why?"

Lang told Sheridan, but left out the gory details.

"Christ." Sheridan shook his head.

"Not a word," Lang warned. "I have too many others to question before the news can break."

"I won't say anything." Sheridan headed back into the crush of people.

Lang set down his empty glass. He wanted another, but his head needed to be clear. Nell wasn't going to like what he had to say.

❖

Several times Lang moved to intercept Nell, only to be foiled by another dancer stopping to talk with her, or Franky strolling up to the bar, giving him a nod of acknowledgment as he looked after the club's business. But finally, a scant half hour before closing, he saw Nell stroll away from their table, alone. He should have been looking for Dooley and questioning him about Scarlett, but that could wait. He caught up with her at the door to the lobby, pulling her aside with a firm hand on her elbow.

"Nice to see you too, Detective," she said. "You should have come and asked me for a dance."

Lang didn't bother to answer her jibe. "What the hell are you thinking?" he hissed, tightening his grasp on her arm. She gave him a puzzled look, one he didn't believe.

"I don't know what you're talking about."

"Do you really think he's going to allow you to have CeeCee stay with you? Have you forgotten what happened to Lina?"

Nell's expression hardened. "CeeCee lost her mother and her home. Franky knows that, and he knows we're friends. That's all."

Lang scoffed. "And how long do you think that's going to last? He's not blind."

Nell tugged her arm free from his grasp. "He won't do a thing. I'm not defenseless."

"Let CeeCee go with Sheridan." Lang found himself pleading, something he rarely ever did.

Nell shook her head. "You're overreacting." She sounded so sure of herself.

"So I put myself in danger, telling you about Lina, and all for nothing," he said bitterly. "I should have taken you to see her in the morgue, blue and bloated from being in the river. That would have sparked some sense into you."

"I won't let her go."

"You need to." First Lina, now Scarlett. And it could be CeeCee next.

"She's mine. Not Sheridan's, not Erven's. Mine."

Nell fixed him with a glare before turning on her heel. So that was it. He'd tried and failed.

❖

Cecilia wet the washcloth and scrubbed at the makeup on her face. The lipstick came off in a smudge of vermilion but her eyes looked like a raccoon's. She rinsed the cloth and took a bit of soap, lathering the cotton. She closed her eyes and scrubbed off the kohl. The movements were mechanical and her mind drifted. She'd bury her mother tomorrow. It seemed surreal, to think of handling the urn the undertaker had shown her. And she'd do it alone. She'd leaned too much on Sheridan and Nell already, and she couldn't bear them seeing her break down yet again.

She opened her eyes. Best not to think of it anymore, or she'd start crying again. She almost wished she could go back to the Orpheus. At least there, she could keep her mind on other things. She rinsed the cloth again and squeezed out the excess water, running it over her face one more time.

When she was through, she went into the bedroom. Nell sat at the vanity brushing out her long red hair. She frowned at her reflection in the mirror.

Cecilia bent to kiss Nell's cheek. "You almost done?"

"Almost." Nell put down the brush and caught Cecilia's hand, pulling her down onto the seat next to her. "I need a real kiss first."

Cecilia clung to Nell as they kissed, feeling the heat of her body through the thin robes they wore. Nell spread Cecilia's robe and cupped her breast. Cecilia mewled in her throat as Nell teased her nipple to an erect peak before stroking lower, along her ribs and over her hips. The seat was too small for much more, and Cecilia broke off the kiss.

"Bed," she said breathlessly, her head swimming with need. She ached to feel Nell's fingers inside her, ached to tease Nell to orgasm with her tongue, even ached to curl up in bed afterward in their post-lovemaking glow. She felt safe there, and loved. She didn't want to be anywhere else in the world but Nell's arms.

CHAPTER TWENTY

At first Lang thought the pounding on the door was his head; he'd drunk enough last night and every night for the past two weeks. Squinting against the morning light, Lang staggered from the bed, grabbing his gun from the nightstand. No one came to visit this early.

The pounding stopped. Lang rubbed the sleep from his eyes and peered through the peephole. He blinked hard and focused. Gabe.

Lang unlocked the door and pulled it open, holding the gun loosely down by his side. Gabe's hand was up, as if he'd been about to start knocking again.

"Come in," Lang said tiredly, turning back into the room. His head ached and he would kill for an aspirin. Instead, he set the gun down and poured himself a glass of whiskey from the bottle he kept stashed in the bookcase.

"I didn't want to wake you," Gabe said. Lang heard the door close. "But Greco insisted."

That got his attention. What could Franky want, especially so early on a Thursday morning? He gulped the whiskey and his headache began to recede.

"What does he want?" Lang turned back to look at Gabe. "And why would he send you—not that I'm not happy to see you." Gabe flushed and Lang drew him into an embrace. It felt strange, with Gabe fully dressed and him in only his undershirt and boxer shorts, still rumpled from sleep. Gabe patted his back and kissed his cheek, then withdrew, shifting uneasily on his feet.

"He wants to see you right away," Gabe said. Lang ran a hand over his hair, feeling it stuck up on one side and flat on the other.

"I need a shower and a shave," he said. "I can be there around noon." He needed to get his head in order and lose the hangover.

"Now, he said," Gabe insisted. "If I don't bring you back with me within the hour, I don't know what Greco will do to me."

From the look on Gabe's face, Franky had meant it. Lang cursed under his breath. He paced to the bathroom and turned on the taps. "Give me a few minutes."

The cold water took the last fogginess from his brain and he slicked back his hair with a comb, peering at his reflection in the mirror. He needed a shave but he didn't have time. He finished washing up and then went into the bedroom to put on fresh clothes. Gabe stood in the doorway, looking anxious.

"Never pegged you for a voyeur," Lang remarked, but Gabe didn't even smile at the teasing. Damn. So it was like that. He straightened his tie and slipped on his shoulder holster, backtracking into the living room to grab his gun. He pulled his trench coat from the hook and put it on, patting the pockets. Keys, wallet, good. The fedora was the last thing, to hide and hopefully flatten his hair.

Gabe looked at his watch.

"Will that do?" Lang asked, his tone sharper than he'd intended. He wanted to take Gabe to bed, not to be taken to Franky.

Gabe only nodded, and Lang followed him out of the apartment and down the stairs. There was a cab waiting at the curb and Gabe opened the door.

They pulled up outside the Orpheus a short time later. Once inside, Gabe led him into the back hallway, avoiding the empty ballroom. They passed the storage closet and Lang felt a frisson of lust. Not the time. Later, perhaps, if he made it out.

Gabe took him right up to Franky's office and knocked on the door. They heard Franky's muffled command and Gabe opened the door. Lang glanced at him and shrugged, then stepped inside.

"Well done, Gabriel," Franky said. "Now get out of here."

Gabe gave a jerky half-bow and left, pulling the door shut.

Lang didn't wait for an invitation; he sank into one of the leather chairs facing Franky's desk. "I knew you were a sadistic guy, but this takes the cake," he remarked. "Why so damn early?"

Franky chuckled, and Lang was relieved that he seemed to be in a good mood. "Best time of the day," he replied. "No one around." His expression darkened and the smile disappeared.

Lang slowly eased himself upright in the chair. He probably wouldn't get to his gun in time but he'd rather die trying. Franky lit a cigarette and Lang relaxed a fraction.

"So, what's so important that you had to get me out of bed at the crack of dawn?" he asked when Franky didn't elaborate.

"I thought I'd be a good citizen and give you some information to help solve a heinous crime in our fair city." Franky started in a serious tone but he couldn't keep a straight face by the end.

"You're turning yourself in?" Lang asked wearily. His headache had returned and set up a slow throb behind his eyes, but he wasn't about to let it show.

"Clearing my name," Franky corrected. "Scarlett was murdered, but not by me."

"Who, then? It certainly wasn't Dooley—the poor bastard's still mourning." He'd finally tracked down Dooley in the days after the murder, and the man had been a blubbering fool when he'd heard the news. Lang, and even Jones, couldn't get a coherent word out of him.

"I had Tony ask around and he found that one of the girls saw Scarlett on the night she was murdered. She was leaving the Orpheus."

"I'm assuming she wasn't alone." Why didn't Franky just get to the point—he was dragging this out as if he were savoring every moment. He tried to think of who else Scarlett had spent time with. "Vogt? O'Brien? Malley?"

"Nell."

Lang sat back, his mind reeling. He couldn't picture it, not at all. "You're joking."

"I wouldn't joke about this," Franky replied coolly.

"But why tell me?" Lang couldn't remember the last time he'd been so dumbfounded. Nell was Franky's girl, had been his through the years, had stood by him. Except for Lina—and CeeCee—that is.

"Even women get death sentences," Franky remarked.

"But she's—"

"A cheating whore." Franky slammed his hand down on the desk, scattering papers and nearly overturning the nearby ashtray.

Lang took a deep breath. To stall for time he withdrew the pack of cigarettes from his pocket and took his time lighting one.

"Did she really do it?" he asked. "Or is this just your way to get rid of her? And why now? She's been cheating on you for years."

"Not like this," Franky growled. "I'm paying for the apartment where she's put her lover, and she thinks I don't know."

"You killed Lina for less than that," Lang observed. He hated having to argue such a point, but Franky wasn't rational. He had to figure out a way out of this.

"I was impulsive," Franky admitted, "but Lina got in my face about it. She deserved it."

"And what about CeeCee?"

"She's a pretty thing, isn't she?" Franky chuckled and the sound made the hair rise on the back of Lang's neck. "It'd be a waste, and Erven would be so upset. He does a lot for the Orpheus, you know."

That was the only thing that made sense about Franky's whole crazed scenario. He wondered if Franky was lying, but it was just too crazy, even for him.

"Why not just get rid of her yourself?"

"And get the book?" Franky scoffed. "You must think I'm a fool."

"Never that."

"Do this for me, Lang, and all the evidence of you and Gabriel goes away. Nell did it, and I want her gone. You'll look good to your boss and the people of Chicago, and you might even get a promotion out of it." He smirked. "The *Tribune* will love you. Imagine the copy."

"I'll have to talk to your witness," Lang said. "I still don't believe it."

"I'll make sure she comes down to the station to see you," Franky replied. Lang didn't answer. He weighed his options and couldn't come to any conclusions.

"Her information had better be watertight," he said. "Otherwise it's not enough to convict anybody." He couldn't recall there being any decent evidence at the scene, but he'd been so sure it had been Franky's work. What if he'd missed something?

"Get a warrant. Search her apartment. Take Nell in once you've heard from my witness." Franky smirked. "I shouldn't have to tell you how to do your job."

Lang took one last drag on his cigarette and rose from the chair. He'd have to go into the station and arrange a review of the evidence, and of the body. And maybe he could stop by Nell's apartment on the way. Franky need not know and perhaps Nell would have an alibi for the night in question.

Franky rose and came around his desk as Lang stubbed out his cigarette in the ashtray next to his chair. He walked Lang to the door, but laid a hand on the doorknob before Lang could let himself out.

"If I find out that you've told Nell, warned her, I'll make sure that every reporter in this town knows about you and Gabriel, and knows that you'd protect a murderer," Franky said.

"Understood."

Franky let him go and Lang strode out into the main room, the place empty and quiet as a tomb. He didn't run into anyone as he left the Orpheus, not even Gabe. The bright morning sun stung his eyes as he stepped out into the street.

Nell. Murder.

He could hardly believe it, but he had little choice. Franky hadn't left him any options. Why would she have done it? It didn't make any sense. If he couldn't go to Nell, he'd have to try someone else. He needed to find Sheridan.

❖

Sheridan was glad the shopkeeper hadn't paid his weekly protection money to Franky Greco. His fist cracked across the man's cheek, and he imagined it was Franky he was beating to a pulp, or Nell. He'd never hit a woman, but he wanted to now. CeeCee still lived with Nell in her fancy apartment and Sheridan saw her less and less. She glanced apologetically across the ballroom on occasion as she danced with Erven Vogt, or sat and gossiped with Nell, but their moments together were few. He wanted more than a stolen few minutes at the back of the ballroom.

Tony thumped him on the back. "That'll do," he said, talking around his ever-present cigar. The shopkeeper lay crumpled against the wall, a hand trying to stanch his bloody, broken nose. Tony gave the man a nudge with his foot. "Next week, Santoro."

Sheridan followed Tony out to the car, his blood still roiling. He rubbed his bruised knuckles. Tony started the engine.

"Can I drop you anywhere?" Tony inquired, shifting the car into gear.

"We have one more stop," Sheridan said. Tony raised a bushy eyebrow. If he couldn't bash in Franky's face, he knew whose he could. He gave Tony the address of CeeCee's old room.

"What's there?" Tony asked, making the turn onto State Street that would take them across the river, down through the Loop and into the South Side. "I don't want my car stolen."

"I have a score to settle," Sheridan answered. "You can stay with the car if you want."

"You know I've got your back, Paddy," Tony said. "Who is this guy?"

"He hurt a friend of mine," Sheridan replied. "He's had this coming for a long time."

When they pulled up outside the sagging old tenement, Sheridan got out of the car before Tony had even killed the engine. Already a score of ragamuffin kids had begun to appear, ogling the expensive car in their midst. Tony stepped out and shut the driver's door, gesturing to one of the older kids, a tough-looking boy with a scowl and a shock of dark hair. The boy swaggered over, but not without a touch of nervousness.

"What's your name, kid?" Tony asked, pulling out a roll of bills.

"Allan."

"So, Allan, here's a buck. If I come out and my car's still here, and untouched, I'll give you another five and you can take the kids down to the diner. Deal?"

"Yes, sir." Allan took up position by the front wheel, tucking the bill safely away.

"Good." Tony came around the car where Sheridan waited. "Lead on, Paddy."

The front door opened easily, and stepping inside, Tony wrinkled his nose. The warm spring day had made the place hot and the smell of unwashed bodies and poor housekeeping was strong. Sheridan stood at the bottom of the stairs, remembering his first time there, taking CeeCee home. He should have taken care of her landlord right then.

"So, why are we here again?" Tony asked. Sheridan didn't answer. He strolled along the hall until he came to a door with a battered wooden sign that read *Manager*. He knocked, and waited. Tony stood back a few paces, looking bemused.

The door opened, and before the man could speak, Sheridan had pushed him back into the room, where he stumbled and fell against a table. Tony followed them inside and closed the door.

Sheridan gave the man a scathing look. "You owe me money," he said. Technically he owed CeeCee the remainder of the rent he'd pocketed when he kicked her out, but they'd get to that in a minute.

"You never lived here," the man scoffed, straightening his shirt collar.

"Do you remember the girl and her mother on the third floor?" Sheridan asked.

"Can't say that I do."

Sheridan saw the barest flash of a smirk on the man's face.

"Let me remind you," he replied, grabbing the man by the front of his shirt and dragging him to the wall. He slammed the man into the wood and the entire building seemed to shudder. The man grunted and Sheridan did it again. This time the man sounded like he was chuckling, though the sound was partly strangled.

"She hadn't paid her rent," he said, shrugging his shoulders.

Sheridan drew back and slugged him, his head cracking against the wood. The man staggered, Sheridan's hand on his shirt the only thing holding him up.

"I told you before not to mess with me. You kicked her out," Sheridan growled, "without warning." He slugged the man again and let go of his shirt. The man slumped to his knees, sputtering blood from a split lip and a broken tooth.

"Not my problem," he slurred through the blood.

Sheridan kneed him in the face and the man collapsed to the floor with a groan. Sheridan stared down at him, the violence having done little to sate his mood.

"Give me a month's rent," Sheridan ordered. "And if you don't, I can make sure it's the last thing you'll ever do."

The man lifted his hand from the dirty floorboards and pointed toward the desk. He slumped back. "Who are you anyway?" he asked, spitting out a tooth.

Sheridan strode over to the desk and opened the drawers. Tony answered for him.

"You had the misfortune to screw over one of Franky Greco's friends," he said, bending over the groaning man. He punctuated the statement with a sharp kick. "Be lucky this is all we're doing."

Sheridan tossed papers on the floor until he found the small lockbox shoved at the back of a drawer. It opened easily and he took out a sheaf of bills, counting them quickly. He pocketed half, then returned to stand over the miserable landlord. "Don't make me have to come back here again," he said. "If I ever hear of you stealing from your tenants, I will, and you'll regret it." The man nodded and Sheridan tucked the cash into his pocket. "Let's go."

Tony gave the kid guarding the car his promised five dollars and the ragamuffins swarmed down the street. Sheridan and Tony drove back downtown, and Sheridan asked Tony to drop him outside Nell's apartment. He needed to see CeeCee.

"You're not even going to get cleaned up first?" Tony asked. "Ladies don't like blood much."

Sheridan glanced down at his clothes. Blood had spattered across his suit jacket and shirt collar and soaked one knee of his trousers. "Home then," he said. "I'll see her later."

The young woman lounged casually in the straight-backed chair in the interview room, her clothing slightly rumpled and worn, her mousy hair starting to slip from her braid. Her gaze roamed to take in Jones, and Lang sighed. He pinched the bridge of his nose, willing his headache to disappear.

Franky had been good on his word; he'd sent the girl over to the station in the early afternoon and she'd flounced in and snootily announced her appointment.

"So, tell me again where you saw Miss Prescott and Miss Ward, Miss Madsen?" he asked.

"I told you, I was coming back to the rooming house, and they came in just before me," she snapped in frustration.

"What time was this?"

"I dunno. Late, I suppose." She shifted in her chair. "I have clients who demand my time."

"Your landlady doesn't like having her tenants coming home at all hours," Lang remarked.

"That old bag." Miss Madsen snorted. "She's just jealous we have people willing to see us. She's always moping around the place."

"Did you see where Miss Prescott and Miss Ward went?"

"Into Scarlett's room, of course." She rolled her eyes. "You got a cigarette, Detective?"

Lang pulled the pack of cigarettes from his pocket and tossed them on the table. She grinned and snagged one. Jones stepped forward to light it for her, and she winked at him. At Lang's look, Jones stepped back to his place.

"And did you hear anything after they went into Miss Ward's room?" he asked.

"Voices," she said, taking a long drag on the cigarette. "Arguing, sounded like."

"What did they say?"

"I couldn't hear exactly," Miss Madsen replied. "Something about the sea, or something? There were a couple of thumps, like maybe someone had dropped something heavy, and then it was just quiet."

Lang doubted the DA would think it enough for a conviction. He stood. "Wait here," he said when the young woman moved to stand. "I'll be back in a moment."

He left Jones waiting with Miss Madsen and he strode down the hall and down the stairs to the basement. The cloying smell of chemicals met him as he opened the door. A body was laid out on the gurney, half-covered by a sheet. The coroner puttered about, placing scalpels into a tray.

"Did you find anything on Scarlett Ward?" Lang asked. "Anything at all?"

"Head wound," the coroner said, turning to the corpse and placing the tray of tools on a nearby table. "Not the work of a professional, and I'd venture to say it's not even the work of a man. Most men are stronger than that. Could be she was struck, maybe with a two-by-four, or maybe something heavier. Doesn't look like a knife wound though, or a bullet."

"You think it was a woman?"

"Could be. It's not an exact science. But I found a few hairs on the girl's clothes that weren't hers. Long reddish ones."

"Any way to identify whose?"

"You said the girl worked at a dance hall. It could be anyone's." The coroner shrugged. "I'll have it all in my report, but it's not done yet. Come back later."

Lang took the stairs up two at a time. Red hairs, possible female killer…had Franky been telling the truth?

When he reached the interview room, Miss Madsen had risen and was arguing with Jones.

"I gotta leave, I can't be late to work."

Jones blocked the doorway with his arm. "You stay until the detective says you can go."

"Leave me your details, Miss Madsen," Lang said. "I'll need to speak with you again."

Jones wrote down her address and her place of work, a saloon on the West Side. When she was done, she pushed her way past him.

"Come with me," Lang said, catching her by the arm. "I'll see you out."

Begrudgingly, she accompanied him from the station. She pulled her arm away when they reached the sidewalk. "Be seeing you." She strode off.

Someone caught him by the arm and he turned, ready to strike.

It was Sheridan.

"What the—oh, it's you." Lang lowered his fist. "I need to talk to you." Lang told him everything he'd learned. When he reached the part about Nell being the killer, Sheridan shook his head.

"That's not possible. She doesn't have it in her to kill anybody."

Lang listened wearily to Sheridan's reply. "I thought he was lying," Lang conceded, "but I have to investigate the possibility, and the witness he found makes it likely." He shook his head.

"Why would she do it? There's no motive." Sheridan looked puzzled. Lang drew him into a diner; they didn't need to be discussing this out on the street. They found an empty booth and ordered coffee.

"At first I couldn't think of anything, but what if Scarlett had something on her?" It had come to him as he'd pored over a list of dancers and employees of the Orpheus. Nell and Scarlett hadn't shared the stage; Enzo's notes were extremely detailed, and it was easy to see when Scarlett had been onstage. They would only have crossed paths professionally.

"Maybe, but murder's taking it a bit far, don't you think?" Sheridan waved to the waitress, who brought them more coffee.

"It'd make things easier for Franky." Lang relayed what Franky had said about getting rid of Nell.

Sheridan gave a low whistle. "She's as good as dead, you know that. He'll pay off the judge and jury, and that'll be it. But what about CeeCee? She's going to get caught up in it, surely."

"Erven Vogt likes her and that's enough for Franky to leave her alone."

"Unless he changes his mind. Pretty easy to set her up as an accomplice." Sheridan lowered his voice so it was barely a whisper. "If we can't take him out, could you get Franky and Nell up on charges? Murder one or murder two?"

Lang pondered as he stirred cream and two sugars into his coffee. It was a tempting thought. Two birds with—well, two *murders* with two stones. Whether Nell had done it or not, trying to get Franky arrested would have the evidence of him and Gabe ending up in the hands of reporters at the *Tribune*. No, Franky had to stay out of prison. But yet…

"I need to talk to Nell," he said. "If she didn't do it, we could go with our original idea, but if she did…" He couldn't let her get away with it, even if he wanted to. He didn't want to be that kind of cop anymore. Bad enough he'd capitulated to Franky's blackmail.

"What about we take them both out?"

Lang choked on his coffee, sputtering and coughing. The waitress hurried over with a napkin and Sheridan clapped him on the back. He dabbed away the spilled coffee and then wiped his watery eyes. His throat burned.

"I'm fine," he managed to wheeze out around another choked cough. He waved the waitress away. "I won't take her out," he said, his voice still ragged. Nell was his friend.

"I still want Franky gone," Sheridan replied. "And I want CeeCee safe. It's too likely that she'll be targeted when Nell's arrested. They spend too much time together for her not to be."

"Convince her to leave Nell's, then," Lang advised. "And soon. My boys will be coming back with more evidence in the next few days and I'll have to make the arrest."

"I doubt she'll believe me—she'll just accuse me of jealousy."

Lang sighed. "I'll find a moment to talk to her. I suppose I can manage that, if I can get her away from Nell."

"And Erven Vogt," Sheridan noted. "Do you think Franky would go visit Nell if she were arrested? We could set up an ambush then. Take out the car and then disappear into the city."

"Let me think on it." Lang tapped his fingers on the checked tablecloth as he considered. It might work, but they'd have to trail Franky from the Orpheus. It would be difficult to know which route he'd take and they couldn't have multiple shooters. He said as much to Sheridan.

"There has to be a way," Sheridan said in frustration. "What if you picked him up?"

Lang pictured himself driving Franky Greco to his death. Literally. He'd never be able to stay in Chicago, not after that.

"I'll need money," he said. "More than what I first thought if you want me to do this. We'd dump him and keep driving, head to Iowa. We couldn't stay here after that. The whole organization would be gunning for us. Capone would make sure of it."

"I won't go without CeeCee," Sheridan said with finality.

"Then she'll have to be in on it," Lang said. "Do you really want to chance that?" It was too easy to imagine a stray bullet wounding her, or Franky hurting her in retaliation.

Sheridan lit a cigarette, looking pensive. Lang wondered what CeeCee had done to inspire such loyalty in a man who seemed to be loyal only to himself.

"Tell her about Nell and then she can decide," he said.

"And the money?" He'd need cash to get himself set up somewhere far away from the Outfit's reach.

"How much?" Sheridan asked.

"Fifty G's," Lang replied. He'd take less, but fifty thousand would set him up anywhere, and he knew some of the gangsters easily had double that amount to play with.

"Twenty," Sheridan said, obviously not about to give in without a show of bargaining.

"It was twenty before," he reminded Sheridan. "Not enough. Forty-five." He took a sip of his coffee, but it had gone cold.

"Thirty."

"Thirty-seven, and that's it," Lang said. He stood. "I'll come see you at the Orpheus after I've talked to CeeCee. You sure you want me to do it?"

"If she won't come along with us, I'll have to try to convince her," Sheridan replied. He looked doubtful. "She won't believe what Nell's done."

"We'll see. See you later."

Sheridan held out his hand and they shook, making the final commitment to their scheme. He couldn't imagine it working, but a world without Franky Greco would be a better one.

CHAPTER TWENTY-ONE

Cecilia could see Nell in the mirror as she lounged casually on the sofa, her foot propped on a cushion and her blue sequined dress gathered up above her knees, revealing high-heeled black shoes and pale stockings. She rested her head in her hand and watched as Cecilia touched up her makeup. Cecilia could hear the murmur of voices outside the dressing room door and she knew it was nearly time to go to work. Erven waited for her, as he did almost every night.

She'd never met a more perfect gentleman. Sometimes she wondered why he didn't invite her home, or to a nearby hotel. He was attentive and charming, but they'd never been to bed. Just as well. Between Nell and Sheridan, the last thing she needed was another lover. Though she'd barely seen Sheridan lately, not since she moved into Nell's.

A knock at the door interrupted her train of thought and she set down her powder puff. Nell didn't move from the sofa, so Cecilia opened the door. Enzo stood there, elegant as always in his tux and tails, but he looked uncharacteristically grim. His mouth had a pinched look and the usual liveliness in his gray eyes was absent. He stepped inside and closed the door.

"There's been terrible news," he said, his voice flat. Cecilia heard the muted sound of crying from the hallway, and Nell sat up, pushing her dress back over her knees. "Scarlett is dead."

Cecilia gasped and Nell clasped a hand to her own mouth, her eyes wide. Cecilia sank back into the chair by the vanity.

"But I just saw her the other day," she said stupidly. Had it been? She really couldn't remember.

"She was found in her apartment." He swallowed and rubbed at his eyes. "She's been murdered."

Nell still hadn't said a word, but her face had gone pale.

"But how?" The words slipped out before Cecilia could stop them. She didn't really want to know all the gruesome details. She shuddered.

"I don't know. Mr. Greco says the show must go on, but I can barely stand it," Enzo lamented. "She was to be in the second act tonight." He shook his head as he opened the door. "How awful. I'll need to rearrange the entire schedule."

Once he'd gone out, Cecilia and Nell looked at each other. Nell seemed to come back to life first, rising from the couch. She embraced Cecilia and Cecilia leaned into her body, closing her eyes. She hadn't known Scarlett well, but she mourned the girl nonetheless. Nell stroked her hair.

"It's almost time to go," she said. "Are you ready, CeeCee?"

"I don't know." It seemed disrespectful to continue on like nothing had happened.

"Come on," Nell urged. "Erven will be expecting you. And we can't stay in here forever."

"I wish we could sometimes," Cecilia replied. She lifted her head and looked up at Nell. "If only it were just you and me."

Nell cupped her cheeks and bent to brush a kiss over her lips. Her tongue teased along Cecilia's lower lip and Cecilia arched upward to deepen the kiss.

They broke apart reluctantly and Nell peered into the mirror, fixing her lipstick. Cecilia did the same and then they went out into the Orpheus. It was showtime.

❖

When Erven pressed her to dance once again, after monopolizing her all evening, Cecilia begged off. Her feet ached and the shoes she wore pinched her toes. He left her at the door to the ladies' room with a promise to see her back at the table in a little while. She knew he'd wander the floor and talk to his business associates, and she'd have a chance to sit down and rest.

She sank down into an overstuffed chair that had been positioned in a little alcove nearby. She toed off her shoes and let her stockinged feet rest against the cool marble floor. The murmur of voices and the dim light made her feel sleepy, though it wasn't that late in the evening. The third show had yet to go onstage.

"I'd hoped to find you alone," said a familiar voice.

Cecilia glanced up. Detective Lang settled himself on the arm of the chair, his outstretched legs a partial barrier to her leaving. Not that she wanted to leave, but he rarely spoke to her, preferring to chat with Nell or skulk about the edges of the ballroom.

"How well do you know Nell?" he asked without any preamble. The question caught her off guard. Why would he even ask?

"Better than most," she replied, at a loss for words. He nodded, looking thoughtful.

"And if I told you to leave her?"

Cecilia bridled at that. He had some nerve. Nell had told her of his tendencies. He should be on their side. "I wouldn't."

"I thought so."

Cecilia shifted in the chair and began to rise, but he put a hand on her shoulder, keeping her in place. "She's accused of murder, CeeCee, and it's looking very likely that she did it."

She couldn't believe it. She didn't believe it.

"Impossible." The word escaped her, barely more than a whisper.

"What do you know of Scarlett?" Lang asked.

"Scarlett? What does she—" Cecilia broke off as things came together in her mind. "You can't be serious."

"I am very serious. Did you know Scarlett well? Did Nell?" His fingers tightened on her shoulder as if to emphasize his questions.

"I didn't know her well at all. She spent time with Dooley, or she was onstage. We didn't talk much."

"Would Nell have any reason to hurt her?"

"No, I don't think so." Even as she uttered the words, she knew them for a lie. She and Nell had been caught in the act by Scarlett, but Nell hadn't said anything threatening. She remembered Nell's grasp tightening on her arm, much like Lang had done on her shoulder just a moment ago. But what did that matter?

"Think hard," Lang said, as if he could tell she'd lied. "But in the meantime, be careful. Spend as little time with her as you can—I don't want you caught up in the investigation."

"I live with her," she pointed out.

"Go elsewhere," he said, sounding frustrated. "Surely you have other friends you can stay with." He shook her, his fingers digging into her shoulder again.

"Go to hell," she snapped, prying his fingers off her shoulder. He'd gone too far. "I won't leave her."

Lang leaned in, pinning her against the chair. "If you won't do it for yourself, then for God's sake, do it for Sheridan."

Cecilia slumped back in the chair. Sheridan. Half the time she didn't know what to feel about him. She was fond of him, but she loved Nell. She couldn't have both of them. And Sheridan kept to himself a lot of the time and she rarely knew what he was thinking. She wouldn't even have known him if it wasn't for Nell.

When she didn't respond, she heard Lang sigh. "Think on it," he said as he rose. "Do you think you'll be safe if she really did murder that girl?"

Cecilia saw Sheridan that night, but she never got a chance to take him aside and ask him about Lang's warning. Erven stayed with her the rest of the night and she couldn't find a way to shake him. When he left to get drinks, Franky leaned over to her, raising his voice slightly to be heard. His dark hair flopped over his forehead, hiding his scar, and his eyes were reddened, his breath reeking of booze.

"What's your secret?" he asked, giving her a wink.

Cecilia sucked in a breath, her mind going immediately to Nell. He knew! "What do you mean?" She tried to keep her voice from wavering and hoped the noise in the club would hide the slight tremble in her words.

"Vogt, of course," Franky replied. "I've never seen the man so in love! And you haven't even—" He cut off his next words, as Erven returned with drinks in hand, passing a whiskey to Franky and glasses of champagne to her and Nell. He settled into his chair and leaned over to give her a kiss.

"What are you doing later?" he asked, resting a hand over hers in her lap.

She smiled. "I don't know," she said, and she had a feeling she knew where this was going. Franky's question had been well-timed, and she wondered if he and Erven had set it up. None of the other girls had held out so long and Erven had become impatient. She glanced at Franky, who wore a smile that was more of a smirk.

"Here's to the lovebirds." Franky grinned and raised his glass, bestowing another wink as she stared at him.

Erven slipped his arm around her. "Come home with me," he said.

"We'll have so much fun." He stroked her shoulder and bent his head to place a line of kisses up her neck until his breath was hot in her ear. She shivered and risked a glance at Nell.

Nell's mouth was frozen in a smile, and she played with the stem of her champagne glass, rolling it between her fingers.

"Don't they make the perfect couple?" Franky was grinning still, and Erven grinned back, like two boys with a secret.

"Of course," Nell replied. Cecilia could hear the cheery insincerity in her tone, but from Franky's and Erven's reactions, they couldn't tell the difference.

"Let's call it a night," Franky said, taking Nell's free hand and bringing it to his lips. Cecilia glanced from Franky to Nell, and back to Erven. Lang's words came back to her. Had he known this would happen? She wavered a moment when Erven rose, before she rose too, taking his hand. She'd stay away from Nell, at least tonight.

❖

Sheridan lingered at the bar most of the night, nursing a pint, and then another, of the Orpheus's cheapest beer. It really wasn't made to linger over; the astringent taste made him wish he'd taken it in one gulp, like most of the others did. But he didn't want to get staggering drunk. He needed to talk to CeeCee.

He watched her as she danced with Erven, sat at Franky's table, and danced with Erven again. It would be closing time before he could speak to her. He'd seen Lang follow her to the ladies' room and she'd come back looking irate, though she'd settled a smile on her face as she crossed the ballroom and returned to her table. He resigned himself to the wait.

When he saw her rise, he became alert, but she took Erven's hand and let him lead her out into the lobby. Sheridan left his warm beer and trailed them, watching as they picked up their coats. Vogt helped CeeCee with her coat and then put a possessive hand on the small of her back, shepherding her outside.

Sheridan managed to slip out the door behind them and he lit a cigarette, trying to look casual. One of the doormen went to fetch Vogt's car.

"Be quick about it," he told the man, who hurried off. He bent close to CeeCee. His voice carried on the wind and Sheridan could hear his words even though he spoke in a low tone. "I can't wait to finally get you home. You'll look beautiful on my bed, my dear."

CeeCee dipped her head, but he couldn't tell if she was shocked or just playing the coquette. Vogt chuckled and tilted her chin up, taking her mouth in a deep kiss for all to see.

Sheridan grimaced and took a drag on his cigarette. He wanted to pull Vogt away from her and beat him to a pulp, but he knew what would happen. He'd end up in the clink and Vogt would get CeeCee. That's the way it always worked with the rich.

He finished his cigarette and flicked the butt into the gutter. At least CeeCee would be away from Nell, though it was little comfort. He was about to step forward when the doorman pulled up with Vogt's silver Rolls Royce. Vogt opened the passenger door for CeeCee, who slid inside, before going around to the driver's side. Sheridan moved away from the wall and CeeCee spotted him for the first time. She stared at him, and in the light from the marquee, he could just see her dismay. Dismay at being with Vogt, or dismay at his having seen her? He didn't know and couldn't ask.

Vogt gunned the engine and the car drove away. He caught one glimpse of CeeCee as she turned her head to meet his gaze one last time, then the darkness swallowed the car.

A taxi drew up and he contemplated following her. Instead, he went back inside. He'd try for Franky first, and when that was settled, he'd return for CeeCee.

CHAPTER TWENTY-TWO

Cecilia woke early, though she couldn't tell if she'd even slept. The last few hours had stretched unbearably and from the moment she'd gotten into Erven's car, the night seemed like it would never end.

Driving kept Erven's attentions from her for the most part. When she'd seen Sheridan, she'd hoped he'd intervene, but he'd seemed reluctant, even emotionless. Her heart had sunk. Erven drove back to his mansion on the Gold Coast. A doorman helped her out of the car and Erven took her cold hand and led her up the marble steps and into the cavernous entryway.

"We need to get you a drink, my dear," he said, rubbing her hands between his. "You're chilled right through."

He led her into a parlor and sat her down on a leather sofa. The fabric of her dress against the slick leather made sitting precarious and she kept sliding to the edge of the seat. Finally she managed to find a half-comfortable spot, perched on the edge of the cushion. Erven came back to her, holding a snifter of amber liquid. He settled beside her, handing her the snifter before he stretched back with a sound of contentment.

"Come sit with me," he said, his hands gripping her waist. Erven lifted her onto his lap, his arm coming around her possessively to settle on her stomach. She let out a squeak of surprise as his other hand slid up and under her dress, coming to rest between her thighs. The stones in his ring pressed against the tender flesh of her inner thigh as she shifted, trying to put a bit of distance between her and his hand.

"Much better now," Erven said, dropping kisses over her bare shoulder and up the side of her neck. "Finish your drink, darling."

Cecilia lifted the snifter and Erven removed his hand from

between her thighs, bringing it up to cup her hand on the glass, tilting the snifter farther. She took a sip, then another, before sputtering. The alcohol burned down her throat and her eyes watered.

"More," Erven said, taking the snifter from her and holding it against her mouth. He didn't stop until she'd drunk the entire glass. It warmed her right through and she felt the flush rise in her cheeks and make its way down to her toes.

"That's better," Erven said approvingly. "I've been waiting for this for a long time."

"Me too," she whispered, just before he kissed her. She could do this, couldn't she? He'd been so generous with her and so patient. All the other girls at the Orpheus were jealous of her, wishing that Erven would pay them some attention, buy them drinks, dance with them all night. She knew how lucky she was, but she knew she was trying to convince herself.

Erven bent her back over his arm and she felt the cool leather against her bare skin. "I've always wanted to see you like this. All mine."

❖

Cecilia lay still in the dim bedroom, Erven's light snoring breaking the quiet. Even in sleep he was possessive and had flung his arm over her, pinning her to the mattress. If she could move without waking him, she would. The thought of her own bed, and a shower, sounded like heaven.

Nell's bed. Not hers, exactly. Nell would have company, she knew. Franky would be sleeping in her place, his head on her pillow, his arm around her. She screwed her eyes shut and willed herself to go back to sleep. She wouldn't think of Nell and Franky in her bed. If she fell asleep again, she could forget that image, forget Lang's words to her last night, forget Sheridan's piercing gaze.

But the time crept by and she couldn't sleep. Though Erven lay next to her, she felt as though the blankets had been pulled away. The sheets imparted no warmth and she slowly stiffened, pressing her lips together to keep her teeth from chattering.

When Erven shifted and rolled over, she breathed a quiet sigh, inching slowly from the bed. Her toes curled against the marble floor and she felt colder still being naked in his vast bedroom. Erven's robe lay tossed over a chair and she snatched it up on her way to the bathroom, wrapping its velvet folds around herself. The hem dragged on the floor and the sleeves were far too long, but it helped.

Cecilia glanced back at the bed as she opened the bathroom door. Erven hadn't moved and if she held her breath and listened, she could just hear his deep, even breathing. Once inside, she flicked on the light and flinched at her reflection in the mirror. Her eyes were ringed with smudged kohl and her hair was flat and limp, lifeless. She needed a bath—craved one—but still she hesitated.

If she dressed and left without waking Erven, she could avoid having to speak to him, or having to indulge him in bed again. Except it was too early and she knew Franky wouldn't have left Nell's. She didn't especially want to come face-to-face with him either. She peeked into the other room. Still asleep. Maybe she'd get lucky and he'd sleep the whole morning away. She silently closed the bathroom door and went to the claw-foot tub set on a pedestal. The hot water gushed from the taps and she let the tub fill, testing the water until it had reached the perfect temperature. She shed Erven's robe and sank into the wet heat, letting the warmth infuse her bones before she began to scrub at the makeup on her face. She'd scrub the entire night away if she could.

❖

Erven staggered into the bathroom just as she drew a towel around herself and stepped out of the tub. He ignored her completely and headed for the toilet, letting loose a stream of piss with a groan. She wrapped another towel around her hair, intending to retreat to the bedroom and dress. She was in the doorway when he caught up with her, wrapping an arm around her waist.

"Where are you going, darling?" he said, his unshaven jaw scratching along her bare shoulder as he kissed her neck. His free hand pushed her towel up in the back and she felt him nestle against her buttocks. He was hard already, insistent. "It's early yet."

"I can't stay long," she said, softly so as not to rile him.

"We have all day." He pressed her forward and into the bedroom and they stumbled toward the bed.

"I have errands," she protested, but he hushed her, bending her over the edge of the bed.

"Later," he said, parting her thighs, his fingers stroking her before he slid inside her to the hilt. She let out a gasp. In this position, spread open for him, he pressed his advantage and went deep, almost more than she could stand. "Oh, CeeCee." He groaned into her hair, pressing her into the mattress, his heavy body covering hers.

He seemed to lose what control he had, thrusting hard and fast into her, keeping her pinned to the bed so she could do little but endure. Finally, he spent himself, pulling out to spurt over her lower back and thighs with a grunt of satisfaction. He fell to the bed beside her, breathing heavily.

Cecilia stared at him as he lay there with his eyes closed. Stiffly, she sat up, pulling the towel from her hair and using it to wipe off her back. She needed a shower.

Erven dropped Cecilia in front of Nell's apartment around noon, leaning over the gearshift to kiss her. She allowed it, but only just.

"I'll see you tonight," he said.

Cecilia kissed his cheek. "Until then." She couldn't wait to get into clean clothes. She'd have to send her dress to the cleaners to get all the wrinkles out. Nevertheless, she smoothed the fabric over her knees as she got out of the car, trying her best to look presentable. Fortunately the street was nearly empty. No one to see her so rumpled.

The doorman nodded to her as she passed, but he didn't comment. She waited for the elevator, tapping her foot on the tile floor and watching the brass arrow above the door make its arc down to 1. The metal gate clattered open and Cecilia stepped back as Franky strode from the elevator. He saw her and stopped abruptly, taking in her dishevelment.

"Looks like you had fun," he said, giving her a leer. "I'm surprised Vogt waited so long with you." He patted her cheek and she flinched at his touch.

"Then why did he?" she asked, straightening her spine and trying to pretend his touch hadn't startled her. She'd learned not to show any weakness around him—he gave no mercy to those who would let him do as he wished.

"Something about you being more innocent than the rest." Franky caught her chin and leaned in close, as if he might kiss her. "We both know that's not true, right, CeeCee?"

His lips brushed hers, strangely gentle. She held herself firm, neither responding nor recoiling. Only when he tried to press his advantage and part her lips did she step back, placing a hand on his chest. Over his shoulder, the doorman watched them with interest.

"I love a feisty girl," Franky said with amused approval. "One of these days, maybe Vogt won't be the only lucky one. Go on up and see Nell." He caught her arm when she went to board the elevator. "But she's been thoroughly fucked, so you won't get much playtime from her today."

Cecilia gaped at him. He laughed and continued on his way. She staggered into the elevator, ignoring the smirk the attendant gave her.

Once inside Nell's apartment, she sank down on the settee.

"CeeCee? Are you back?" Nell came from the bedroom, wearing a robe and mules. "What is it?" She perched on the settee and her perfume enveloped them.

Cecilia closed her eyes and took a deep breath. "It was a long night," she said. Did she dare to tell Nell that Franky knew? She'd been foolish to think otherwise. Why hadn't she taken Sheridan up on his offer? She would have been safer by far. Yet she didn't regret one minute of her time with Nell. She rested her head against Nell's shoulder.

"I need a shower," she said, feeling weary. "And we need to talk."

"The boss wants to see you." Tony stopped at Sheridan's table in the diner, puffing on his cigar and ignoring the nasty looks he was getting from a table of busybodies. He settled into the chair across from Sheridan.

"What for?" Sheridan lit a cigarette, his mind whirling with possibilities, most of them brutal. Lang could have ratted him out, and he'd be a dead man. He leaned back in his chair.

"Big meeting," Tony replied. "He needs a couple of the boys to back him. He asked me, and I want you."

"All right. Now?"

Tony nodded.

Sheridan stood, leaving his lunch unfinished. He left a couple of dollars on the table and grabbed his fedora from the chair beside him. He moved with relaxed ease; he was doing a favor, not ending up at the bottom of Lake Michigan.

"I've got the car out front, then we can go for a beer after," Tony said.

"If we get a chance," Sheridan agreed.

Franky sprawled on the sofa in his office, a half-naked dancer pleasuring him with her mouth. His fingers were tangled in her dark hair and for a moment Sheridan thought it might be CeeCee. But then Franky grunted and came and the girl drew back in disgust. Not her. Franky sat up and rearranged his clothes before handing the girl a few bills.

"Go on," he said brusquely. She stumbled to her feet and gave Sheridan and Tony a wide berth as she left. "Come on in." Franky chuckled. "I always concentrate better afterward."

Tony smirked and Sheridan forced a smile. "Pretty girl," Tony said.

"She's all right. Now, about this weekend. Capone wants us there early, to make sure Hymie's boys don't get the drop on us, but we can't take too many boys or it'll look like we don't trust them."

"Should I bring in a couple others?" Tony settled into a chair across from Franky and Sheridan followed suit.

Franky eyed them both. "A couple more, one for each car." He frowned. "We're to bring a few girls too, to make things more casual."

"And Hymie loves the ladies," Tony said, winking at Sheridan.

"Who will you bring?" Sheridan knew this could be his chance. He had to tell Lang.

"Nell will go, as always. The Irishmen like her, though I can't imagine why." Franky made a face. "And if Nell comes then she'll want to bring CeeCee. It doesn't really matter." He focused on Sheridan. "You're Irish," he said abruptly. "What do you know of Hymie Weiss and that lot?"

"He's nervous, not like O'Banion," Sheridan replied. "At least, he was when I knew him. I spent the last few years in prison and wasn't there when he took over."

"We'll scare him," Tony said confidently.

"He wants to weasel in on our turf," Franky said. "Capone might let him, if he pays enough, but I don't want him anywhere near my bars and clubs."

"Will Capone listen to you?" Sheridan asked.

"If he won't, I'll get Nell to whisper in his ear. She's good at that."

"When do you want us?" Tony asked.

"Thursday, about four o'clock. We'll have dinner with Hymie at one of his restaurants on the West Side, and then we'll talk."

Sheridan lit a cigarette. He could let Lang know and they'd have a good chance at Franky. But CeeCee...he didn't like putting her at risk. He'd have to do something about Tony as well. Tony was loyal to a fault; he couldn't be bribed and he'd be quick to shoot anyone who made an attempt on Franky's life.

"We'll take two cars," Tony said. When Franky raised a brow, Tony continued. "I want more men with us, and we can head off any attempts to run us off the road."

Franky laughed. "You're a bit paranoid, don't you think?"

"Can't be too careful with the Irish," Tony retorted. "Present company excepted."

"It's not like it was in O'Banion's day," Sheridan remarked. "I'm surprised someone hasn't tried to take Hymie out and bring the gang back to full strength."

"Maybe you?" Franky suggested.

"I'd rather be here on the up and up," Sheridan replied. "I took the rap for a bust and they abandoned me in the clink. I don't want anything to do with them."

Franky's gaze had wandered to the door and Sheridan could just hear the chatter from a pair of girls outside.

"Good, that's settled," Franky said. "Tony, get it sorted. And send in the blonde when you leave."

Sheridan rose with Tony and they left Franky, now half sprawled again on the sofa. Tony jerked a thumb at the blonde smoking a cigarette. Her hair lay over her shoulders and her dress was snug against her curves. Almost the exact opposite of the previous girl.

"Boss wants to see you," Tony told her. She ground out the cigarette in the ashtray and, plastering on a come-hither look, sauntered into the office. The door closed behind her.

Tony chuckled. "I don't know how he does it—all those girls."

Sheridan shrugged. "Wonder what Nell thinks of it all." He followed Tony down the stairs and out through the quiet lobby to the car.

"Don't think she gets a say," Tony said, "for all that she and Franky go back forever. She told me once he'd freed her from an orphanage workhouse. She's been with him ever since."

"That's loyalty for you."

❖

Cecilia felt sick with worry as she stepped out of the shower. She'd run over several variations of how she'd ask Nell about Scarlett, but they all ended in anger and pain. She put on her robe and took her comb from the vanity. She couldn't delay any more.

Nell sat on the settee, one leg crossed over the other, the mule dangling from her toes. She flipped through a magazine, skimming the articles.

CeeCee perched on the edge of the settee and began to comb out her hair. Finally she broke the silence. "Can I ask you something?"

Nell put down the magazine. "What about?"

Cecilia swallowed down her nervousness. "Scarlett," she said, her hand dropping to her lap and the comb shedding water on her robe.

Nell shrugged one shoulder. "What about her?" She began flipping through the magazine again, but Cecilia pushed on.

"That detective spoke to me," she began, "and he said you were under suspicion."

Nell lowered the magazine. "Is that so?" Her features seemed to harden, her eyes chilled, but she bit her lip. "Why anyone should care about a trashy dancing girl like her is beyond me."

"She was nice." The statement came out weakly but it was the best Cecilia could do.

"She was a sneak and a whore," Nell bit out. With surprising ferocity, she chucked the magazine across the room. "She would have told everyone about us—she threatened to tell Franky, and she tried to blackmail me." Her breath caught and Cecilia thought she heard a sob.

"So, you—"

"I didn't mean for it to happen. We fought, and she fell." Nell rose on her knees before Cecilia, reaching out to clasp her hands. Cecilia felt the teeth of the comb bite into her palm. She couldn't stop staring at Nell's hands, the crimson nails, the pale flesh. There had been blood on those hands not long ago.

"I didn't know what to do, so I left her," Nell said. "I knew I'd be blamed and knew no one would back me, or believe me. Please, Cecilia, look at me."

Cecilia lifted her gaze from their hands reluctantly, glancing to the line of Nell's robe against her cleavage, a reddened mark on her collarbone, the surprisingly delicate line of her neck and jaw, her full lips, her slim nose. And finally her eyes, gray and soft.

"She threatened to give us away, and she would have," Nell said. "I hate that it happened, but trust me, it was for the best."

Cecilia shuddered, imagining Scarlett's horrible last moments. And it was such a waste. Franky's words echoed in her mind.

"We should leave," Nell suggested, stroking her thumb across the back of Cecilia's hand. "Go to San Francisco, or better yet, to France, far away from here. I have no ties, and neither do you, anymore."

Cecilia let out a moan. If only. "It's too late."

"What do you mean? We can leave tomorrow, take the train to New York and the boat over a few days later. We'll be fine. I have money."

"He knows," Cecilia confessed miserably. She wanted to sob, but the pain of the comb digging into her palms kept her coherent.

"How?"

"I don't know, but he knows. He said as much to me in the lobby." As she related Franky's words, the horror of it all overwhelmed her and she broke down, her shoulders shaking with the force of her sobs. Nell let go of her hands and caught her up in a tight embrace.

For all Nell had done, this was still Cecilia's safe place, in Nell's arms, surrounded by warmth and the scent of her perfume.

"We'll leave," Nell murmured against her hair. "We'll leave this all behind. Trust me, CeeCee. I'll take care of you."

Chapter Twenty-three

Detective Lang came up the stairs from the coroner's office and was headed out the door of the station when Jones caught up to him.

"Detective, you have a call," he said, catching Lang by the elbow.

"Who is it?" He needed to go back to the scene, go over the evidence one more time. The guys had done it, but he needed to be there, to walk through the small apartment.

"He didn't say."

"Take a message," Lang replied, irritably shaking Jones's hand from his arm. "I'm busy."

"But he said he'd only talk to you," Jones protested. "It might be a tip."

Lang sighed. "All right." He followed Jones back into the offices, a place he tried to be as infrequently as possible. Jones indicated the phone and Lang waved him off, but he still hovered. "A little privacy, officer, if you please."

Chastened, Jones retreated. Lang lifted the receiver. "Lang here."

"I need to see you." The voice was male, familiar.

"What about?" Lang asked.

"What we spoke of recently." He placed the voice. It was Sheridan.

"Not the usual place," Lang said. He rattled off the address of Scarlett's apartment.

"I'll see you there." The line went dead. Lang replaced the receiver and headed toward the door, where Jones shifted from foot to foot.

"Was it a tip?"

"Maybe. I want you to gather up the witness statements for me, order them by time on the night of the murder. I'll need to look at them when I get back."

"Yes, sir."

He didn't need to look at them, but that would keep the young man busy and out of his hair. Lang retraced his steps through the station and strode out the door. Instead of taking a patrol car, he hailed a taxi. He didn't feel like accounting for his whereabouts to Navarra. Sheridan was on to something—he had to be.

❖

The taxi dropped Lang in front of the run-down apartment building. At first glance, he didn't see Sheridan, but when he moved toward the door a familiar figure detached itself from the shadowed nook beneath the stairs. Lang ushered Sheridan inside and Sheridan followed him to Scarlett's apartment.

"We can talk inside. Just don't touch anything." As soon as he'd closed the door behind them, Sheridan spoke.

"We have a chance," he said, and related his earlier meeting.

"It's possible," Lang agreed, "and better then anything we would have tried before. Do you have my money?"

Sheridan held out a roll of bills.

"That's quick."

"It's not all of it," Sheridan replied, "but it's what I had to hand."

"Since when do you carry around this kind of cash?"

Sheridan smirked. "Went to get it after Tony dropped me off. I haven't had much to spend it on, thanks to Franky's occasional bonuses for the Orpheus men."

Lang tucked the roll into the inside pocket of his suit jacket. "I'll count it later."

"There's twenty G's there," Sheridan said. "The rest will come after. Now, why are we here instead of at the diner or someplace else?"

"This is Scarlett's apartment," Lang answered. "Nell—well, someone—killed her here and it's somewhere safe to talk. Only cops can come in here for now."

Sheridan gave a wry laugh. "If you don't need me, I'll go. I'm expected at the Orpheus tonight, as always."

"I'll come by later," Lang said. Sheridan left the apartment and Lang turned back to the clutter. He could hardly picture Nell in the shabby room, much less murdering Scarlett, but everything pointed to her.

❖

Cecilia couldn't stand to stay seated, not when her mind was so uneasy. Erven had yet to arrive and Nell was still primping in the dressing room, so Cecilia moved through the thin crowd of the ballroom. As she passed near the door to the lobby, she saw Detective Lang checking his coat. He gave her a wink before lighting a cigarette and heading toward the men's room. Cecilia followed him.

She lingered as close to the door as she dared, wishing she smoked or had something to do so she didn't feel so conspicuous. Finally the door opened and he emerged, straightening the jacket of his plain dark suit. His gaze fixed on her and she stepped out from the wall to meet him.

"Can we talk?" she asked. "Somewhere private?"

He took her arm and they strolled casually into the ballroom.

"I have a place," he said, and he took her through a doorway behind the bar, leading her through a plain hallway to a storage room. "It's not much, but it should be private enough."

"Are you sure?" She gave the room a doubtful glance. Surely someone would need the cleaning supplies.

"We'll be fine for a while yet," he replied. "I've been here before." He ushered her inside and pulled the string that hung from the bare bulb in the ceiling above. The door swung shut and he leaned against it.

It was now or never, Cecilia realized, but how could she admit that he'd been right?

"We don't have all night," Lang reminded her.

"You were right."

He raised a brow and gave her a questioning glance, but didn't speak.

By telling him, she could be giving Nell over to the Chicago PD, and their perverse justice. Or was she? Most cops were bent; Franky had joked about greasing palms and getting his boys out on a technicality. That could happen to Nell too. It had been an accident, though she knew it didn't look good.

"Nell told me. She's not a murderer, Detective." She met his impassive gaze before dropping her attention back to her hands. "I don't know what to do." Nell had begun to plan their escape, but how could she flee with a murderer? She'd been convincing at first, but as

Cecilia had paced the ballroom tonight, she wasn't sure if she could do it after all.

"She told you what?"

"About Scarlett. It was an accident. They were fighting, and Scarlett fell."

"Christ." He turned away from her, his shoulders sinking, then straightening. "I don't believe it. She's lying."

"You don't know her like I do. She's not lying."

"Either way, you need to leave her," Lang said, turning.

"But—"

"Franky's gunning for her, and if you stick around, you'll get caught up too."

"He might get me anyway," Cecilia replied, shivering. She wrapped her arms around herself as she thought of Franky's words.

"Why do you say that? Because of you and Nell? He told me outright he had no score with you, CeeCee."

"I don't believe it."

Lang glanced down, looking as if he were pondering something, scraping the toe of his shoe on the dirty floor. "We're leaving on Thursday if you want to come with us," he said finally.

"Us?"

"Sheridan and I."

Pain lanced through her. Sheridan hadn't said a word. He would have left without her.

"How?" She wanted to storm out, to find Sheridan and demand to know what he was doing. She moved toward the door and Lang put his hands on her shoulders to hold her back.

"It's a long story," he said, "and it'll take strength and gumption if you dare to join us."

❖

"I convinced Tony we only needed one car," Sheridan remarked as Detective Lang lingered nearby. They didn't look at each other; Lang fumbled in his jacket pocket for his cigarettes and lighter, and Sheridan kept his gaze on the ballroom, doing his job.

"How'd you manage that?" Lang asked, finally locating his cigarettes.

"Told him I figured two cars was asking for trouble. Besides, he and I could take care of anyone who tried."

Lang let out a derisive laugh. "Playing to his pride—well done." "Franky still wants to bring Nell." Sheridan rested his gaze on the couple as they sat drinking and carousing at their table.

"And Nell will bring CeeCee, of course," Lang commented. "She's in, by the way."

"What?" Sheridan forgot himself and glanced toward Lang.

"Eyes front," Lang reminded him, taking a drag on his cigarette. "I had a little chat with her earlier and I know you wanted her safe, but she wouldn't be safe for much longer anyway."

"What do you mean?"

"Franky knows all about her and Nell, and now that she knows, it's spooked her. Franky's sore and I wouldn't put it past him to hurt her. I'd rather have her there with us."

Sheridan let his gaze drift back over the crowd. It'd be dangerous with a full car, even if Lang was careful and didn't run them off the road. Franky would come out blazing, furious and deadly. His gaze came to rest on CeeCee, dancing with Erven Vogt. The man held her close—too close—as if they were alone in a more intimate setting. It made his blood boil. He couldn't go over there and call Vogt out, but he'd be damned if he'd let her stay in Chicago to be pawed by a man like that.

"All right," he said finally. "She comes. The girls will have to hunker down out of the way and we'll just pray they don't get shot."

"And you'll take CeeCee with you?" Lang asked. "She looked stricken when I said you were pulling up stakes."

"I'll take her," he replied. "But what about Nell? I won't take along my competition."

"Maybe I'll drop her at a police station on my way out of town," Lang replied.

"Is that safe?" He couldn't imagine Nell taking such betrayal lying down.

"We're not coming back," Lang reasoned. "And she has a murder rap to beat, though CeeCee says Nell didn't do it on purpose."

"I don't care whether she did it or not. It's your call. If anything changes, I'll let you know." Sheridan strolled away, heading toward the back bar, where a pair of men had begun a shoving match, probably over the dancer who stood there with her arms crossed, looking peeved. She shot him and the other bouncer an appreciative glance as they swooped in to break up the fight.

Sheridan took the taller man by the collar and dragged him back.

The man struggled and cursed, trying to get free and take a swing at him.

"How dare you?" he shouted. "Don't you know who I am?"

Sheridan shoved him through the swinging door into the back of the Orpheus and let the man go. The man stumbled and caught himself against the wall before turning. Balling his fist, he rushed Sheridan and took a swing.

Sheridan sidestepped the blow and sent his own fist crashing into the man's face, hearing a satisfying crack. He wanted to do the same to Vogt, but this man would be a fine substitute.

CHAPTER TWENTY-FOUR

Sheridan checked his pistol one last time before sliding it into the holster under his arm. He shrugged on his suit jacket and then his coat, loosely buttoning both so that he'd still have access to the gun when the time came. His switchblade rested in his trouser pocket and he could feel its heaviness against his thigh. If he had to grab it to protect himself, he'd be better off dead, but he wasn't about to leave it behind.

There was a honk from the street and he settled his fedora on his head, scanning the tiny apartment before he left. He wouldn't miss it, this small dim room, but he hated leaving his possessions behind. He wore his nicer suit and a clean shirt, and his good leather shoes. His first suit, the brown serge, hung on a hook, alongside half a dozen clean shirts. The landlord would probably sell the lot once he realized Sheridan wasn't coming back.

Sheridan rested a hand on his breast, feeling the roll of bills under his palm. He didn't have enough extra to pay Lang the full promised amount, but he hoped Lang wouldn't count the roll. The rest of his money was distributed carefully through his clothing, so he wouldn't be broke if he had to make a run for it without his coat or suit jacket.

He closed the door, leaving it unlocked, and started down the hallway. Time to begin.

❖

"Ready?" Tony tapped his fingers on the steering wheel, a cigar between his teeth. Sheridan settled into the front seat. His foot nudged a hard leather case.

"As I'll ever be."

"I don't like this," Tony muttered as he drove along, turning onto South Halstead Street.

"What do you mean?"

"Your idea of one car."

"You thought it was fine before." Sheridan glanced at him.

"I don't know—meeting the Irish, and only one car...what were we thinking of? Bad enough Franky's bringing the dames."

"That why you brought the typewriter?" Sheridan tapped the Thompson submachine gun case with his foot.

"I'd never be without it," Tony replied. "Especially not with those Irish bastards." He chuckled and gave Sheridan a punch to the shoulder. "Except you, of course."

"So, not a bastard then?" Sheridan kept his tone light, trying to pretend that this was nothing but a job.

Tony snorted. "Didn't say that," he quipped. The car pulled up in front of Nell's apartment building. "You go up, fetch the girls and Franky. I'll keep watch down here."

"Hope they're ready," Sheridan remarked, drawing another chuckle from Tony.

"Hard to know with dames," he said.

The doorman eyed him as he went past but he'd obviously been expected, as the man made no move to intercept him. He took the elevator up and strolled down the hallway to knock on Nell's door. Franky opened the door, looking irritated.

"Damn women, they take forever," he muttered. "Come in. Maybe you can convince them to hurry it up."

Sheridan stepped inside and moved toward the bedroom door, giving it a crisp knock. The door opened and CeeCee stood there, her eyes wide and worried. She breathed a sigh when she saw it was him.

"Nell's not quite ready," she said, loud enough for Franky to hear.

"Are you?" Sheridan asked.

"I have everything I need," she replied and gave him a nervous smile. She came out into the living room and Sheridan couldn't help but admire her, even as he noticed Franky doing the same.

Her dress wasn't as glittery and revealing as what he'd seen her wear to the Orpheus, but it suited her well, the black satin clinging to her slender form and falling loose from her hips, ending at her knees. She wore dark stockings and low-heeled shoes. As she moved forward, a slight jingle and shine brought his eyes to her chest. She'd put on several long, beaded necklaces to distract from the simplicity of her dress.

"Packing for an expedition?" Franky remarked when he saw the purse she'd slung over her shoulder. It was a little larger than her usual clutch, and Sheridan caught his breath, wondering if such a slip would be their undoing.

"It's not like we're going to the Orpheus," CeeCee chided Franky. "A girl has to fix up her makeup now and then." She gave him a wink and he chuckled.

"Very sensible of you," he said. "I'll go drag Nell out and meet you down at the car." He strode past her into the bedroom and Sheridan let himself relax just a fraction.

"Let me help you with your coat," he said, resting his hand on the small of her back. At the closet, she pointed wordlessly to a simple yet expensive black coat with a delicate fur muff.

"That's the better one," she said.

"Much more sensible than the others," he agreed, pushing aside several lighter coats and wraps, most of which looked to be Nell's.

"I'm sensible when I need to be," she replied, her voice surprisingly sharp. He glanced down at her as he took her coat from its hanger.

"Are you sure you want to go through with this?" he asked quietly as he held the coat out, helping her as she slid her arms into the sleeves. She gathered her purse from where she'd let it fall to the floor.

"I can't stay here, not with him around," she answered, her gaze moving past him, taking in the luxurious apartment. Her saw her blink hard. "It would never work in the end."

"It might have," Sheridan offered, opening the outer door and leading her into the hall. The words sounded empty to his ears—they were little more than a platitude, and they both knew it.

"If it wasn't for him." CeeCee glanced at Sheridan as they waited for the elevator. "I hope whatever you have planned works, or we're all going to end up dead."

He bent and kissed her gently as the elevator drew up. He couldn't promise, so he didn't say anything, but as he drew back, she seemed to understand. She gave him a brave smile.

"Let's go."

❖

Cecilia tucked her bag by her feet and tried to relax into the Packard's luxurious leather seat. Sheridan had opened the door for her and helped her in, but now he stood, leaning against the car and smoking a cigarette, waiting for Franky and Nell. The driver, Tony, tapped his hands impatiently on the steering wheel. Suddenly he stopped and turned to look at her, resting his arm on the back of the seat.

"You be careful in there tonight," he said, startling her. She nodded, but he wasn't finished. "Them Irish are tricky bastards—pardon my French—so don't go anywhere alone."

"Thank you."

He meant well, but his words ratcheted up her nervousness and fear. She had enough to worry about without adding Irish gangsters to the mix. She bent to touch the handle of her bag. She'd packed a change of clothes, rolled as small as she could manage, her teacup and her mother's, and the bottle of Chanel No. 5 Nell had given her. She wished she could have brought more.

The car door opened and Nell slid across the seat until her thigh was pressed full against Cecilia's. Had this been any other time, Cecilia would have reveled in the touch, but the warmth was still comforting.

"Sorry we took so long," Nell said breezily. Franky settled in next to Nell and Sheridan closed the door before rounding the car to sit on the passenger side up front next to Tony. Cecilia studied his dark hair where it just about touched his collar. He'd need a haircut soon.

"Next time I'm going to leave you behind," Franky said.

"You wouldn't," Nell replied, leaning her head against Franky's shoulder. She'd left her hair loose tonight, and her red curls spilled down over his dark trench coat. Instead of chastising her, he chuckled, and Cecilia wondered what had gone on between them while she, Sheridan, and Tony had waited. It wasn't fair that Franky could publicly flaunt his attachment to Nell when she couldn't do the same.

"Don't push it," he said, tugging on one of Nell's curls. He glanced up at the men in the front seat. "Is everything ready?"

"Yes, sir," Tony replied. "I drove by the restaurant earlier and checked it out, and I arranged for a few men—freelancers, if you will—to be having a meal while we're there. I didn't like us going in with so few numbers."

"Well done," Franky said and leaned back in his seat. "I'll do the talking once we're there, but no matter what Capone wants, I have no intention of letting Hymie Weiss in on my beer rackets." He gave a derisive snort.

Cecilia knew little about the gang's business, but she'd never heard anyone talk that way about the big boss, Al Capone. The usual tone for Capone was one of respect. What was he thinking? She glanced at Tony and Sheridan, but neither of them made any further comment. Tony was expressionless, but as Sheridan turned to look out the passenger-side window, light from the street lamps rolled over his features. His mouth was a tight line, and he looked hard, unforgiving.

"If you didn't want to work with him, why bother with a meeting?" Nell asked. She stroked Franky's knee until he put a hand over hers to still her touch.

"We'll look like team players," he explained, likely as much to Sheridan and Tony as to Nell and her. "And when things don't work out, I can say I tried. Capone doesn't trust those Paddies anyway."

Sheridan didn't say anything about the slur and Cecilia wondered at that, though she knew she wouldn't have the courage to confront Franky Greco. She leaned her head against the back of the seat and let her gaze roam out the window, watching the city go by. The night seemed long already, and it had only just begun.

The Packard pulled up before a two-story brick building. Sheridan could just see the sign above the door. The street lamp nearest the building was out and he wondered if that had been purposely done. He wouldn't put it past Hymie to take every advantage. He patted his jacket, reassuring himself that his gun was there and ready should he need it, and then exited the car.

The street itself was quiet, though he could hear faint music coming from the restaurant, and the grumble of the car's engine. An old Model-T trundled by and he tensed, but the people inside were all farm folk, not hoods like him. The restaurant sat near the outer North Side, and he knew he shouldn't be surprised to see folks like that about. The rest of the street was dark, with several warehouses and storefronts all locked for the night. Aside from the restaurant, it seemed a desolate place. Safe though, as far as he could tell.

He opened the back door, and Franky got out, followed by Nell. He rounded the back of the Packard as Tony killed the engine, opening CeeCee's door. He gave her a hand up and she leaned against him as her foot slipped on the uneven pavement. Sheridan kept his gaze moving over the street, but he couldn't see any hint of Lang. The man had better not welsh on their deal.

The front door of the restaurant opened and Sheridan turned slightly, putting himself between CeeCee and the wide-shouldered man who lumbered out, peering into the dim light.

"Hymie's waiting for you," the man said, surprisingly genial given his grim expression. Franky strolled to the door with Nell on his arm and Sheridan followed with CeeCee. He glanced back at Tony, who hadn't moved from his spot by the car door.

"I'll stay here," Tony said, lighting his cigar.

"The car will be fine," the man said, but Tony shrugged.

"I'll stay here," he repeated.

That would make it easier for Lang, Sheridan thought. Or harder, if Tony interfered. But he couldn't worry about that now. He entered the restaurant.

The place was more than half-full and the conversation flowed with the liquor. Some of the men looked familiar, though it had been nearly a decade since he'd been a grunt in O'Banion's gang, now Hymie's. He doubted most of them, if any, would recognize him now. He wasn't the same young hood eager to prove himself. If he could, he'd go back and tell his younger self to stay clear of O'Banion's gang and especially of the robbery and chaos that resulted in his stay in the clink.

The man who'd greeted them, a ginger-haired giant, led them through the restaurant to a back room. Franky strode through as if he owned the place and Nell matched him stride for stride, bestowing flirtatious glances on a number of the men as she passed. Sheridan could see them preen when she laid eyes on them, only to slump back into their seats when she passed without a word.

Next to him, CeeCee kept her head high and proud, though her gaze never left Nell's back. She held on to his arm and if he hadn't been wearing a coat and jacket, he was sure her nails would have left little half-moons in his skin.

The back room was nicer than the restaurant—the seats were comfortable low-backed leather armchairs—and the tables had been polished to a high gloss. A half-dozen men ringed the room, sitting in pairs; one pair flanked Hymie Weiss, who had the seat of honor, his back against the wall. The other men seemed relaxed, one pair even playing cards, but Sheridan knew better. They'd be dead in an instant if anyone made a move on Hymie.

Franky took the seat across from Hymie without waiting for an invitation. Hymie smiled, but there was no humor. Nell made to sit beside Franky, but Hymie pointed to her.

"Girls over there," he said, motioning to one of the other tables.

Nell pouted prettily, but when she saw that both men were unmoved, she flounced over to the empty table. CeeCee let go of Sheridan's arm, and he gave her hand a reassuring squeeze before she went to sit next to Nell.

"Have a seat," Hymie said, indicating the chair next to Franky. Sheridan removed his hat as he sat down, resting it on his left knee. He rested his right hand on the arm of the chair, ready to go for his gun, not that he expected to need it here.

Hymie directed his gaze to Sheridan, completely ignoring Franky. "You're playing for the wrong side there, son," he said. "You should be with your own."

Sheridan leveled a look at Hymie. "So I could take the fall a second time?" For a moment Hymie looked as if he might lose his temper; his face grew red and his eyes were flinty, but then he chuckled.

"As you will. So, Greco, let's get down to it so we can get back to the more pleasant things. I'm sure the ladies don't want to spend all their time listening to their men jawing."

"Yes, let's," Franky replied, desultory as he lit a cigarette, his movements slow and measured. He made no move to say more, and after a few moments, Hymie shifted in his seat irritably.

"Here's my proposal," Hymie began. "We need more clients for the liquor we've got coming in from our distillery outside the city, and you've got the clubs."

"My clubs don't need another supplier." Franky took a drag on his cigarette and stared Hymie down. "If I let you in to sell, what's in it for me?"

"A good price," Hymie said. He leaned forward and gestured to one of his men, who brought over a crystal decanter and a pair of tumblers. "And a product unmatched by anything made in Illinois. Top-quality booze cheaper than bringing in the Canadian stuff." He poured a measure into each glass.

Sheridan leaned forward to take the glass Hymie proffered. He brought it to his nose. The booze had an almost spicy scent. He took a sip and held it in his mouth, savoring the flavor. Spicy, yet almost caramel. It was probably one of the better whiskeys he'd had since getting out of prison.

Franky picked up the other glass and took a sip. "Not bad."

"Gerry, pour the girls some so they don't feel left out."

The ginger giant came and took the decanter, setting tumblers before Nell and CeeCee. He gave them each a splash of whiskey, then brought the decanter back to Hymie, who had pushed forward a tumbler for himself. Gerry poured Hymie a generous portion.

"In return," Hymie continued, "we'll pull back on our activity in the South Side and leave it for your boys, aside from a couple of clubs."

Franky considered the offer. "Let's talk numbers," he said. He gave Sheridan a glance. "The girls look lonely," he said.

Sheridan rose without a word. He didn't care about their deal. Franky would try to screw Hymie and Hymie would try to screw Franky. He didn't know what Capone had suggested to either man, but it could be a long night.

❖

He didn't have as long to wait as he'd expected. Hymie waved him over an hour or so later.

"Greco here tells me you're a stand-up guy," Hymie said. "We're talking expansion, but we need a guy to organize."

"Why me?" How had it come to this, when he'd begun by hauling crates for Sal?

"Someone has to stump around to all those towns," Hymie remarked. "And better an Irishman than an Italian. Not that I mean any insult," he added as an aside to Franky.

"We've been talking numbers, and profit," Franky said. "For a half cut in the distillery's profits, we'll expand distribution west. What do you think?"

Sheridan wanted to laugh in Franky's face, to pull his gun and tell him he was through and that he'd put his trust in the wrong man, but he couldn't, not with all of Hymie's thugs there. He'd never get out alive and neither would CeeCee. But if he made a deal with Hymie, it might hold even after Franky's demise.

"I'll do it," he said.

"Excellent." Hymie poured another round. "We'll talk details later. To us."

Sheridan toasted with the rest but he merely wet his lips with the whiskey. He needed a clear head. Hymie waved Nell and CeeCee over and told Gerry to open the door and let in his lovelies. Several young women, all somewhat slatternly in appearance, sidled into the room. A thin blonde went straight to Hymie and perched on the arm of his chair, leaning over to whisper in his ear and give him an eyeful of her cleavage.

Nell settled in a chair to Franky's left and shot the blonde a derisive look, which the blonde returned. Sheridan bit back a smile. Nell would never make many friends among the women. Except CeeCee, of course. She'd taken the chair closest to him but had said little.

One of Hymie's men sat down on her other side and leaned forward. "Hello, darling," he said. "Can I get you another drink?"

Sheridan put his hand on CeeCee's knee and gave the man a pointed look.

The man grumbled but rose. "Figures," he muttered, retreating to sit with one of the others.

CeeCee laid her hand over his, gripping his fingers. She looked pale in the dim light and her hand was like ice.

"Drink up," he encouraged and handed her his glass. It held a finger of whiskey still. "It'll do you good."

CeeCee took the glass obediently but didn't drink. Her gaze moved past him, and he knew if he turned his head a fraction, he'd see the object of her gaze. Nell. If he could keep them apart, he would. Forever.

"Drink up," he said again, "and relax. We'll be here awhile." She sipped the whiskey and he put a finger under the glass, tilting it up. CeeCee swallowed the last of the liquor and gave a little cough. Her pale cheeks went pink.

"Go spell Tony for a bit," Franky said, clapping a hand on Sheridan's shoulder. His tone was jovial but the hand on Sheridan's shoulder was firm.

Sheridan gave CeeCee's knee a light pat, then stood.

Nell leaned over. "Come sit next to me, CeeCee," she said, reaching out a hand. CeeCee rose at the summons and her gaze caught Sheridan's. He knew she'd be careful but he worried about leaving her. He went to the door and glanced back. CeeCee sat beside Nell, who poured more whiskey from Hymie's now nearly empty decanter into their glasses. She'd be all right.

The main room was becoming raucous as the evening wore on and he didn't recognize any of the clientele. Whoever Tony had hired to be here, they were unknown to him. He went outside where Tony still leaned against the car, now smoking a cigarette.

"Deal done?" he asked, straightening.

"Seems to be. Go have a drink. I'll stay out here for a while."

Tony grinned at that. "Finally. Any ladies in there worth the trouble?"

"Not especially, unless they're already occupied."

"Pity." Tony headed inside and Sheridan found himself alone on the dimly lit sidewalk. He lit a cigarette and leaned back against the car. It would be a long wait until Franky was ready to leave.

He'd been there perhaps fifteen minutes when a figure detached itself from the shadows. The man wore a trench coat and fedora, much the same as him, and Sheridan tensed, withdrawing his hand from his pocket.

"Got kicked out, did you?"

It was Lang. Sheridan lost some of the tension. "Tony needed a drink."

"Just as well," Lang remarked. "I've got a car down the alley nearby, just waiting for when Franky leaves. Do you have the rest of the money?"

"Not now," Sheridan replied. "I wouldn't trust us not to get jumped in this neighborhood."

Lang chuckled. "Later, then."

"You can take his roll after I kill him," Sheridan replied.

"How much?"

"Probably a few grand. Hard to say. But that's not a worry—it's the extra men that will be."

Lang shot him a sharp glance. "What extra men?"

"Tony had some guys come to stake out the restaurant, buddies of his."

Lang swore. "Did he say if they'd be riding with you on the drive back?"

"Nothing. But it's not like there's an extra car." Sheridan glanced about. The street was still quiet. "What about your car? You're not afraid of someone stealing it?"

"Someone's watching it," Lang replied.

"Who?" This hadn't been part of the plan.

"Friend of mine—don't look so surprised. Anyway, you won't have to pay him, if that's what you're worried about."

Sheridan checked his watch, angling the face so he could see the time. "You'd best go back there, then. This could be a long wait."

"It's already midnight," Lang reasoned. "I can't imagine Franky really wants to stay around that long and rub elbows with Hymie. He's always hated those North Side bastards."

"Oh, I know," Sheridan said. "And I'll give him another reason to."

The door of the restaurant opened, spilling light onto the sidewalk. A familiar form lumbered out. Sheridan cursed under his breath.

"Boss'll be coming out in a little while," Tony said, striding up to the car. He peered at Lang through the gloom. "Detective?"

Lang threw Sheridan a pointed look. "Just passing by on a case and saw your man here," Lang replied smoothly.

"A case? Out here?"

Lang shrugged. "Got called in."

"What on?" Tony was curious now, probably because he knew most of the policemen by name and Lang was way out of his territory. Even Sheridan knew that much.

Lang leaned in and Sheridan wondered what sort of game he was playing. He gestured to Tony to lean closer. "I can show you," he said, "but you can't tell anyone. You and Sheridan. Come on." He started back the way he came.

Tony glanced at Sheridan.

"Let's go take a look," Sheridan suggested. Lang had something in mind.

They kept a step behind Lang as he went into a nearby alley. It was dark back there. As the walls of the buildings closed in the deeper they went, Sheridan strained to see. If Lang had something planned, he hadn't said a word.

There was a grunt and then the clatter of a garbage can being knocked over. Tony careened backward, bent almost double.

"Bloody copper," Tony gasped. "Paddy, get that bastard."

Sheridan caught Tony as he lurched to one side, staggering under the man's heavy weight. Lang emerged from the shadows, looking furious.

"Come on, you fool!" Lang reached for Tony, grabbing him by the lapels. He shoved Tony into the brick wall. "Give me a hand!"

Sheridan was frozen on the spot. Tony was the closest thing he had to a friend. The man had taken him under his wing after he'd gotten his revenge on Angelo. He couldn't do this to him. "Stop it, Lang. You don't—"

Tony pushed off the wall and launched himself at Lang, burying him under two hundred pounds of muscle and fat. Sheridan grabbed Tony by the shoulders and tried to pull him off.

"You—" Tony began.

"Wait," Sheridan said, desperate to stop what Lang had started. Tony looked up at him, loosening his hold on Lang. "I don't know what's going on—let him explain."

"He's a corrupt cop and a faggot," Tony snarled. "He deserves all he gets."

Sheridan caught a glint of metal and heard the sickening thud. Tony pitched sideways, his eyes rolling back into his head. Lang staggered to his feet, clutching his pistol. He glowered down at Tony's unconscious form.

"Bastard," he spat. "Take him out and let's go."

"I can't kill him. This wasn't part of the plan."

Lang swore again. "What kind of fucking thug are you? What did you think we were going to do? You want to get Franky Greco? You won't if his man here manages to raise the alarm."

"Just tie him up," Sheridan argued. "We'll leave him here." Tony began to groan and come around.

"Oh, for fuck's sake," Lang growled. He pointed his pistol at Tony's head. Sheridan grabbed his arm.

"Not him," he said. "Only Franky." Tony was his friend. Tony hadn't been the one who'd set his family's apartment on fire. Only Franky deserved to die.

"You think he wouldn't take you out?" Lang pulled his arm away.

Tony looked up, blood running down his cheek. Sheridan could just see its damp shine in the gloom. "Don't—" Tony croaked, trying to get to his feet.

Lang lifted the pistol again. Sheridan grasped his wrist, forcing it upward. With his free hand, he loosened his tie, pulling it over his head.

Lang sneered. "We're going to run out of time." He lowered the pistol reluctantly. Sheridan knelt beside Tony, looping the necktie around his wrists, tying the bindings tight.

"Paddy, what the hell?" Tony sounded shocked, but his voice was gaining in strength, and it was apparent he was becoming fully conscious. Sheridan didn't know what to say. In a sudden burst of movement, Tony shoved him backward, rising to one knee. Sheridan sprawled back on the pavement.

Lang didn't wait for Tony to regain his feet. The pistol flashed again and Tony crumpled, blood pouring down his face. Sheridan scrambled to his feet.

"He's out this time," Lang said with disgust. "It would've been easier to kill him. But still…can't have him following us." The gunshot echoed off the brick and a dark stain spread from Tony's knee.

CHAPTER TWENTY-FIVE

Cecilia heard the shot as they came out of the restaurant, and she clutched Nell's hand. Franky stepped in front of them and she cowered behind him.

Nell tried to shove him aside. "What's going on?"

Sheridan emerged from the shadows.

"Sher," she breathed. Franky's attention went to him immediately.

"What's going on, Paddy?" he snapped.

Sheridan shrugged. "Car backfiring," he said. "I'll get ours started." He headed toward the car, opening the back door. "Ladies."

Cecilia slid inside and Nell followed.

"Where's Tony?" she heard Franky ask.

"Taking a leak."

"Idiot," Franky muttered. "Shove over," he said to Nell, who slid over on the seat until she and Cecilia were snug together once again. Nell glanced at Cecilia. Their faces were close enough that if Cecilia stretched, she could kiss her.

"Hello, darling," Nell said, giving Cecilia a flirty wink. Franky snorted. "We need to find some way to pass the time," Nell said.

"Limericks?" Cecilia suggested, trying to distract Franky from Nell's flirtatiousness. She'd heard one of the men inside make one up on the spot and it was the first thing that came to mind.

Nell laughed. "I have no talent for that."

"Get in the car!" A commanding voice cut across Cecilia's next words and she saw Sheridan being shoved into the car by a man whose face was obscured by the brim of his fedora, pulled low.

The man held a gun, and he got into the passenger seat before they could react. He leaned over the back of the seat, his gun pointed at Franky. "Your gun," he demanded.

"Go to hell," Franky replied, reaching for his own weapon.

The retort of the gun was loud in Cecilia's ears. The shot echoed and the whole world seemed muted. She heard a muffled shout but she didn't dare move. The car rumbled and swerved into the street.

"Faster."

She could just hear the words, or was she reading the man's lips? He swung his pistol over to Nell, who froze. "Don't move," the man commanded. "And don't you dare help him."

Franky clutched his right shoulder, his hand scarlet with blood. He gritted his teeth but didn't cry out. His dark gaze was grim.

The car swerved again and Cecilia was thrown back against the seat. The street lamps were receding and the close-knit buildings of the city faded into the distance, in their place, farmland and trees. Headlights flashed in the rearview mirror. Was that help?

"Brilliant." The man laughed and removed his fedora.

Cecilia gaped and Nell let out a curse. "You bastard!"

Lang chuckled. "Now, now—if it wasn't for me, you'd probably be dead," he remarked, "or in prison. So I'd be careful if I were you."

"Stop this car!" Nell commanded. Sheridan slowed the car, but Lang turned to him.

"Take a left at the next crossroads," he said. "It'll be perfect."

Cecilia watched as Sheridan kept his eyes on the road, speeding up again. Lang seemed to have taken over. She didn't understand. What Lang had told her earlier hadn't prepared her for this.

"Where are we going?" she dared to ask.

Lang's attention moved to her. "Somewhere private."

"Don't hurt us," Nell said.

"Shut up!" Franky hissed at her. He looked furious but pale and the blood still ran sluggishly between his fingers. "What do you want, Detective?" He sneered this last word.

"Money," Lang said. "But that's not the only reason we're here." He glanced at Sheridan, who slowed to take the turn. The car rattled along a rutted dirt road and Cecilia thought she might be ill.

"How much do you want?" Franky bit out. "You know I'm good for it."

"If it were up to me, I'd just take the money and leave you out here. Or maybe not," Lang said. "Pull up here."

They'd stopped in a clearing before an old half-rotted house just visible in the moonlight. The other car pulled up behind them, illuminating the clearing with its headlights.

"Out," Lang commanded. "And leave your piece in the car. Nell, take it off him, if you would."

Nell reached into Franky's jacket as he glared at Lang, drawing out his revolver.

"Leave it on the floor," Lang said. "Is that your only one?"

"Yes." Franky grimaced as he pressed harder on his wound. The blood slowed to a trickle and then seemed to stop. Nell set the gun on the floor and Cecilia felt the warm metal brush her foot. She opened the door and stepped out into the clearing, the heels of her shoes sinking into the muddy ground.

Sheridan came around the car and took her arm, guiding her to stand by the back bumper, in view of the headlights from the other car. "Don't get in the way," he warned her. "This could get dangerous before long."

"More than it already is?" She wrapped her arms around herself, trying to keep off the chill from the breeze. She shivered.

"Trust me," he said, his voice low. She looked up at him and he cupped her cheek. A flash of worry crossed his face before he became stoic and stern again, turning away from her.

She'd be fine if she stayed there, Sheridan thought, out of shooting range. He'd leave the Thompson gun in the car, away from it all. He turned back to face Franky, striding over to where he stood, leaning against the Packard.

"What's this all about?" Franky snarled. He flexed the hand of his injured arm and winced, though he tried to hide it. Nell stood at his side, looking as defiant as she'd always been. Interesting. Would she stand by him if she knew Franky was going to turn her in?

"Ask him," Lang said, gesturing to Sheridan.

"Settling old scores," Sheridan said. He kept out of arm's reach—he knew Franky had it in him, and he wouldn't go down without a fight.

"What scores?" Franky pushed away from the car. Sheridan drew his gun.

"Stay right where you are," he said. He envisioned a bloody hole appearing in Franky's forehead, the spray of brains and skull; it would hit the car if he did it now. He backed up and Franky kept coming.

"You really think I'd listen to you?" Franky asked. He seemed to straighten and grow taller as he moved forward, his steps becoming more sure. "You're nothing. I worked my way up and a stupid Paddy's not going to be the one to bring me down."

"I'm not just any Paddy," Sheridan replied. He leveled the gun at Franky's chest. "Remember the fire on South May Street, back in 1911?"

"What about it?"

Sheridan tightened his finger on the trigger. "That was my family."

Franky laughed. "You're that scrawny little runt? I thought you'd likely died in juvie, pathetic little boy that you were. Suppose I should have known better." He lunged, one hand out for the gun, the other flashing silver.

Sheridan squeezed the trigger and felt the retort of the gun, then Franky bowled him over. There was blood dripping onto his face, but he didn't know from where. Franky's knife flashed and Sheridan felt a fiery pain in his side. He struggled to throw Franky off but the man was easily his size, and heavy. Vaguely he heard a scream, and then a pale, thin hand came over Franky's shoulder, grasping at his coat.

The movement distracted Franky, and it was enough for Sheridan to lash out with the gun, clocking Franky on the side of the head. Sheridan managed to get to his knees and then stagger to his feet. He wiped the blood from his face and tried to ignore the painful twinge in his side.

CeeCee sat up shakily, a hand to her head. Franky lay sprawled beside her, his face and arm bloody. Jesus, the blood. Lang stood where he had been before and he looked on impassively. He made no move to help or hinder anyone. And Nell, where was she?

As he turned to help CeeCee, Nell flew at him from out of the darkness. Her nails caught his cheek and he threw up an arm, shoving her away. Through his haze of anger, he heard a shriek cut off in midcry, but it wasn't Nell's.

Franky held CeeCee by the throat, his hand dark and red against her pale skin. She scrabbled at him but he ignored her as if she were a fly buzzing near. The blade flashed again in his hand and he laughed, his face a grotesque, bloodied mask. The gunshot had grazed the side of his head. A pity it hadn't been just a few inches over.

"Drop the gun," he commanded.

Sheridan didn't move. If he dropped his gun, he'd be dead.

Franky tightened his grip and CeeCee made a noise somewhere between a gasp and a choked cry. "She must not mean very much to you, if you won't even try to save her."

"Franky, don't." Nell came forward, her hand outstretched. She ignored Sheridan. "Please."

"Of course you'd plead for her," Franky growled. "She'll end up just like Lina, and all because you couldn't resist another girl."

CeeCee struggled against his grasp, her body convulsing, flinging her arms out, desperate to get free. She was going to die, strangled by Franky, if he didn't do something. "All right," Sheridan said. "Let her go." He raised his gun and lowered it carefully onto the rutted ground in plain view.

Franky loosened his grip just slightly and CeeCee gasped for breath, the color beginning to return to her cheeks.

"Bring me the gun," Franky ordered, gesturing to Nell with the knife.

"Let her go," Nell said, "like you said you would."

"The gun," he repeated. Nell stooped to pick it up. At first Sheridan thought she was uncomfortable holding it, but then her grip shifted and he could see that she handled the gun as easily as any man.

Nell kept it by her side and stood. "Let her go."

"Not yet," Franky replied. "Maybe not ever. Why shouldn't I punish you both, since you seem so attached to this pretty little thing? You've never learned your lesson, Nell, and I've been lax in reminding you of your place. Oh, and poor little Scarlett—she told me what I needed to know. You didn't need to kill her."

"I didn't kill her. She fell. And I'm not yours, Franky," she said, raising the gun.

"Oh, but you are," he replied. "Who got you out of that workhouse? Who raised you up out of the gutter? You are mine, Nell. Always have been. You'd be dead if it wasn't for me, worked to the bone or starved. Now give me the gun."

Nell sighted down the barrel.

Sheridan grabbed her by the shoulder. "You'll hit CeeCee—don't risk it."

She sneered at him. "Fool." She took aim and fired.

"Bitch." Franky grimaced and dropped the knife, loosening his hold on CeeCee. A red stain spread from his shoulder. She'd winged him.

CeeCee squirmed and struggled; her elbow connected with Franky's chin and he let go. She scrambled away, crawling over the muddy ground, her black dress caked with dirt.

Lang hauled her away from Franky, putting her between him and the car. He strode forward. "None of you can do this right," he said in disgust. He waved to the other car and Sheridan heard a door slam.

A young man walked toward them, his features silhouetted by the glare. "What should I do?" he asked. He seemed familiar but Sheridan couldn't place him.

"Gabe, take Nell to the car. I don't want her trying to shoot me too."

"Don't you dare touch me," Nell snapped.

Gabe hesitated.

"Gabe, she's not invincible, for God's sake," Lang said.

Nell turned on him. "You think I care about your little toy?"

"Not in the least, but unless you want me to take you in for Scarlett's murder, you'll do as I say."

"For God's sake, Lang, she fell. I didn't kill her."

Gabe held out his hand for the gun. Nell seemed to be hesitating, torn between Franky and Gabe.

Sheridan left them to their standoff. He caught a glimpse of metal near his left foot and stooped to pick up Franky's knife. He lunged toward Franky, so suddenly that Lang and Nell were caught off guard.

He hit Franky and the impact nearly knocked the breath from him. The hilt of the knife jammed against the heel of his hand, but he could feel it puncture and slide deep into a heavy, warm body.

Blood slicked the blade and his hand. Franky grunted under him. He pulled back and the knife came clear of the wound in Franky's chest.

"You...fucking...Paddy," Franky wheezed, blood bubbling from his lips. He collapsed backward into the dirt, his eyes rolling back into his head. Nell let out a shriek. Franky shuddered, then lay still.

"Finally," Sheridan heard Lang mutter under his breath. He stooped to feel Franky's pulse, then glanced at Sheridan. "Did that make it all better? You owe me."

Sheridan unbuttoned Franky's coat and dug into his pockets. He pulled out a roll of bills and tossed it to Lang. "All yours." He took a handkerchief from Franky's pocket and wrapped it around the knife, wiping off his prints. He dropped the knife beside Franky's corpse as he stood. "Now what?"

"I'm headed out of town with Gabe," Lang said. "I don't care where you go, or with whom."

Nell pushed them aside, looking down at Franky. Her gaze was stony and cold and Sheridan wasn't sure if she was grieving or angry. Probably both.

He gave her a wide berth as he went to CeeCee's side. She sat on the running board of the Packard, her throat mottled with bruises and blood. He went down on one knee. "Time to go," he said, taking her hand. Her gaze met his, then slid past him and upward.

"You're not going anywhere with CeeCee."

The cold muzzle of a gun rested against the back of his neck.

CHAPTER TWENTY-SIX

Lang pocketed the thick roll without bothering to count the bills. He ignored Nell and threw his arm over Gabe's shoulder. Gabe grinned at him. "Let's go," Lang said. "I've always wanted to see the West Coast." He glanced back to see Sheridan on his knees before CeeCee and Nell behind him, resting a gun against his neck. He let go of Gabe.

"Nell," Lang called out. She turned but kept the gun at Sheridan's neck. "I wouldn't do that if I were you. Bad enough to have one murder rap."

"Go to hell."

"The DA's making up his charge sheet and you'll be a wanted woman," Lang continued. "You really shouldn't have killed Scarlett. It gave Franky just what he needed."

"They won't do anything to me. I'm innocent."

"You really believe that?" Lang asked. "All your power's lying right there in the mud." He gestured to Franky's bloodied corpse. "Even if you're innocent, they'll take you down anyway without his protection." He'd thought about taking Nell with him when he left Chicago, but now he didn't want to be anywhere near her.

Nell's bravado faltered and he could see the gun shaking as she lowered it. CeeCee rose to her feet and came to Nell's side, though she brushed a hand over Sheridan's cheek as she went. She took the gun from Nell's slack fingers, and Lang watched as she slipped her arm around Nell. Incredible. Nell would have killed Sheridan without a thought and yet CeeCee still treated her with loving kindness.

Lang fingered the roll of bills tucked into his pocket. Nell wasn't his problem now. "San Francisco awaits."

❖

From the hard set of Sheridan's mouth, Cecilia knew he wanted to leave Nell there, but she couldn't bear the thought. She stared at him over Nell's chignon; for once Nell clung to her, needed her. Cecilia wouldn't let her down now. She heard the gunning of a car's engine and turned her head. Lang was leaving, without any good-bye. The car backed up and made a U-turn before heading out to the highway. Without its headlights illuminating the clearing, the night was very, very black.

"Get in the car," Sheridan said gruffly.

"Not without Nell."

"Right now, we need to get out of here. Just get in the car."

Cecilia took Nell to the passenger side of the Packard. Her tears had stopped but she still trembled. Cecilia closed the door and went back to Sheridan. He reached out to open the driver's side door. She set her hand over his. "We can't just abandon her."

"That wasn't part of the plan, CeeCee."

"To hell with your plan." Cecilia tightened her grip on his hand. She'd seen him kill a man, had seen the ferocity with which he'd lunged at Franky, yet she knew he wouldn't hurt her.

"We can take her back into the city, but that's all."

"She's not safe there."

"Neither are we." Sheridan's arm came around her, surprisingly tender.

"What if we gave her money, helped her leave?"

"I don't have enough for us all, CeeCee."

"We can manage. She has money in her apartment." Cecilia thought of Nell's wealth of clothes and jewels, and of the small safe secreted at the back of her wardrobe. She wouldn't be destitute.

Sheridan's gaze moved past her. "Did Franky trust her with the combination to his safe at the Orpheus?" He broke away from her and went back to the corpse, digging through its pockets. She heard the jangle of keys and shuddered. She didn't know how he could do that, matter-of-factly searching a dead man's pockets. Sheridan drew out Franky's billfold and flipped it open, taking the few bills there before tucking it back into Franky's pocket.

"What if she doesn't know?" Cecilia asked. Her voice seemed loud in the gloom.

"Then she doesn't," he said. "Get in the car. I want to be out of Chicago for good by sunrise."

Cecilia opened the door and slid across the bench seat next to Nell. Sheridan got in and slammed the door. He turned the key and the car rumbled to life, the headlights flickering on. Nell didn't say a word, but her eyes were glassy and her face was puffy from crying. Cecilia blinked back her own tears. Without Nell, she'd be destitute, cold, and probably dead, like her mother. She took Nell's chilled hand in hers.

"Everything will be all right," she whispered as Sheridan turned the car around and drove back toward the city.

"No, it won't," Nell replied, her voice flat. But she squeezed Cecilia's hand as if she could take the sting from the words.

Sheridan drew the car around the back of the Orpheus, parking it just beyond the concrete staircase. The last of the dancers would be leaving out front, going home with clients. There would be a lull before the cleaning staff came in. He gave CeeCee a gentle nudge. She'd fallen asleep between him and Nell, her head resting on Nell's shoulder.

She came awake with a start. "Where are we?"

"The Orpheus. I need you to stay in the car, make sure no one steals it. I'll take Nell up to Franky's office and we'll be back before you know it."

"But I—"

"We can't leave the car," he interrupted, though he kept his tone gentle. "I won't be long. I promise." He killed the engine and handed her the key. She gave him a worried look.

He and Nell exited the car and climbed the stairs to the back door. He gave it a tug—locked. He took Franky's keys from his pocket, flipping through them until he found a match.

The back halls of the Orpheus were quiet, as he'd hoped. They took the stairs to the second floor.

"I might not be able to get into his safe," Nell said abruptly.

Sheridan turned on her. "He never told you the combination?"

She shrugged. "I might not be able to remember it—it's not like he let me have full access whenever I wanted." She gave him a challenging stare, as if daring him to contradict her.

"I'll split what's there, if you can open it," he said tersely. Perhaps that lure would help her remember.

"You're so gracious," she mocked. "I can see why CeeCee loves you." A drunken man lay sprawled on one of the sofas, fast asleep. Sheridan moved past him and unlocked the office door. Nell followed close behind, closing the door behind her.

"I could have left you out there," Sheridan remarked. He wished he had. He and CeeCee would be gone from the city by now if he had. But yet, he couldn't deny CeeCee.

"I'm surprised you didn't," she replied. "But then, CeeCee wouldn't have let you."

"Just get the safe open," he said. Instead of trying the safe, Nell sidled up to him, looking up at him from under her lashes, a smug smile on her full lips.

"Does it bother you that she was mine before you had her? That she'll always be mine?" She pressed full against him, her lips brushing his cheek. "You'll never be enough for her. But maybe with the two of us…" She reached up, running a finger along his jawline.

He caught her wrist. "I thought you loved CeeCee."

"I do," she retorted, "but why should that limit me? Or you? Or CeeCee? You're so staid, Sheridan."

"Staid?"

"Old-fashioned, then. I know you want to leave me behind. I would, if I were in your position."

"Would you?" He tried to ignore the press of her body against his, then gave up.

"Maybe. But CeeCee loves you."

"You'll be dangerous to her, with Scarlett's death on your record."

"And you've killed Franky Greco—you think you'll be any less dangerous than me?" She pulled her wrist free of his grasp. "*I* won't have Capone's men after me. The cops will be far more merciful than gangsters. You should know that."

She turned her attention to the safe, bending down to pull the handle. To his surprise, the door creaked open. "Well, that was easy." She smirked and pulled the door wide. Plain manila envelopes were stacked inside. Nell snagged the top one and opened it, drawing out a stack of photographs. He looked over her shoulder. Detective Lang leaned against a shelf, a man on his knees in front of him. On his face was a look of ecstasy. Nell slid the photos back into the envelope and took the next one from the stack. More photos, this time of a grimmer nature.

Sheridan didn't recognize the woman in the photos, but it was apparent Nell did. She stiffened, and her knuckles whitened as she clutched the envelope. He saw a glimpse of a bared and bloodied limb before she shoved the photos back into the envelope.

"Who was that?"

"No one," Nell retorted. She wiped her eyes. "There's no money either, just these. Let's get out of here. I'm glad the bastard's dead."

Sheridan leaned past her and scooped out the rest of the envelopes. Methodically he tore them open, but each contained only photographs. Blackmail, or evidence…but no money. He tossed them on the desk in disgust.

"Those are worth money, you know," Nell said. "If you had the balls to use 'em."

"And get myself killed?"

"Coward."

Sheridan glanced at the pile of envelopes. There had been a familiar face in one of those envelopes. He sorted through them again until he found the one he wanted. Erven Vogt stared out of the print, sprawled on a bed hung with velvet curtains. At first glance it didn't seem important, but the girl in bed beside him was slim and tiny, and impossibly young. Her makeup was smeared, and her hair had been done up like one of the dancers, all glossy and pulled back from her delicate face. How Franky had managed to get these shots, he didn't even know.

"Amazing what you can do with cameras these days, isn't it?" Nell remarked.

"He let Erven in here, knowing this?" Sheridan's stomach roiled.

"He's rich. Of course he did. He let the rich ones do whatever they wanted." Nell looked at him as if he were an idiot. "Are you coming or not? We need to get out of here."

Sheridan tucked the envelope into his pocket and followed Nell out. The drunken man still snored on the sofa and they went past him, heading down the stairs. As they reached the bottom, a man turned the corner.

"Miss Prescott!" He looked startled. "You're back. Where's the boss?"

"We're going home," she told the man. "It was a long meeting."

"Did the boss stick it to those Paddies?" the man asked with a chuckle.

"I'm sure he'll tell everyone the score," Nell said. "Now, if you'll excuse us."

"Sure thing. I should get back to my spot out front."

Sheridan breathed a sigh of relief. Nell opened the back door, and he heard a familiar voice.

"But why would they leave you out here?" Erven leaned against the open car door, his gaze fixed on CeeCee. He wore a dark woolen jacket and his bow tie dangled loose around his neck. He glanced up at them. The strong scent of whiskey tickled Sheridan's nostrils. "Is Franky with you?"

"He's at home," Nell said without missing a beat. "We just had a few things to do first."

"If you're done, I can take CeeCee home," Erven said, giving CeeCee a wink. CeeCee didn't move from the passenger seat of the car. Her gaze flicked up to Sheridan.

"I promised to take her home," Sheridan said, coming down the steps to stand next to the car. He saw CeeCee's shoulders relax a fraction. He wouldn't let her leave with him, especially not with the photographs he'd seen.

Erven shrugged. "I wasn't there then. Come on, darling, let's go." He took CeeCee's hand, bringing her to her feet with a sharp tug. She tried to pull her hand free, but he held her fast, wrapping an arm around her waist. "They haven't been taking care of you, my darling," he said to CeeCee, taking in her muddied clothes. Under the dim light from the open back door, he squinted. "What on earth happened to you?"

CeeCee shook her head. "Nothing." She tried to twist from his grasp, but failed.

Erven turned on them, his speculative gaze taking in Sheridan and Nell. "And where's Franky? Nell, tell me the truth."

"He's at home," she said again.

Erven shook his head. "If that were true, you'd be with him," he replied.

"Not always," CeeCee spoke up. "She's usually with me."

"And I'd love to watch." Erven leered at Nell. "If you let me, I won't tell Franky that you've been cheating on him with this thug, either."

Nell scoffed. "You seriously think I'd cheat on him with Sheridan?"

"Why else would you be here with him and not Franky?"

Sheridan shouldered Erven aside and bent back the man's arm. CeeCee slipped free and Erven swore.

"How dare you!" He took a swing at Sheridan, but Sheridan was faster than the whiskey-sodden businessman. Erven staggered, blood pouring from his nose.

"Best get out of here," Sheridan threatened, "unless you'd like me to let the cops know about your taste for little girls."

Erven wiped the blood from his nose, shaking his hand. Dark drops rained on the pavement. "You're bluffing."

"Try me." Sheridan drew the envelope from his pocket. Erven seemed to pale, then he reached for the envelope. Sheridan slid it into his pocket again. "Best you head home, Mr. Vogt." He kept his anger under tight control; as much as he wanted to hurt Erven further for even daring to touch CeeCee, he couldn't. It'd be bad enough getting out of Chicago without the death of a wealthy businessman to add to his crimes.

Erven's hand closed over his wrist, his fingers digging in. "Give them to me!"

"For God's sake, we need to go." Nell pushed between them and shoved Erven aside, away from the car. Sheridan went to the driver's side and pulled open the door. CeeCee tried to grab Nell and get her away from Erven, but he had her now. Sheridan leaned over CeeCee and pulled the passenger's door shut, grunting with the effort.

"What are you doing?"

"Keep the door shut, lock it. I'll deal with Vogt."

CeeCee gaped at him. Outside, Nell struggled with Erven, and he heard a thump as one of them hit the side of the Packard.

He pushed away from the car and came around the hood, grabbing Vogt by the back of the jacket, pulling him away from Nell. The man struggled and Sheridan slammed him against the car.

Vogt's knees seemed to buckle, but he straightened. "You bastard." He came at Sheridan, but his movements were nearly as slurred as his words. Sheridan sidestepped the punch, though it clipped him on the shoulder, and let Erven fall. Sheridan kicked him in the ribs, drawing a grunt as he collapsed.

"You done?"

Sheridan looked up. Nell wiped a hand across her mouth, and he was pretty sure he saw blood.

"Let's get out of here."

"I need my things."

"It's too risky. Someone's bound to raise the alarm now that Vogt's here. We need to leave the city," Sheridan said tersely.

"I have money."

Sheridan thought of the roll in his pocket. They'd manage, at least for a while.

"It's not worth the risk. Do you want us all to end up in jail?"

"That wouldn't—"

"It would, and jail's no fun. Worse than the workhouse, believe me."

Nell glared at him, but when he didn't waver, she finally relented and turned to the car. The passenger door of the Packard opened and Nell slid in next to CeeCee. Sheridan went to the driver's side door. He still wasn't sure of this, bringing Nell with them, but it seemed he didn't have a choice.

Sheridan drove across the bridge and into the West Side.

CHAPTER TWENTY-SEVEN

As they left the city behind, Cecilia's fear and exhaustion turned to numbness. She hunkered down next to Nell, her valise on the floor in front of her. Her feet were cold and the mud had dried on her dress, though the black fabric hid a lot of the damage.

"Where will we go?" she whispered, lifting her head from her knees.

Sheridan glanced over at her. "Out of Illinois," he said. "Once we're across state lines we have a better chance. We're not important enough for the FBI."

"They'll track us if they really want us." Nell's cynical voice cut through the noise of the engine.

"They wouldn't, would they?" Cecilia asked.

Sheridan snorted. "You don't know cops very well. If there's a sap to take the fall, that's what'll happen. We're not going to be the saps."

They fell into silence. As the sun rose over the horizon, they passed over the border into Wisconsin. They drove through a small town and Cecilia was surprised Sheridan didn't stop. She was hungry and cold, and she wished for nothing more than a hot bath and some sleep. The only parts of her body still warm were those bits pressed against Nell. Everywhere else felt like ice. The last of the adrenaline faded from her system. Her entire body ached. She cautiously pressed a hand to her neck and winced. She couldn't see the bruises but knew they were there.

"We'll stop soon," Sheridan said. "If we get into Milwaukee, it'll be easier to keep from attracting attention."

"Whatever you say," she said listlessly.

Nell squeezed her shoulder. "He's right, you know."

Sheridan slowed the car and pulled over onto the shoulder. "Cecilia," he said, his voice kind, even sympathetic, "we'll stop when we can. Be strong just a while longer." He reached over and cupped her cheek, seeming to ignore Nell, who flicked a glance at him.

"You all right, Paddy?" Nell asked.

Cecilia looked more closely at Sheridan. He'd gone pale and had tucked his left hand under his jacket, pressed tightly against his right side. She recalled his struggle with Franky. Had he been hurt? It had happened so fast.

"Sher?" She inched back across the seat and laid a hand on his arm.

"I'll be fine," he said. "I just need to rest. When we get to Milwaukee we'll find a hotel."

She studied him. He avoided her gaze, his face expressionless, his eyes focused on the road, but his body was stiff with tension. She slid across Nell to sit next to him, then drew away the side of his trench coat. His suit jacket seemed darker, and when she touched the wool, there was a tackiness that caught at her fingers. When she lifted her hand away, her fingers were red.

"Sher—you're hurt." She pulled the suit jacket away and finally saw the shirt underneath. His spread fingers were reddened where he held them against his side and his shirt clung to his ribs. She drew in a breath.

"It's not serious," he said. "It had almost closed until Erven roughed me up."

"Why didn't you say something?"

"And what would you have done?" His sharp tone stung. "Gone with him? I'm sure he offered to set you up in style."

"I don't love him," she replied. That wasn't the only reason, but she didn't want to discuss Erven. Their recent evening flashed in her mind. Lavish, but cold. She could never have lived like that.

Sheridan didn't answer.

"I'll drive," Nell said. "You're liable to pass out on us, and then where would we be? Shift over." She got out of the car, walked around, and nudged Sheridan aside to claim the driver's seat.

"Keep to the limit," Sheridan warned.

Nell snorted. "I've been driving for years. Don't you worry."

When they reached the outskirts of Milwaukee, Nell slowed, following the few cars on the road into the center of the city. She pulled into a hotel a couple of streets away from the train station.

"This'll do for now," Nell said, killing the engine.

"One of you will have to go in," Sheridan said, pulling a small roll of bills from his pocket. "I'll attract too much attention."

"I'm covered in mud," Cecilia said, pulling up her coat's collar to hide her neck. "And I can't rent a room. They'll think I'm a prostitute."

Sheridan lifted his hand away from his side and tugged at the gold ring on his pinky. He slipped it onto her ring finger. "Go on then," he said, looking amused. "We'll be Mr. and Mrs. Smith. And Miss Smith, I suppose."

"They won't even notice that there's three of us," Nell said. "Try to get a room with two beds though. We won't all fit in one."

Cecilia turned the ring around on her finger. It was a bit loose, but it would pass muster. She took a few small bills from the roll and gave the rest back to Sheridan. No need to flash their money in front of strangers.

"I'll be right back."

❖

Sheridan leaned his head back and closed his eyes. Nothing had gone as planned. Franky was dead, but that was small consolation. Tony could be dead too, and he regretted that. The man had been a friend, of sorts. He shifted in the seat and the knife wound in his side burned like fire. He was sure his ribs were cracked. At least he'd kept CeeCee from harm, though he hadn't planned on taking Nell along. He thought Lang would have taken her and saved him the trouble.

Where was Lang now? Probably across two states and counting his cash. The cash. Damn Franky Greco for thinking his blackmail more important than cash in the safe. The money he had would keep them for a few weeks, at best, if they found somewhere cheap to stay. He frowned. They couldn't stay here long.

"We'll get you cleaned up soon, I suppose."

He glanced at Nell. "I'll manage. You're a good driver, by the way."

"I got Franky to teach me. Told him if I could drive, he wouldn't have to fuss over me so much." She smiled briefly. "Didn't think it'd come in handy like this." She paused. "Look, we'll have to play this as best we can. I think CeeCee loves us both, but we don't much care for each other."

Sheridan chuckled, then grimaced at the pain in his side. "When

I first saw you, I thought you looked like a glamour girl, all cold and above everyone. But you're not so bad."

"Glad we've got that sorted."

A tap on the window startled him, but it was only CeeCee. He opened the door and shoved the car keys in his pocket.

"Do you have anything?" she asked, going around to the passenger side to fetch her bag. She hefted the case with the Thompson submachine gun. "Is this yours?"

He took it from her. "It is now. Did you get a room?"

"It's tiny, with two beds, but it has a bathroom," she replied. "I paid for two nights, though I don't think he believed me when I said it was for me and my husband." She frowned and he wanted to reassure her. Any other woman he'd known would have fallen to pieces by now, but CeeCee was calm as could be.

"He won't fuss since he has his money," Nell said, pulling her coat tight around her as they headed toward the hotel and up to their room.

Sheridan slid the Thompson behind the single chair, out of the way. CeeCee dropped her bag at the foot of the closest bed. The bed itself creaked as she sank down onto it, her shoulders drooping. Nell sat down beside her.

Sheridan made sure the door was locked. "Get some rest," he said. He removed his coat and hung it on the hook on the back of the door. The sun streamed in through the streaked window and he saw how stained his suit had become.

CeeCee stared too. "Do you have any other clothes?" she asked. "You can't go out in those."

"Nothing. I couldn't pack without making Tony suspicious. I'll wash it in the sink."

CeeCee pushed her jacket off her shoulders and rose, coming toward him. "And your shirt…" She trailed off when he removed his suit jacket.

Sheridan pushed open the bathroom door. The room was the size of a postage stamp. He dropped the jacket into the sink and began to unbutton his shirt. There was a bar of yellow soap on the side of the sink.

"I'll wash it," he said, pulling his shirt from the waistband of his trousers. The blood had soaked all down his side and the shirt was a dark crimson. Washing wouldn't be enough.

"Give it here," CeeCee said, squeezing into the bathroom next to him. "I'll see what I can do. You need to clean that wound." She took the shirt from him and he let her take his spot in front of the sink. He stepped out to strip off his shoes and trousers, leaving on his underclothes as Nell looked at him speculatively.

"Don't let me stop you," she said, leaning back on her elbows on the bed.

Sheridan let his trousers drop to the floor. "You'll have to use your imagination." He heard the water running and went back into the bathroom.

CeeCee had lathered up his shirt and the water was already scarlet. She bit her lip in concentration as she scrubbed at the stains.

He bent and kissed her cheek. "Thank you," he said, and turned to run the bath. He washed the blood from his torso, exposing the jagged line of the knife wound. It didn't look so bad now, though the edges were red and slightly swollen. He cleaned himself off as best he could.

CeeCee turned to him, holding up his sopping-wet shirt. "It's not going to work," she said. The shirt was still tinged pink and the cotton torn.

"I'll make do," he said. He'd have to buy a new shirt.

CeeCee wrung the shirt out over the sink and hung it from the doorknob. "Is the water hot?" she asked.

"Not really."

She sighed and rubbed her eyes. "I'd so hoped for a hot bath."

"Have a bath anyway—you'll feel better."

Sheridan watched as CeeCee pulled off her dress, folded it, and placed it outside the door, on the chair. In her slip and underwear she was a vision, even tired as she was. He started to rise from the water and reached for a towel as she removed her slip and then her bra. He tried to concentrate on wiping his face and chest as he stepped from the tub, but his eyes were drawn to her.

CeeCee unclipped her stockings and rolled them down, exposing her pale legs. She unhooked her garters and let them fall. Sheridan wrapped the towel around his waist. They stood inches apart on the damp floor and he had to shuffle around her. Her breast brushed his chest and he willed himself not to react. His body ached but he still wanted her. It didn't matter that his ribs were cracked or that he'd just been covered in blood, not even that he'd been awake for an entire day. He closed his eyes and took a breath.

A gentle hand rested on his abdomen, perilously close to the edge of the towel. His eyes snapped open.

"Sher, I forgive you," CeeCee said.

He let out the breath he'd been holding in one great whoosh. He was speechless; he could only stare at her, so beautiful and standing so close. She embraced him and then he took her in his arms. He bent his head, and his lips brushed the soft flesh at the intersection of her neck and shoulder. His kiss was gentle, only lightly touching her bruises. He wished he could have done more to stop Franky.

Even after a night on the run, he could still smell her perfume, faintly floral. He lingered, his lips brushing her skin again. The scent was comforting, even as she finally withdrew and gave him a gentle kiss. He missed her touch, the feel of her warmth against him.

"Rest," she said, gently pushing him out of the bathroom. "I'll be out soon."

He retreated into the bedroom, securing the damp towel as it started to droop. On the bed, Nell dozed, deep shadows beneath her eyes, her red hair bright against the sheets. He pulled the worn velvet drapes across the window. Rather than settle into the other bed without CeeCee, he picked up his trousers and dug into the pocket, bringing out the rest of his cash. He drew back the striped coverlet, sat on the edge of the bed, and counted it carefully.

Not enough. Not for long. And they'd have to ditch the car. When he woke, after he got a new shirt and maybe a new jacket, he'd sell the car. They could buy train tickets west. They weren't without hope yet.

He glanced up as CeeCee emerged from the bathroom, wrapped in the remaining towel. Beads of water glistened in the hollows of her collarbones and she'd washed off the remains of her makeup. She looked younger than her age, and aside from the shadows under her eyes and the bruises mottling her neck, she didn't look like she'd been through hell and back.

She glanced at the money in his hand. "Will we be all right?" she asked, her voice barely a whisper, as she came to sit next to him on the bed.

"Don't worry," he said. "I'll take care of you. We'll manage." He tucked the bills back into his trouser pocket and let them fall to the floor.

"What will we do? We can't stay here long. And what about you and Nell?"

He told her his idea of heading as far west as they could get. "And Nell and I have an understanding," he said. "We'll work things out as we go."

"Are you sure?" she said, resting against him. "I've never been west."

"We'll go until we want to stop," he said.

"San Francisco," Nell murmured, turning on her side to face them.

"Maybe," Sheridan allowed.

"I want to see the sea," CeeCee remarked, her mouth widening into a yawn.

"I promise."

When she lifted her head, he kissed her. Her soft lips opened under his and she moaned into his mouth, though they drew apart when Nell coughed.

"I'll be in the bathroom," she said, sounding amused as she rose from the bed. She gave them a glance. "But it's my turn when I come back."

The bathroom door closed and Sheridan tugged CeeCee's towel free. They would be all right, as long as they had each other. And Nell would grow on him.

CHAPTER TWENTY-EIGHT

Cecilia woke in the midafternoon, feeling only somewhat rested. Nell lay beside her, her arm flung out and the sheet bunched below her breasts. In the other bed, Sheridan slept on, snoring lightly. It seemed strange to be with both of them at once, to have both of them here. She'd never thought it possible. Cecilia rubbed her eyes and sat up. The ugliness of the old and worn hotel room stared back at her. The ceiling sagged in one corner and the molding was stained with damp, the striped wallpaper faded and peeled at the edges. The whole place seemed sad.

She pushed back the covers and slid from the bed, pulling the sheet back up to Nell's chin, and then padded across the floor. Her underwear hung in the bathroom. It was a bit damp still, but it would have to do. She dressed quietly, then took Sheridan's shirt from the doorknob.

He could never wear it. The blood had stained the cotton beyond repair. She spread it opened and measured the length of the sleeves and the size of the collar. She would slip out and buy him a few new shirts. Then they would leave. She didn't want to spend any longer here than she had to.

The man at the hotel front desk, a different one than when they'd arrived, helpfully directed her to a shop a few blocks away.

"I'd like a couple of shirts please," she said to the young man in the tailor's shop. She gave him Sheridan's measurements. "Do you have anything ready to go?"

"Just a moment." The young man went into the back of the shop and Cecilia paced to the window. A newsboy had just set down a stack of papers and a huge headline blared across the front of the broadsheet.

GANGSTER FOUND DEAD

"Ma'am?"

She turned back to the young man, but her mind wasn't on the purchase. Once she had the shirts, she rushed from the shop. The newsboy was doing a brisk business and he sold her a paper along with the rest. She clutched the dirty newsprint in her hand. GRECO'S MOLL MISSING, blared the subheadline. Cecilia stopped dead. She turned the paper over and below the fold was a photo of Nell standing next to Franky at the Orpheus. Her heart contracted.

Oh, Nell.

She realized she'd been standing in the middle of the sidewalk and forced her feet to move. She found the hotel once more and took the stairs in a daze. She let herself into the room. Nell was gone from their bed, but Sheridan was pacing.

"Where have you been?" Sheridan took her by the shoulders, looking furious. "I was worried sick."

Cecilia wordlessly held up the newspaper.

"So fast," Sheridan muttered to himself. He took the paper, reading the story to himself. "Christ."

Sheridan flung the paper on the bed and Cecilia scrambled to read it. "We have to get out of here, especially Nell," she whispered.

"And quick," Sheridan said. He'd put on his trousers but was bare-chested. "Why did you go out?"

She tore her eyes away from the page. "You needed shirts." She handed him the wrapped parcel. He said something, but she didn't hear him. The last paragraph of the story caught her eye. "Oh God." Nell could face execution if found guilty of murdering Franky Greco and Scarlett.

"I know," Sheridan said. Half-dressed, he took her hand. "There's nothing we can do now except get out of here. Get your things." He finished buttoning up his shirt and put the spare into her bag. He pulled on his suit jacket and trench coat and put on his fedora.

Nell came out from the bathroom and saw them ready to go. She wore only her slip and stockings but had her dress in her arms, and her hair and makeup were done.

"What's going on?"

Cecilia handed her the paper, and she read, her lips pressed together.

"We're heading out of here," Sheridan said. "Get dressed. The sooner the better."

"How the hell can they think I murdered Franky?" Nell crumpled the paper in her hand and tossed it into a corner. "Those bastards." She hurried to pull on her dress.

Cecilia didn't know what to say. In a daze she picked up her bag and gave a last glance around the room, wondering if she'd forgotten anything. Sheridan picked up his case.

"We'll have to leave the car," he said. "They'll be looking for it now and we can't risk it. If someone gets our descriptions and links us to it, we're done for."

The lost money didn't matter to her. All she could think of was Nell.

"I have some money," Nell said. "I never leave without it. We'll be fine, even without the car." She gathered up her things and put on her coat.

The three of them walked from the hotel to the train station. Sheridan bought three tickets to Saint Paul, the first train leaving the station. They didn't have to linger long on the platform.

"Will we ever come back?" Cecilia asked. She thought of her mother's ashes in the cemetery at Rose Hill. She should have said good-bye.

"I don't know," Sheridan replied. The train chugged into the station. "Maybe in a few years, once things die down."

"Maybe a decade." Nell sounded cynical to Cecilia's ears. "Gangsters have long memories."

Sheridan helped Cecilia up the steps, a hand on her back. How had it come to this? She never once thought she'd be on the run. But at least she had her two loves with her. That's what mattered.

The train's whistle blew.

About the Author

Alyssa Linn Palmer is a Canadian writer and freelance editor. She splits her time between a full-time day job and her part-time loves, writing and editing. She is a member of the RWA, the Calgary RWA, and RRW (Rainbow Romance Writers). She has a passion for Paris and all things French, which is reflected in her writing. When she's not writing lesbian romance, she's creating the dark, morally flawed characters of the Le Chat Rouge series and indulging in her addictions to classic pulp fiction.

Books Available From Bold Strokes Books

Cold to the Touch by Cari Hunter. A drug addict's murder is the start of a dangerous investigation for Detective Sanne Jensen and Dr. Meg Fielding, as they try to stop a killer with no conscience. (978-1-62639-526-8)

Forsaken by Laydin Michaels. The hunt for a killer teaches one woman that she must overcome her fear in order to love, and another that success is meaningless without happiness. (978-1-62639-481-0)

Infiltration by Jackie D. When a CIA breach is imminent, a Marine instructor must stop the attack while protecting her heart from being disarmed by a recruit. (978-1-62639-521-3)

Midnight at the Orpheus by Alyssa Linn Palmer. Two women desperate to make their way in the world, a man hell-bent on revenge, and a cop risking his career: all in a day's work in Capone's Chicago. (978-1-62639-607-4)

Spirit of the Dance by Mardi Alexander. Major Sorla Reardon's return to her family farm to heal threatens Riley Johnson's safe life when small-town secrets are revealed, and love may not conquer all. (978-1-62639-583-1)

Sweet Hearts by Melissa Brayden, Rachel Spangler, and Karis Walsh. Do you ever wonder *Whatever happened to...*? Find out when you reconnect with your favorite characters from Melissa Brayden's *Heart Block*, Rachel Spangler's *LoveLife*, and Karis Walsh's *Worth the Risk*. (978-1-62639-475-9)

Totally Worth It by Maggie Cummings. Who knew there's an all-lesbian condo community in the NYC suburbs? Join twentysomething BFFs Meg and Lexi at Bay West as they navigate friendships, love, and everything in between. (978-1-62639-512-1)

Illicit Artifacts by Stevie Mikayne. Her foster mother's death cracked open a secret world Jil never wanted to see...and now she has to pick up the stolen pieces. (978-1-62639-472-8)

Pathfinder by Gun Brooke. Heading for their new homeworld, Exodus's chief engineer Adina Vantressa and nurse Briar Lindemay carry game-changing secrets that may well cause them to lose everything when disaster strikes. (978-1-62639-444-5)

Prescription for Love by Radclyffe. Dr. Flannery Rivers finds herself attracted to the new ER chief, city girl Abigail Remy, and the incendiary mix of city and country, fire and ice, tradition and change is combustible. (978-1-62639-570-1)

Ready or Not by Melissa Brayden. Uptight Mallory Spencer finds relinquishing control to bartender Hope Sanders too tall an order in fast-paced New York City. (978-1-62639-443-8)

Summer Passion by MJ Williamz. Women loving women is forbidden in 1946 Hollywood, yet Jean and Maggie strive to keep their love alive and away from prying eyes. (978-1-62639-540-4)

The Princess and the Prix by Nell Stark. "Ugly duckling" Princess Alix of Monaco was resigned to loneliness until she met racecar driver Thalia d'Angelis. (978-1-62639-474-2)

Winter's Harbor by Aurora Rey. Lia Brooks isn't looking for love in Provincetown, but when she discovers chocolate croissants and pastry chef Alex McKinnon, her winter retreat quickly starts heating up. (978-1-62639-498-8)

The Time Before Now by Missouri Vaun. Vivian flees a disastrous affair, embarking on an epic, transformative journey to escape her past, until destiny introduces her to Ida, who helps her rediscover trust, love, and hope. (978-1-62639-446-9)

Twisted Whispers by Sheri Lewis Wohl. Betrayal, lies, and secrets— whispers of a friend lost to darkness. Can a reluctant psychic set things right or will an evil soul destroy those she loves? (978-1-62639-439-1)

The Courage to Try by C.A. Popovich. Finding love is worth getting past the fear of trying. (978-1-62639-528-2)

Break Point by Yolanda Wallace. In a world readying for war, can love find a way? (978-1-62639-568-8)

Countdown by Julie Cannon. Can two strong-willed, powerful women overcome their differences to save the lives of seven others and begin a life they never imagined together? (978-1-62639-471-1)

Keep Hold by Michelle Grubb. Claire knew some things should be left alone and some rules should never be broken, but the most forbidden, well, they are the most tempting. (978-1-62639-502-2)

Deadly Medicine by Jaime Maddox. Dr. Ward Thrasher's life is in turmoil. Her partner Jess left her, and her job puts her in the path of a murderous physician who has Jess in his sights. (978-1-62639-424-7)

New Beginnings by KC Richardson. Can the connection and attraction between Jordan Roberts and Kirsten Murphy be enough for Jordan to trust Kirsten with her heart? (978-1-62639-450-6)

Officer Down by Erin Dutton. Can two women who've made careers out of being there for others in crisis find the strength to need each other? (978-1-62639-423-0)

Reasonable Doubt by Carsen Taite. Just when Sarah and Ellery think they've left dangerous careers behind, a new case sets them—and their hearts—on a collision course. (978-1-62639-442-1)

Tarnished Gold by Ann Aptaker. Cantor Gold must outsmart the Law, outrun New York's dockside gangsters, outplay a shady art dealer, his lover, and a beautiful curator, and stay out of a killer's gun sights. (978-1-62639-426-1)

White Horse in Winter by Franci McMahon. Love between two women collides with the inner poison of a closeted horse trainer in the green hills of Vermont. (978-1-62639-429-2)

Autumn Spring by Shelley Thrasher. Can Bree and Linda, two women in the autumn of their lives, put their hearts first and find the love they've never dared seize? (978-1-62639-365-3)

The Renegade by Amy Dunne. Post-apocalyptic survivors Alex and Evelyn secretly find love while held captive by a deranged cult, but when their relationship is discovered, they must fight for their freedom—or die trying. (978-1-62639-427-8)

Thrall by Barbara Ann Wright. Four women in a warrior society must work together to lift an insidious curse while caught between their own desires, the will of their peoples, and an ancient evil. (978-1-62639-437-7)

The Chameleon's Tale by Andrea Bramhall. Two old friends must work through a web of lies and deceit to find themselves again, but in the search they discover far more than they ever went looking for. (978-1-62639-363-9)

Side Effects by VK Powell. Detective Jordan Bishop and Dr. Neela Sahjani must decide if it's easier to trust someone with your heart or your life as they face threatening protestors, corrupt politicians, and their increasing attraction. (978-1-62639-364-6)

Warm November by Kathleen Knowles. What do you do if the one woman you want is the only one you can't have? (978-1-62639-366-0)

In Every Cloud by Tina Michele. When Bree finally leaves her shattered life behind, is she strong enough to salvage the remaining pieces of her heart and find the place where it truly fits? (978-1-62639-413-1)

Rise of the Gorgon by Tanai Walker. When independent Internet journalist Elle Pharell goes to Kuwait to investigate a veteran's mysterious suicide, she hires Cassandra Hunt, an interpreter with a covert agenda. (978-1-62639-367-7)

Crossed by Meredith Doench. Agent Luce Hansen returns home to catch a killer and risks everything to revisit the unsolved murder of her first girlfriend and confront the demons of her youth. (978-1-62639-361-5)

Making a Comeback by Julie Blair. Music and love take center stage when jazz pianist Liz Randall tries to make a comeback with the help of her reclusive, blind neighbor, Jac Winters. (978-1-62639-357-8)

Soul Unique by Gun Brooke. Self-proclaimed cynic Greer Landon falls for Hayden Rowe's paintings and the young woman shortly after, but will Hayden, who lives with Asperger syndrome, trust her and reciprocate her feelings? (978-1-62639-358-5)

CPSIA information can be obtained
at www.ICGtesting.com
Printed in the USA
LVOW08s2116090117
520367LV00001BA/6/P